FRINGE
THE ZODIAC PARADOX

COMING SOON FROM CHRISTA FAUST AND TITAN BOOKS

FRINGE
THE BURNING MAN (July 2013)

CHRISTA FAUST

FRINGE

THE ZODIAC PARADOX

TITAN BOOKS

FRINGE: THE ZODIAC PARADOX
Print edition ISBN: 9781781163092
E-book edition ISBN: 9781781163108

Published by Titan Books
A division of Titan Publishing Group Ltd
144 Southwark Street, London SE1 0UP

First edition: May 2013
1 3 5 7 9 10 8 6 4 2

Copyright © 2013 Warner Bros. Entertainment Inc.
FRINGE and all related characters and elements are trademarks of
and © Warner Bros. Entertainment Inc.

Cover images courtesy of Warner Bros.
Additional cover images © Dreamstime.

This is a work of fiction. Names, characters, places, and incidents either
are the product of the author's imagination or are used fictitiously,
and any resemblance to actual persons, living or dead, business
establishments, events, or locales is entirely coincidental.

No part of this publication may be reproduced, stored in a retrieval
system, or transmitted, in any form or by any means without the prior
written permission of the publisher, nor be otherwise circulated in any
form of binding or cover other than that in which it is published and
without a similar condition being imposed on the subsequent purchaser.

A CIP catalogue record for this title is available from the British Library.

Printed and bound in the United States.

Did you enjoy this book?
We love to hear from our readers. Please email us at readerfeedback@
titanemail.com or write to us at Reader Feedback at the above address.

To receive advance information, news, competitions, and exclusive
offers online, please sign up for the Titan newsletter on our website
www.titanbooks.com

PART ONE

1

SEPTEMBER 1968

He liked to kill the young men first.

Not because he was afraid of an act of retaliation, or heroism. This particular kid was a cocky little bastard, arm around the dull, dumpy blonde in the passenger seat like he owned her, but he'd be no match for Allan's superior physical strength and mental acumen.

They never were.

No, Allan Mather would kill the young man first because he wanted to show the blonde that no one could save her. He wanted to give her time to live inside that terrible moment of understanding before she met her own, inevitable end.

Just thinking it, about sharing that special, intimate moment with a new girl sent a flush of heat over the surface of his skin, warming the cool barrel of the Whitmer 9 mm he had tucked into the waistband of his faded fatigue pants.

It was an unexpected Indian summer night, probably

the last hot night of the year. Yet there was just this one car. Just this one couple. When Allan first started hunting here, a popular make-out spot like Reiden Lake would look like a drive-in on a Saturday night. Dozens of cars, all packed with sweaty human vermin, offering shallow promises in exchange for meaningless animal copulations.

Now the cocky kid's souped-up '66 Edsel Lynx was the only vehicle parked at the eastern scenic overlook. Which showed just how cocky he was—and how stupid his date was. Because the "Lover's Lane" murders were all over the papers, and anyone with a lick of sense would have stayed home. It was almost like they wanted to be there. Almost like destiny.

A pair of young graduate students sat side by side on a rocky outcropping at the western edge of the lake, a small open cooler at their feet and a brand new red Coleman lantern casting a gentle glow across the rippling water. The autumn night was brisk, but comfortable.

The one on the left was clean cut and well dressed, his dark hair neatly combed into a mathematically perfect side part. Tall and rakish, he had a strong profile and a deep baritone voice that made everything he said seem weighty and significant. Particularly to female undergrads.

The one on the right looked like an unmade bed. With his long, frizzy, light brown hair, he might have been mistaken for a stylish British rock star, but in reality he only looked that way because he couldn't be bothered to cut or comb it. His clothes, on the other hand, were square and schizophrenically whimsical. A moth-eaten tweed Norfolk jacket that might have been new in 1929, worn over a hand-me-down athletic shirt featuring the name of a Catholic high school he never attended. His pants were too short, revealing wildly mismatched socks, one solid brown and the other bright blue argyle. Both of his scuffed dress shoes were untied.

"Listen, Belly," the one with the mismatched socks said. "While your argument for the inclusion of caffeine to provide an additional generalized arousal of the senses is both well reasoned and valid, I would counter that the unique balance between phosphoric acid and citric acid in grape Nehi will better complement the biosynthetic ergoline compound in our newly formulated pharmacological launchpad."

"Forget it, Walter," Bell replied. "I'd rather drink Denatonium Benzoate than grape Nehi. Besides, we must remain consistent in what we use as a supplement, so that the findings will be accurately measurable."

"Fine," Walter said. "I reluctantly capitulate to the cola option… this time." He grabbed a bottle of RC Cola from the cooler and popped the cap. "However, I want it on record that I felt it was *not* the ideal combination."

"Duly noted." Bell removed a tiny vial and a capped syringe from the inner pocket of his sport coat. "We're going with the usual five hundred micrograms, right?"

"Right," Walter replied, taking a swig. "The dosage also must remain consistent, so that any observable differences in the effect will be clearly attributable to variations in the formula."

Bell nodded, uncapping the syringe and piercing the rubber top of the tiny vial. He tipped the vial upside down and drew out the correct quantity of the clear liquid. Walter held out his cola, and Bell inserted the needle into the neck of the bottle, squirting the contents of the syringe into the fizzy beverage.

Walter balanced his bottle on the rock beside him and opened a second cola for Bell. Bell dosed it like the first, and then took the bottle from Walter, pocketing the vial and syringe.

Walter raised his bottle.

"To paraphrase the great German physicist Max Born," he said. "'Here's to building our road behind us as we proceed.'" He frowned and looked out over the dark water. "Or maybe that was Donovan."

"*L'Chaim*," Bell replied with a crooked grin, clinking his own bottle against Walter's.

Walter nodded, and they lifted the bottles to their lips.

The sky above Allan's head was starless and blank, like the gray, dead screen of an unplugged television.

The still surface of Reiden Lake was the sky's twin, just as dead.

Once the young man and woman were dead, the tableau would be perfect.

Allan's night vision was already superb—sharp and clear, almost like that of a nocturnal animal—but now he was beginning to see and hear things even more clearly. The trees whispered, gossiping behind their crisscrossed branches. The rich, loamy dirt seemed to breathe under Allan's boots, and shadows were gathering behind him like shy children. The acid he had dropped was just starting to kick in.

He'd calculated the dose so that he would be peaking right around the time when the murder was complete, and he'd returned to the safety of his own hidden car to bask in the afterglow, relishing and reliving each perfectly executed moment. He kept a notebook in his glove box, and that's where he would compose his next epic letter for the local newspaper, describing the killing in glorious detail and taunting the hapless authorities.

If he was lucky, he might even get to watch the discovery of the bodies, and the investigation in process. That was his favorite part, watching the police and their pathetic, ineffectual flailing. It was like watching insects drowning in a gob of his spit.

It was time.

He was ready.

He pulled on his gloves, then slid the gun from his waistband and strode purposefully over to the passenger-side door of the Lynx.

The windows were down, and an infuriatingly banal pop song was bubbling out of the radio. The girl was wearing an unflattering, baggy floral print dress that looked like she'd borrowed it from a maiden aunt. Up close, it was clear that her blond bouffant was a cheap wig. Its coarse, synthetic texture was deeply disturbing to Allan's chemically enhanced mind, reminiscent of dead insect legs and abandoned cocoons.

The shadows around his ankles struck up a high-pitched keening. Something was wrong.

Run, the shadows cried.

The girl turned toward him in horrible, unnatural slow motion and he was frozen, riveted, unable to look away.

"Police," she said. "Drop your weapon."

There was a gun in her thick, hairy hand. She wasn't a girl at all. She was a man. A police officer. And so was her cocky date. Both of them were staring him down with steely eyes as cold and professional as the bores of their guns.

He was the one who'd let himself get too cocky, and now he would have to pay for his arrogance.

2

Walter looked longingly into the cooler, at a bottle of grape Nehi. Its gracious, almost feminine shape shimmered with lush condensation and he was suddenly convinced that this particular bottle contained an elixir of perfect, exquisite refreshment the likes of which had never been experienced by mere mortals. Its mysterious deep purple hue seemed profoundly significant.

Ordinary purple was at the very bottom of the CIE 1931 color space chromaticity diagram, and represented one of the limits of human color perception. Yet *this* purple seemed to contain elusive, twisting glints of a color that was just beyond the normal range. If he were to ingest such a color, he felt sure that it would instantly bond itself to the rhodopsin inside the photoreceptor cells of his retina, and endow him with a new, unprecedented kind of vision.

He reached for the bottle and it slipped, mercury-like, out of his grasp. Taunting him.

"Note," Bell said, writing in a small red notebook. "Initial onset of hallucinogenic effect observed at…" He looked down at his watch. "10:17 p.m."

"Fifty-four minutes from ingestion," Walter said.

"That's almost twenty minutes faster than the previous formula."

He looked back at the seductive bottle of grape Nehi and saw that it had transformed into a small, purple-skinned woman with white, finger-waved hair and a hat shaped like a bottle cap. She undulated gracefully amid the ice cubes, seemingly unaffected by the cold beneath her tiny bare feet. The other bottles became women, too, and within minutes the entire cooler had become a miniature Busby Berkeley musical number, complete with synchronized swimming in the water from the melted ice.

While such a hallucination was cute and charming, it wasn't particularly significant, or unusual. Walter needed to focus, to meditate and look inward, to try and elevate his consciousness to a higher level.

He turned away from the cooler and looked out over the surface of Reiden Lake.

A searing beam of light from a stealthy police zeppelin flooded the scene, half blinding Allan and causing a nauseating burst of agitated color around the edges of everything. His mounting anxiety was amplifying and intensifying the effect of the acid, but he had to keep it together. Had to use his superior intellect to beat these animals.

He knew what he had to do.

He dropped the gun and held up his hands.

"That's it," the cop in the wig said, reaching for the handle of the Lynx's door. "Now go on and back up. Nice and slow."

"Yes, sir," Allan said, smirking inside.

This was his chance.

He did as he was ordered, but cheated his step toward

the overlook. There was a low log rail edging the parking area, then a thirty-foot drop down an eroding bank to the sand dunes and sawgrass of the small public beach below.

The two undercover cops started shouldering out of the car. For a split second, their attentions were divided. Their guns lost their aim in the shuffle.

Allan jumped.

A lesser man, a weaker man, might have broken his leg falling down that cliff. Or maybe even his neck.

Allan was not a lesser man.

He was in peak physical condition. Strong, powerful, and at the top of his game. Even in his altered state, he maintained perfect balance and presence of mind. As heavy as he was, he could be as graceful as a cat when he needed to be.

The slope wasn't entirely vertical—more like an eighty-five percent grade, he judged. He went down facing inward, hands crossed in front of his eyes and the steel toe tips of his combat boots digging into the crumbly clay to slow his descent. Still, it was a hard landing, buckling his knees and jarring his brain, and he crouched, gasping in the sawgrass for precious seconds.

His heart pounded unnaturally loud in his ears, Mandelbrot patterns spiraling in the corners of his eyes.

Not very catlike at all, he thought with irritation.

Above him, he could hear the pigs swearing. The dust kicked up by their frantic feet drifted out over the edge of the drop, transformed into glowing white ectoplasm lit by the dirigible's searchlight. Then a bewigged head peered over the edge, silhouetted in the luminous cloud.

"Where the hell is he?" one gruff voice called.

"I can't see a damn thing down there!" the other replied.

Just as Allan had planned. The blinding glare of

the searchlight had turned the shadow of the cliff into impenetrable blackness. Within it, he was invisible.

"Come on, Charlie," the first pig said to the other. "We gotta find a way down."

Allan rose to his feet as the cop thudded off to the left, heading for the curving railroad-tie stair that led from the overlook to the beach. His knees sent spinning purple and red pinwheels of glowing pain into the night, lighting him up. He froze, suddenly certain that the police would be able to see his every step.

Keep it together. It's just the acid. They can't see you. He was the only one who could see the pain.

He limped to the right, hugging the base of the embankment and heading for cover of the pinewoods on the south edge of the beach. Before he got halfway there, the *basso profundo* rumble of the dirigible's engines fired up, sending throbbing black pulses through his brain. The police blimp was on the move, edging out over the beach. His sheltering shadow began to narrow.

Then there was no more shadow except for the lurching black shape directly below him. The white beam of light smashed down on his shoulders with the weight of a waterfall, slowing him, trying to crush him to his knees.

"Stop or we'll shoot!" a distant voice called, faint and nearly lost under the deep hum of the dirigible's engine.

Allan glanced back the way he had come. The cops had reached the beach and were running toward him, guns out, kicking up the sand with their piggy cloven feet.

There was a loud *crack*, then another. He heard something thump into the sand close to his left.

He picked up his pace, fighting through the pain in his battered knees.

▲

"There's something special about this place," Walter said. "Ever since I was a boy, I always felt this lake was... for lack of a better word, *magical*. That's why I brought you here, Belly. I wanted you to feel it, too."

"I..." Bell said, his forehead creasing. "I do. I feel it."

Walter had been a loner as a kid, singled out as weird and uncool, but not unhappy with his isolation. Social interactions always left him feeling anxious and awkward. He'd never really understood the point of friendship as defined by books and movies, and preferred to spend time alone in the woods or the library. Or here, at Reiden Lake, where his Uncle Henry had a cabin.

When he'd first met Bell, they'd clicked instantly, bonded by their love of organic chemistry, and of chess. But while Walter was grateful for the company, and enjoyed having someone with whom to share his more controversial theories on the use of consciousness-expanding drugs, he never felt like he really understood William.

Bell was charming. He knew what to say to girls and, more importantly, what *not* to say. He knew which tie would go with which shirt. He had a cool car and never got lost. He was Walter's only real friend, but he still seemed kind of like an alien, or a member of a different species.

Until that night.

That night, with their latest psychotropic formula coursing through their brains, Walter felt closer to Bell than he'd ever felt to anyone. Siamese twin close. The Hollywood cliché—of army buddies so tight they would take bullets for each other—suddenly made perfect sense to Walter.

Not only did Walter feel like he finally, truly understood his friend, but in that moment, he also felt completely understood by Bell. A feeling so monumental and unprecedented that it almost brought him to tears. Never once in his twenty-two years of life had he ever felt that level of understanding from another human being.

Not from family. Not from a woman. Not ever.

It was as if their skulls had become transparent, allowing the secret patterns of their thought processes to sync up in a mirrored burst of neurological fireworks. He looked at Bell, and heard that deep, distinctive voice even though his lips weren't moving, except for the slightest hint of a Mona Lisa smile.

Unlike the previous blend, this formula seems to induce a profound empathy, bordering on telepathic.

Still clinging to the rigid guide rails of scientific method, even at the height of his trip, he forced himself to double-check his own slippery perception.

"What did you say?" he asked Bell.

"I said," Bell replied, his lips moving normally, "That unlike the previous blend, this formula seems to induce a profound empathy..." But he didn't finish his sentence. Instead he stared toward the lake, a look of awestruck wonder washing over his face.

Another bullet cracked off of a nearby rock.

"Ten more bodies," Allan called out over his shoulder. "Ten more victims. Kill me now and you'll never find them! Think of their families, never knowing what has become of their loved ones!"

It was a lie, of course. Allan *never* hid his work. But the police were fools, and easily manipulated.

"Sir?"

The voice was questioning, its owner desperate to be told what to do by someone in a position of authority. Hopeless without orders, like they all were.

"Awaiting orders, sir." Another voice, another pig, equally flummoxed. Just like Allan knew they would be.

Pathetic.

"Hold your fire!" This new voice stronger, more cocksure. The boss pig. "Take him alive!"

And then there he was—a fat, pig-snouted silhouette, squealing orders from the cliff top, police lights edging everything with red and blue. Reinforcements had arrived. The bait had been taken.

With the police bullets held momentarily in check, Allan took advantage and broke for the pines at a dead run, keeping to the hard-packed sand and shale near the cliff. Behind him, the cops floundered in the loose sand of the beach, their sty-mates stumbling and squealing as they came stampeding down the steep embankment as if herded by predators.

In twenty strides Allan was under the sheltering shadows of the trees, pushing his way through the scratchy undergrowth. Above, the searchlight shattered into a thousand shining spears stabbing through the interlaced pine boughs like the shafts of light in a religious painting, shining down on the messiah.

He laughed softly to himself. While he was unquestionably superior—even God-like, in his own way—he certainly wasn't on this earth to save anyone. Quite the opposite, in fact.

More like an Angel of Death.

Now that he was out of their line of sight it would be easy to evade the bumbling porkers and return safely home. By the time he reached the southern edge of the woods and returned to his hidden car, he would be nothing but a ghost, vanished into thin air, just like he always did. Laughing and taunting the flat-footed swine from the safety of the ether.

Behind him he heard his pursuers crashing through the undergrowth like the fat hulking beasts they were. But then there came a new volley of animal sounds, agitated barking, growling and baying that crackled like forks of blue lightning across his vision.

He looked back. Hunched and snouty pig shadows lumbered through the trees behind him, swinging flashlights in hoofed hands as they snorted and oinked to one another in their sub-human speech. But running ahead of them was an entirely different pack of animals. Predators, not prey. Allan could see little but the menacing, low-slung shadows with gaping, slathering maws flashing vicious teeth and lolling tongues. But he knew what they were, and that knowledge was like ice water in his belly.

Dogs. He hadn't counted on dogs.

Humans were abysmally stupid, soft, pampered and useless, their ancient instincts atrophied by modern convenience. But hounds, they'd never strayed far from their natural state as hunters, gleefully free from the limitations of morality and civilization. They posed a genuine threat, ugly and amplified to nightmarish proportions by the acid surging though his synapses, and for a terrible moment, Allan found himself nearly paralyzed with fear.

Must think.

Yes, he needed to rely on his superior mental acumen. He might not be strong enough to single-handedly overpower a pack of hunting dogs, but he could easily out-think them.

Water. That was the answer. He could wade into the lake to throw them off the scent.

So he leapt over the mossy hulk of a fallen tree and veered left, heading for the shoreline. The trees and undergrowth grew denser and he had to force his way through. Pine branches and blackberry vines clutched at him like grasping, clawing hands, leaving tingling patterns of sensation on his body that glistened in the corner of his eyes like snail trails.

The trees seemed to be twisting and shifting to block him, deliberately getting in his way, then opening up again behind to let the howling hell hounds through. All of nature was working against him, jealous of his abilities.

Ahead, through the pulsing tree trunks, he saw the glimmer of water.

Almost there.

Without thinking, Walter turned to see what his hallucinating friend was staring at, expecting to see nothing, or some figment of his own chemically enhanced mind.

What he saw was a small slit in the air above the surface of the lake, approximately six feet from where they sat. About twelve inches long, it pulsed with a strange, shimmering glow around the edges. As he watched, the slit elongated and bulged slowly outward, until it was first the size of a child, and then the size of a tall man. It gaped open, disturbingly wound-like, and dark water began to flow through it like blood, creating strange spiral currents in the surface of the lake.

This wasn't unprecedented. He'd seen glimpses of these kind of glowing "wounds" during past experiments. But this time he felt sure that Bell could see it, too.

"Tell me what you see, Belly," he said, whispering without knowing why.

"An opening," Bell said, staring transfixed at the shimmering slit. "Like a kind of... gateway."

"Yes," Walter said. "Yes, that's it exactly." He gripped

Bell's arm. "Do you realize what this means? Our minds have become perfectly synchronized! We are sharing the exact same vision. It's incredible!"

"Incredible," Bell repeated, although it was difficult for Walter to know if he had actually said that out loud, or just thought it.

Bell rose to his feet and waded into the lake, utterly unmindful of his designer trousers and expensive shoes. Walter never let go of his friend's arm, wading in beside him without a moment's hesitation. He barely noticed the chilly water and thick, clinging mud sucking at his own shoes.

"But if it's a gateway," Bell whispered. "What's on the other side?"

3

Allan battled his way through the last rank of trees then caught himself on the edge of the lake, ready to slip silently into the water. But the bank was undercut. It gave way beneath him and he splashed awkwardly into the water in a shower of dirt and rotten leaves.

The dogs bayed louder, frenzied by his closeness.

He cursed. Betrayed again by spiteful nature. Finding his balance, he started right, hunching into the undercut, knee deep in water with his ankles tearing clinging reeds up from the mud with every step.

There was a boat landing just around the next point—nothing more than a dirt road that went into the lake so weekend sailors could back their boat hitches into the water. There were always a few rowboats and canoes tied off or turned upside down and stored to either side of it. With his strength, they would never be able to catch him if he took one.

Behind him, the dogs reached the bank, snuffling and milling around, reluctant to dive in. The squeals and grunts of their pig masters echoed their confusion, and the piercing beams of their flashlights darted everywhere. Except in his direction.

He laughed and, as silently as he could manage, headed for the closest canoe, only a few yards away. It was floating in the high tide, its tether submerged under the lapping waves. He squatted down in the cold water and reached for the knot, fingers groping blind in the weeds and mud until he found it. The wet rope was swollen, the knot slick and tight. Methodically, he went to work, pulling and teasing it apart.

As he did so, a dancing light on the surface of the water around the tether was mesmerizing. It carved swirling arabesque calligraphies into his retina, a cursive cuneiform that seemed almost decipherable, if only he could concentrate on it long enough. It was trying to tell him something—a story of other worlds, of pathways between realities, of an endless, ever-repeating, never-repeating pattern of possibilities. He thought he heard a clear deep voice, speaking directly into the vibrating cortex of his tripping mind.

A profound empathy, bordering on telepathic...

The ripples turned jagged, and began jumping. Baying filled his ears. He looked up to see dogs and grunting, two-legged pigs splashing down from the pine bank and racing toward him as red and blue lights screamed and sirens bounced off the trees along the dirt road that led to the launch.

The water had tricked him! Made him forget the knot. He'd been crouching in the water just staring at the hypnotic patterns.

Enraged, he surged upward, tearing the canoe's iron mooring stake out of the mud, using it to swipe around at the dogs that churned the water around him. But there were too many of them, all around him now. The pigs were among them, grabbing his arms, his shirt, his throat.

A hundred piggy hoof-hands groping him and violating every part of his body as dog teeth tore at his pants and the flesh beneath.

His head was plunged maliciously into the water and then wrenched back out again.

"Cuff him!" This from one of the gleeful pigs. Their laughter and squealing swirled around them like thick, choking smoke from a grease fire.

"Careful!" one pig said. "We wouldn't want him to accidentally drown while resisting arrest, now would we?"

"That would be terrible, wouldn't it?" another replied.

"We have to take him alive!" This from a cop standing on the shore and calling over the shoulders of his more aggressive brethren. "What about the missing bodies?"

"Shut up, Jensen," the first pig snapped.

Again, Allan's head was shoved beneath the surface of the lake. Water filled his nose and throat, and blinded his eyes. The thrashing bites of snarling dogs tore at his wildly flailing limbs, then the bright bite of steel as a handcuff closed around his left wrist.

He lost his grip on the mooring stake and kicked out with a boot heel instead. The response was more piggy squealing, and a lessening of the crushing weight that was holding him down.

Allan fought his way to the surface, retching and gasping and swinging as dogs and pigs fell away all around him.

"Son of a bitch broke my damn kneecap," an injured piggy cried.

"I told you not to…" the other began. Then his voice trailed off. "Wait… what… what the hell is that?"

Allan backed away from them, snarling and tearing at the dangling handcuff. He waited for them to charge again, wary and ready to fight to the death. But they didn't. They were staring at something behind him, their snouted, pig-eyed faces bathed in a pale flickering light.

He looked back over his shoulder. The dented canoe was floating away from him in the knee-deep water, drifting further into the lake, but that wasn't what had caught the eyes of the gaping, awestruck cops.

A strange shimmering fissure hung in the air, just a few feet away, like a rip in the night. As he looked, it seemed to grow. He thought he saw movement within it. He heard voices, whispers.

Was it another hallucination?

No. The pigs were seeing it too. Unless his visions were somehow bleeding into reality? Impossible. But yet...

"What are you waiting for, knucklehead?" one of the pigs bellowed. "Get him!"

Allan turned back around to face his pursuers. The swine and the hounds were coming for him again with renewed fervor. He took a sloshing step backward, instinctively reaching to catch the drifting canoe. His hand passed right through the plane of the shimmer and didn't touch the canoe. Instead he felt a swirl of cooler water and a chilly breeze. Curious, because the air around them had been warm, still, and dead all night.

Then the pigs were reaching out for him. The dogs leapt, snarling and snapping. He had to act, and fast.

Allan threw himself backward, screaming defiance, falling.

The shimmer surrounded him, engulfed him. It's curious, clinging glow filled his eyes, filled his lungs, filled his mind. A sickening disorientation overwhelmed him, obliterating any sense of up or down. All of a sudden, the squealing pigs and snarling dogs looked like salvation to him.

He reached for them, bellowing for them to pull him back, save him from this terrible spinning nothingness. His arms pinwheeled, trying to stop his fall, and then...

Walter and Bell each reached out a hand toward the undulating gateway, doing so at the exact same moment, as if they were two arms attached to one body. The edges of the gateway seemed to respond to them, sending out glistening tendrils in all directions, like the tentacles of a sea anemone.

A millisecond before their fingers touched the strange, shimmering substance of the gateway, a stocky, heavy-set man with a reddish brown crew cut came tumbling backward through the opening. He staggered against Walter and Bell, knocking them back so the three of them fell together, flailing in the shallow water.

A flood of terror and shock raced through Walter, induced by the sudden, inexplicable appearance of this strange man. As quickly as it manifested, it began to dissipate in Walter's racing brain as he registered how utterly ordinary the man really was. This wasn't some kind of trans-dimensional alien or spiritual messenger from a higher plane of existence. It was just a regular, everyday kind of man, about 5'10," thick and barrel-chested. In his late 30s or early 40s. Unremarkable but for his muddy clothes and thick, chunky-framed glasses.

Walter couldn't imagine that an extra-terrestrial being would need glasses. Besides, this man was likely a manifestation of the acid.

He was genuinely amazed that his own mind could create such a realistic, flawlessly rendered vision, down to the slight stubble on the stranger's beefy jowls.

"Belly," Walter said, helping his shivering friend

find his footing in the slippery muck of the lake bed. "Do you see…?"

"Yes," Bell said. Leaning against Walter for footing, he reached out a hand to help the wet stranger. "Who are you?"

Without responding, the stranger looked back over his shoulder at the swiftly shrinking gateway behind him, as if he expected something to follow. He turned again and narrowed his eyes at Bell, his gaze suspicious in the glow of the lantern, before reluctantly accepting Bell's help to get back to his feet.

"Who are *you*?" the stranger echoed. His voice was as mundane as his looks, with just the slightest hint of a New England accent around the "r."

Walter reached out to help steady the disoriented stranger and found a pair of handcuffs dangling from the man's left wrist.

Before he could register the significance of the handcuffs, however, Walter felt the sudden brutal intrusion of a third mind into the warm, empathic connection he'd formed with Bell. The profound telepathic loop between the two friends was wrenched into a shrieking, distorted triangle by what felt less like a human presence than a howling void filled with jittering coded symbols and bitter, black rage.

Then the bottom seemed to drop out of the world, and Walter was suddenly plummeting into that terrible void inside the stranger's mind, like a helpless Alice down a rabbit-hole filled with dark, violent imagery.

He saw page after flapping page of letters, many seemingly written using some kind of complex cipher or code.

He saw a pretty young brunette, no more than sixteen years old, her big blue eyes wild with terror as she ran away from a parked station wagon. She seemed to be reaching out to him, but before she could grasp his outstretched hand, she was gunned down, shot repeatedly in the back.

He saw the stranger pull a squared-off black hood over his head, repositioning his glasses over the roughly cut eye-holes. On his chest was a crossed circle, like the crosshairs of a gun sight. The afternoon sun flashed off a bright edge of a blade that was gripped in his bulky fist.

Walter saw a blood-spattered car door that had been removed from the vehicle to which it had once belonged. On that door, the handwritten words "Vallejo" and "by knife." Then that same crossed circle seemed to burn like an all-seeing eye above a list of dates that twisted away before Walter could read them.

He saw the skyline of an unfamiliar city, a grim pale tower on the top of a hill, like the barrel of a gun pointed at the foggy gray sky, looming over a quaint cluster of homes.

He saw a yellow cab, the friendly, mustachioed driver talking casually over his shoulder to the stranger in the instant before the driver was shot, point blank in the head, his glasses flying off and clattering against the dashboard.

He saw the stranger tear a young blond woman's brightly patterned blouse, his hands crawling with unnatural, flickering sparks that burned the fabric and the flesh beneath, but somehow left him whole and untouched by flame.

The burnt woman's agonized screams followed Walter down deeper into the tunnel of bleeding wounds and charred flesh and anguished mouths until he abruptly hit bottom, a gritty cement floor inside some kind of industrial building. He couldn't see Bell, but he could feel a deep, almost cellular awareness of his friend—close at hand, sharing his vision as he got slowly to his feet.

He was inside what appeared to be a warehouse of some kind. There was a Ridgid Tools calendar on the wall beside him, featuring a photo of a well-endowed blonde with strangely styled hair that looked like wings around her face, and the smallest bikini Walter had ever seen.

The date on the calendar was September 1974. All the days had been crossed out, up to the 21st.

The large, multi-paned window at the far end of the room was mostly blacked out, except for a single missing pane on the bottom left that let in a pale gray wash of daylight. The stranger stood beside the broken pane, the delicate snout of a shouldered rifle poking through the window frame and a mesmerizing dance of sparks swarming over the surface of his hands and forearms.

The stranger didn't seem to notice Walter or the unnatural sparks. He was utterly focused on whatever he had in his sights. Walter walked over to the window and looked out over his shoulder, through the missing pane.

A city bus with a blown tire had pulled up to the curb across the street, in front of a disreputable, shuttered bar with an unlit neon sign that read *Eddie's All Niter*. The narrow rectangular screen above the windshield displayed the number 144 and three letters; PAR. The rest of the letters that would have spelled out the name of the route were missing or broken.

A chubby, anxious man was helping a group of frightened senior citizens off the incapacitated bus. The first one out was a tiny, ancient black woman with a multicolored scarf tied under her chin and thick cat-eye glasses. She had on a red cloth coat and was holding a library book with one gnarled finger stuck in between the pages to hold her place. She was leaning heavily on a chipped wooden cane and looking like she was trying very hard not to cry.

The window Walter was looking through had to be at least three stories up and on the opposite side of the street, yet some how he was able to see every little detail of that woman, with disturbing clarity. Her heavy brown orthopedic shoes and thick, swollen ankles. The title of her book, *The Other Side of Midnight*, and the peeling library sticker scotch-tapped on the spine. A gold toned musical note pinned to the left lapel of her coat. Her handmade canvas totebag with colorful felt letters that spelled out the words:

LINDA'S GRANDMA.

Then it dawned on Walter what was happening.

The stranger had shot the tire. He was going to shoot the woman. And all the other passengers from the bus.

In that instant, Walter couldn't breathe. He felt as if he was underwater, tangled in seaweed and unable to move his cold, sluggish limbs. He was desperate to get to the stranger and knock the rifle out of his sure, steady hands, but even though they were mere inches apart, somehow Walter just couldn't seem to reach. All he could do was watch, helpless as the stranger squeezed the trigger.

On the street below, the old woman seemed to look right at him, her dark eyes silently asking *why*.

Why is this happening?

Then a bullet smashed into her high, round forehead, driving her back in a gaudy spray of blood and shattered bone. Her book flew from her outstretched hands and landed open in the gutter, pages fluttering in a sudden wind.

Then the scene at the warehouse disintegrated into fragile ash, whirling away and leaving Walter floating in a vast abyss of nothingness.

Still he couldn't breathe. Now he was drowning, a crushing weight on his chest as his limbs went numb and useless. Spangles of greenish light swarmed across his vision and he realized that he could no longer feel any attachment to Bell. He was utterly alone in that abyss, heart like a small panicked animal scrabbling to escape from his aching chest.

Bell was lost, gone forever, and Walter was alone.

Alone.

Then he felt a hand on his arm, pulling him roughly upward.

Walter broke the surface of the lake with the desperate gasp of a newborn, hands clutching at Bell's soaking wet shirt.

"God *damn* it, Walter," Bell said. "When you went under... Man, I thought I'd lost you."

He hugged Walter way too hard.

"Where is..." Walter sputtered, pulling back from the embrace, coughing and spitting algae-tainted water out of his burning throat. "...that man...? Was he real?"

"I saw him, too," Bell said. "A truly remarkable shared hallucination, unlike anything I've ever experienced." He slung his arm around Walter's shoulders, helping him to the shore. "But then, out of nowhere, the trip turned dark and heavy, with all these images of blood and murder.

"And then you went down, under the surface of the water. By the time I was able to find you and pull you out, my adrenalin must have burnt off any residual effects of the drug. Right now I feel pretty damn straight." He shook his head. "Too straight. How about you? How do you feel?"

Walter looked around. The lake was quiet, pristine and calm. Their cheerful little Coleman lantern on the shore was burning low, nearly out of fuel. The cooler was still there, too, sitting right beside the lantern, filled with perfectly ordinary soda. No sign of any tiny women. No kind of cosmic gateway, and no one there but him and Bell.

But the gateway, the stranger, and those awful bloody visions. They'd all seemed so real.

"Belly," Walter said. "We are *never* using that formula again."

4

Allan was cold, wet and terrified, and was having an extremely hard time distinguishing reality from hallucination. At first he had imagined that he'd fallen through some kind of gateway into another dimension, but now that he was starting to come down off his trip, the very concept sounded absurd. He found himself in the same old ordinary world.

Same dirt, same trees, same lake.

He took a moment to lean against the rough bark of a massive oak tree and collect his disjointed thoughts. How much of what had happened to him that night was real, and how much was pure hallucination?

Had he imagined the couple in the car? The entire encounter with the cops? There certainly was no sign of them now. No zeppelins overhead, no prowlers on the overlook, no baying dogs. Nothing. Even the crickets had fallen silent.

As much as it humiliated him to picture himself running alone through the woods, striking out against imaginary attackers, he was certainly happy to find himself a free man.

That's when he noticed the handcuffs.

One manacle was clamped tight around his left wrist, and the other dangled, open. The metal was cool to the touch, and as solid as the ground under his feet. He must have had some kind of encounter with the police, at some point during all that madness. He certainly hadn't handcuffed himself.

But where the hell were they now?

And what about those two kids in the water, the ones who seemed to be able to read his mind. He could still see their faces, so vividly—particularly the soft, almost girlish face of the long-haired hippie in the baggy tweed jacket. It was as if the kid had looked right into his brain, and barged his way in to Allan's most treasured fantasies. That sense of unexpected intimacy was more than he could take.

And he could still feel the tactile sensation when he had shoved the kid away, plunging his frizzy-haired head down into the water before bolting for the shore.

But now, he couldn't help but wonder if he'd imagined that, too.

Clearly the only option was to return home and get some sleep. He was chilled and frazzled and running on fumes as he trudged down the long, winding deer path that would take him back to the spot where he'd hidden his car. Tomorrow, he would check the papers and scan the police band, and see if he could piece together what the hell had happened.

His car was gone.

It wasn't just gone, it was as if it had never been there. There were no tire tracks. The place were he had parked was overrun with lanky, fragile white flowers that couldn't possibly have grown up in the time he'd been gone.

Yet there had to be an explanation.

Could he have forgotten where he had left his car?

No, he didn't forget things. And he could never have forgotten something like that. After all, Allan was a meticulous man, who prided himself on the attention he paid to the smallest details. His rigid adherence to each plan was what allowed him the freedom to drop acid in the midst of a murder, because he knew that no matter what happened, he could always count on the careful preparations he'd made while he was sober.

But there was no other place to hide a car on this side of the lake. He hadn't seen it along the side of the deserted road, or at the overlook where he'd first spotted—or thought he spotted—the young couple who turned out to be cops.

No, his car must have been stolen.

The notebook.

His notebook was in the glove box of his car.

He felt a deep throbbing panic rise up in his guts. If his car had been stolen, then the notebook was stolen, too. That notebook was everything to him. It was the place were he gave voice to all his private demons and dark fantasies, and kept a meticulous record of every aspect of each one of his killings.

There was absolutely no way he could be incriminated by the contents of that notebook, because the police were far too intellectually inferior to crack his ingenious private ciphers. But just the thought of a random stranger turning those pages and holding the repository of his most private and sacred thoughts in their grubby little hands—it made him physically ill.

I'm starting to lose it.

Hands trembling, sweating, heart racing. Although he was no longer actively hallucinating, he couldn't shake the feeling that everything around him was *abnormal*.

The acid he'd taken must have been tainted somehow. That was the only logical answer to explain the bizarre, impossible events of the evening. All he could do now was to find a way to get himself home safely, and ride out the rest of this awful trip until the poison had run its course. He could come back out to Reiden Lake and look for his car in the morning.

For now he just needed wheels. Any wheels.

There was one lonely vehicle parked on the side of Lakeshore Drive. It had Massachusetts plates, but looked foreign. The unfamiliar brand name on the bumper, "Chevrolet," sounded French or something. But the design of the car wasn't entirely unlike the kind of standard American muscle cars made by Edsel or Hobart.

But that was irrelevant. What *was* important was that the door wasn't locked, and he found the keys under the driver's side visor, so he didn't have to figure out how to hotwire a foreign car. Lucky for him, everything else about it was relatively normal, though curiously designed.

He redlined it all the way home.

It was nearly dawn by the time he made it to his house in Remsen. He ditched the stolen car several blocks away and walked the remaining distance home, left hand in his pocket to hide the cuffs.

First things first. He went directly in to the garage, planning to remove the handcuffs with a hacksaw. But inside the garage, everything had been rearranged. His tools, which he'd kept for years hanging on a custom built pegboard on the western wall above his workbench, were gone, replaced by floor-to-ceiling shelving full of what looked like gardening supplies. Big dusty sacks of grass seed, fertilizer and vermiculite.

Panic wrestled with confusion. There was no way someone could have broken into his garage, stolen all his tools, and built those shelves in the time he'd been at Reiden Lake. Even if it *were* possible, the shelves looked weathered and ancient, as if they'd been there for decades.

The acid. Clearly the tainted acid was still affecting him, making ordinary things seem strange. He *knew* there was a hacksaw in this garage. There had to be. It was just his mind playing tricks, telling him things were different.

He made himself search slowly and methodically, as if he were sifting through the garage of a stranger. Eventually he found a hacksaw inside a large rusted toolbox, although it was smaller and more narrow than his own. At least that's how it appeared.

He told himself it didn't matter. He had to get the cuffs off, and no amount of residual hallucination was going to stop him. He couldn't seem to find his workbench—or anything even remotely similar—so he just squatted down on the floor and braced his left wrist against the stained concrete.

Once he'd sawed through the single cuff around his wrist, he hid the broken handcuffs inside a half-empty box of Slug and Snail Death, promising himself he'd dispose of them properly later, once he'd gotten some sleep and gotten his head back on straight.

When he took his keys out of his hip pocket and went to let himself into the house, he discovered the door that led from the garage to the kitchen was unlocked.

He never left any door in the house unlocked.

Never.

Inside his house, the feeling of wrongness ratcheted

up even higher. All the furniture seemed different. Strange rugs and tables in unexpected places. Magazines with titles he'd never heard of. Panic set in again, making his heart race, but he squashed it down.

It's not real. None of this is real.

Forcing himself to breathe, he pressed his palms against the wall, holding on like it was the only thing keeping him from flying into a thousand pieces. At least the walls were the same, rooms and hallways unchanged in their layout.

Familiar.

Safe.

Fighting to keep his breath slow and even, he followed the wall to his bedroom door. Grasping the doorknob, he paused, suddenly afraid. Deeply, irrationally afraid of what he would see if he opened that door.

He made himself turn the knob, and eased the door slowly open.

Inside, his dim bedroom looked relatively normal. The bed was in its normal place, though the room was small enough that there was really only one place a bed would fit. It was unmade, and the blanket looked slightly different, but nothing too jarring. His dresser was in its normal place too, though it seemed taller and narrower.

The window was open, allowing a light breeze and a spill of faint lavender twilight into the room. Strange, because he always kept the windows shut at night, but it wasn't impossible that he might have forgotten to close it.

There was something on his bedside table. Something that was also completely normal, yet the sight of it evoked a profound icy dread.

His glasses were on the bedside table.

His hands flew up to his face. No, his glasses weren't on the bedside table, they were on his face, where they belonged. His mind was playing tricks again.

But they looked so real, those glasses. So humble and ordinary and familiar. Nothing trippy or psychedelic about them. They were just his regular glasses, sitting right were he always set them when he went to bed each night.

The toilet flushed in the bathroom down the hall.

There's nothing abnormal about the sound of a toilet flushing either, but Allan couldn't have been more terrified if he'd heard a gunshot.

Someone else was in his house.

The bathroom door opened and a man came out, backlit by the light, face in shadow. He was the same height as Allan, but a little bit paunchier around the middle, dressed only in clean white boxer shorts.

When the man saw Allan, he let out a startled, wordless sound and staggered back, bracing himself against the doorframe.

Allan didn't hesitate. He charged the intruder and wrestled him to the hallway floor. They fell together into the rectangular pool of light emanating from the open bathroom door.

The intruder was *him*.

Only, like everything else in the house, this him-that-wasn't-him was just a little bit off. His hair was a little longer and styled differently. He was maybe ten pounds heavier, and looked soft all over, like he'd never done a hard day's work in his life.

It looked like he had cut himself shaving the day before, leaving a small, healing nick on the right side of his jaw.

"Wh-who are you?" the intruder asked, breathless and stuttering with fear.

Who are you? Just like that kid had asked him back at the lake.

Objective rationality deserted Allan in that moment. Confronted with this impossible doppelganger—who was so like him but yet not quite an exact replica—Allan felt himself finally snap inside. In a strange way, it was almost a relief, not to have to fight against the wrongness anymore. Raw animal instinct took over as he closed his shaking hands around the doppelganger's throat.

As he watched the intruder's face—a face so like his own—flush and distort, eyes bulging and lips twisted into a gasping rictus, he let out an involuntary shriek of horror and fury.

At least he thought it came from him.

He slammed the doppelganger's head against the floor, over and over again, until his arms and shoulders ached from the strain of it. Until the intruder was dead.

Until *he* was dead.

He'd killed himself.

Sobbing now, he struggled to his feet, unhinged by a soul-destroying terror beyond anything he'd ever experienced. He looked down at his own murderous hands and saw that they were crawling with tiny sparks, as if electric insects were crawling beneath the surface of his skin.

The flesh of the intruder's throat was charred black and lit from within by some kind of grotesque and unwholesome glow, like a deep-sea creature or the poisonous numerals on a radio-luminescent watch.

He staggered into the bathroom, slamming and locking the door, as if the other him might spring back to life and attack with renewed fury.

Nothing happened for several minutes. All was silent. The sparks dancing in spirals around his fingertips began to fade, leaving behind perfectly ordinary, unremarkable hands.

Hallucinations. Terrible, terrifying, but still just hallucinations, rapidly fading as his body processed out the toxins.

None of this is real.

Utterly exhausted and unable to keep his body upright for a minute longer, he collapsed first to his knees and then, curling on his side, went fetal on the soft bathroom rug.

He fell almost instantly into a deep dreamless sleep.

5

When Allan woke, stiff and horribly dehydrated on the bathroom floor, it was already nighttime again. The little window above the bathtub was black. He'd slept through the entire day without even realizing it. Clearly his body and brain needed the downtime.

He got cautiously to his feet and leaned heavily on the edge of the sink, turning on the cold water and drinking deeply for several minutes, right from the faucet. He splashed the icy water on his face and neck, running his fingers over his bristly crew-cut hair. All things considered, he didn't feel all that bad. Looking over his blurry and haggard reflection in the mirror, he made himself a promise.

I'm done with acid. Clearly the risks were too great.

Toweling his face dry and stretching his sore muscles, he began to feel in control again. He felt around on the floor until he found his glasses where they had fallen the night before. He stood and wiped the lenses with a fold of his shirt, making a mental list of tasks to triage after whatever mess he must have made the night before.

Once that was done, he'd close up shop as quickly

and efficiently as possible. Clearly, it was time for another move. Rural New York State was no longer viable.

A new state, a fresh start.

New girls. New victims.

He felt almost cheerful, with a spring in his step as he put on his glasses, unlocked the bathroom door and turned the knob.

The door wouldn't open. Something was blocking it from the other side.

He put his shoulder to it, forcing it with all his strength. He could feel the heavy mass on the other side yield to his efforts as it was slowly pushed out of the way. When the door was open about six inches, Allan could see something on the other side.

A pair of naked, hairy legs, tinged a dark bruised blue along the bottom.

The corpse of his murdered doppelganger was still in the hallway. Worse, the doppelganger clearly hadn't been quite dead after all, and had somehow managed to crawl a few feet across the floor before finally expiring against the bathroom door.

It was real. It was all real.

Allan slammed the door again, pressing his back against it and then sliding down to a sitting position. He drew his knees up to his chest as the panic bloomed inside him, threatening to send his sanity spinning away into oblivion.

Now that he had his glasses on, everywhere his eyes went inside the claustrophobic bathroom, he saw things he didn't recognize. Brand names he'd never heard of on the toothpaste and shaving cream. A framed painting of a happy frog holding an umbrella—he never would have chosen that. Even the rug he'd slept on, a garish, burnt orange and olive striped monstrosity that was totally unlike the simple navy blue one he'd chosen for his own bathroom.

He wasn't tripping anymore. He really *was* somewhere else. Somewhere that looked very much like the real world, but was filled with mirrored doubles of everything.

This wasn't his house, it was a double of his house, complete with another him who lived there and chose that god-awful rug and that god-awful frog. He really *had* gone through some kind of gateway the night before.

A gateway to a parallel universe.

It was hard to believe, theoretically impossible, yet there he was.

So he began to gather his thoughts. A lesser mind might have been crushed by this kind of paradox, but Allan was better than that. He had no choice but to take this bizarre new world in stride.

He had to start formulating a plan.

Because there was no doubt in his mind that the corpse on the other side of the door was real. Which meant he needed to get away from the scene of his crime, as quickly as possible.

West. He would go west. Would the cities on the crazy mirror version of the West Coast still be the same as the cities in his old familiar universe?

Only one way to find out.

6

AUGUST, 1969

Allan sat at the cheap, second-hand desk that came with this, the latest of several furnished rooms he'd rented. A forgettable room in a long line of forgettable rooms in forgettable neighborhoods in and around his new hunting ground of San Francisco.

After that strange, twisted nightmare he'd left behind in upstate New York, Allan had adapted quickly and efficiently to this new, slightly different version of the world, settling right back in to his familiar routines. Being mechanically inclined, he'd picked up a variety of odd jobs to pay the meager bills while pursuing his true mission.

The result was that his life was better than ever.

His last escapade had been a little problematic, and the boy had somehow managed to survive the attack, but Allan wasn't worried that he would be identified. After all, he was a ghost in this funhouse mirror world, a man who had never been born. He had nothing to fear.

In retrospect he was starting to think that he might

be getting over the concept of preying on couples. Outgrowing that scenario. He fingered the crude, handmade black hood sitting on the desk beside his gun, thinking of the next murder he had in mind. He'd planned to find a couple enjoying a romantic date in the park, and had no intention of abandoning his plan. But he decided that this would be his last couple, and it would be his finest work yet.

After that, who knew what he would do next?

He found himself suddenly thinking of Betty Lou, the pretty and vivacious teenager that he would forever think of as the Lake Herman girl. He'd tortured and killed several bums and hobos on his journey across the country, but she was his first female victim in this new world. He could still picture the terror in her big blue eyes when she saw her hapless boyfriend shot in the head at point blank range, knowing she would be next.

There was something so special about her, because her death had proven to him that although everything around him was different and strange, some things never changed. The sacred perfection of that moment when a young girl realizes that she is about to die—that never changed.

Maybe he ought to start focusing entirely on single women, he mused. Allowing himself more time with each individual girl, indulging in a more hands-on kind of methodology.

But for the moment, he had other business to attend to. On the desk was a clutter of crumpled papers and an open notebook. There were several different ciphers, and experiments with substitution codes of various kinds. It had been a real chore for Allan to devise a code that would be basic enough for unevolved mongoloids like the police and local newspapermen to solve. And, unsurprisingly, they had failed even then. It had required a pair of clever civilians—a teacher and his wife—to crack it, no matter how elementary it was.

The pigs in this universe were just as stupid as their counterparts in his own world. That didn't surprise him in the slightest.

It was hot and oppressively stuffy in the little room, but he still kept the thick, cigarette-scented drapes tightly shut on the single window. To combat the swelter, he'd discarded his clothing and sat naked on the rickety wooden folding chair. Naked, except for a pair of leather gloves.

He checked and compulsively rechecked a 9 mm semi-automatic pistol, then set it down on the desk and picked up a pen. He turned to a fresh page in the notebook and began to write.

Dear Editor, This is the Zodiac speaking.

7

OCTOBER, 1969

The cabbie was chatty.

Allan didn't mind. He planned to kill the man as soon as he arrived at the Presidio Heights street corner he'd selected as his destination. This had no effect on his willingness to engage in casual, friendly dialog along the way. It was actually somewhat enjoyable. Freeing, almost, because he knew that any memory of this conversation would soon be decorating the taxi's dashboard, along with the rest of the cabbie's brain.

"Tell me," Allan said, "do you believe in alternate realities?" He closed a gloved hand around the grip of the 9 mm pistol in his jacket pocket.

"Say what?" The cabbie pulled up to a red light, signaling a left turn.

"Other universes," Allan said. "Universes, not unlike this one, but just a little bit different."

"You mean like a place where I'm four inches taller, four inches longer and married to Jane Fonda?" The cabbie let out a husky, sandpaper laugh. "Sign me up!"

Allan persisted.

"Do you believe it's possible, through the use of mind-altering chemicals, to open doorways and travel from one universe to the other?"

"Say, you don't look like one of them hippies," the cabbie said. "But you sure sound like one."

"Surely you're familiar with Schrodinger's cat?"

"Whose cat?" The cabbie shrugged and made the turn. "I got a pet cat myself. Cute little Siamese. I guess you could say I'm more of a cat person than a dog person."

"It's a theory," Allan continued, ignoring the digression. "A kind of paradox. It posits that if you were to put a cat in a box containing an automated mechanism that had a fifty-fifty chance of releasing a poison and killing it, the cat would be simultaneously alive and dead inside the box until you open it and observe the outcome. At that point, your perception would lock it down into one state or the other, but until that solidifying moment of observation, the cat would exist in two universes at once."

"Jeez, that's terrible," the cabbie said. "Who would do something like that to a poor little cat?"

"Don't you see?" Allan said, looking out the window at the passing houses. Nice, upscale houses, lights on to chase away the night. "I'm like that paradoxical cat. A creature of two worlds, alive and dead at the same time."

"Whatever you say, mister."

Allan could see that the cabbie was becoming uncomfortable with their conversation. His shoulders hunched down, eyes locked on the road. Allan was about to try another, more mundane conversational gambit when he realized that they were arriving at their destination.

"Just a little farther down," he told the driver. "There, at the corner of Cherry."

"You got it."

The cabbie pulled over.

"Do me a favor, would you?" Allan said, gripping the gun a little too tightly. "Put the car in park."

"Sure." The cabbie shrugged and did what was asked. "But what for?"

Pressing the barrel close, Allan shot the cabbie in the back of the head.

He pocketed the gun and got out of the back of the vehicle, casting a quick glance around him. The quiet, classy street was deserted. Only just before 10 p.m. and all the little human animals were already tucked into their upscale beds. Allan felt fine. Calm and warm inside, as if he'd just taken a slug of good whiskey.

He swiftly pulled the front passenger side door open and got in. He dragged the lifeless cabbie across the seat by his bloody shirtfront until the corpse slumped across his lap. He took the man's wallet and keys and then, using a small folding utility knife, he cut a large square of fabric out of the back of the cabbie's striped shirt.

Then, as he was holding that blood-stained trophy in his gloved hand, it started to happen.

The hot, unbearable itch in his hands, burning between his fingers. Like insects crawling under his skin.

Maddened by the sensation, he dropped the swatch, stripped the smoking gloves off his hands and threw them away, into the back seat, sure they were about to burst into flame. Once his hands were bare, he saw to his horror that the sparks were back. Just like that terrible night back in New York.

Just like every time since then. No matter how he tried to deny it. But this time it was more intense than ever.

He made himself breathe deeply, struggling to remain calm. Nothing was on fire. Nothing was hot or burnt. He would be able to control it this time. With each breath, the terrible sparks faded, their strange energy dissipating until they were gone.

He reached down and plucked his trophy off the floor of the cab, tucking the bloody fabric into his jacket pocket. He was about to push the dead cabbie back over to the driver's side and exit the cab, and he actually had his right hand on the door when he suddenly realized the implication of having taken off his gloves.

Fingerprints. He'd left fingerprints.

It was too late just to get the gloves out of the back seat and put them back on. It'd be like closing the barn door after the horses were out, anyway. No, the only option was to wipe down the surfaces of the cab as best he could.

He took out his handkerchief and wiped down the dashboard, the seat, and the interior of the door. Then he got out and wiped first the outside of the passenger door and then the driver's door. He was fairly certain he hadn't touched the driver's door, but he couldn't be too careful.

He heard sirens in the distance. Growing closer.

Time to go.

He walked away, heading north on Cherry Street. When he made a right on Jackson, he spotted a police prowler driving slowly toward him.

His heart stopped, then revved like a race car. His throat constricted, suddenly dry and parched. The sparks flared in his hands, and he shoved them deep into the pockets of his slouchy blue jacket, terrified that the pigs would see the glow.

One of them turned toward him, looking right at him. Allan wrapped his fingers around his pistol. There was no way he was going to surrender without a fight.

The cop turned away, and the prowler continued down Jackson without slowing.

He felt a surge of elation so powerful it was almost sexual. He'd beaten them again. He imagined the young pig being forced to explain that he'd seen the legendary Zodiac Killer in the flesh, but hadn't bothered to stop him. A small, private smile played over his lips as he turned on Maple and headed north, into the Presidio.

PART TWO

1

SEPTEMBER 20, 1974

Walter stood alone beside a small, cheaply produced poster for the paper he and Bell had just presented—*Use of Fluorescent Probes to Investigate Hepatic Microsomal 'Drug'-Binding Sites.*

The paper had been very well received, although he couldn't help but notice that more than half the audience was female. Striking odds when contrasted against the fact that the attendance for the annual conference of the American Biochemical Society tended to be more than 75 percent male.

But Walter was an enthusiastic supporter of women's lib and was pleased to see so many vigorous and inquisitive female minds seeking to embrace and decode the intricacies of the natural world. He stood by, ready, willing and able to discuss the finer details of sigmoidal reaction velocity with any one of these eager young scholars.

Yet for some reason, they all ignored him and clustered around Bell.

Maybe Bell was right about Walter's jacket. He had only one jacket, which he had worn every day for ten years. It had originally belonged to his father, a tweed Norfolk that had a few moth holes and was a little frayed around the cuffs, but was still perfectly serviceable. It had deep pockets that could hold up to a dozen rolls of Necco wafers, as well as his notebook and several spare pens. He seemed to lose pens like a shark loses teeth.

Yet Bell had repeatedly threatened to throw that jacket away or set it on fire while Walter was sleeping. He had even gone so far as to buy his friend a new jacket, a snazzy plaid double-knit sport coat like the ones that Bell favored, but the pockets on the outside were fake, sewn shut and just for show, and the one inner pocket could barely hold two rolls of Necco wafers and a single pen. So that jacket stayed in his closet back at MIT, and Walter had worn the Norfolk jacket again to U. C. Berkeley, just like last year.

And none of the women wanted to talk to him, just like last year.

Bell, on the other hand, was holding court in the center of a crowd of enraptured females. Bell, with his sharp sport coat and rust-colored turtleneck and charming smile. The scientist in Walter liked to believe that he could replicate the results by duplicating the methods, but in his heart he knew there was something about Bell that couldn't be duplicated.

Off to the left, he noticed an older, slightly mannish woman and her chubby friend deep in conversation. They were the only two females who seemed unaffected by Bell's charisma, and Walter found himself eavesdropping on them.

"Can you believe he's back?" the older one was saying, pointing to an article in a folded newspaper. "I swear I was just starting to feel safe at night."

"But how can they be sure the new letters are from the same guy?"

"They used handwriting analysis. It's him, alright. I wonder if the killings are going to start back up again."

"Jesus," the older woman said. "I took a cab to work for two years after I saw that letter where he threatened to shoot senior citizens on a city bus."

Walter's blood suddenly felt like liquid nitrogen in his veins.

"Excuse me," he said, stepping closer to the two women. "I'm sorry, I couldn't help but overhear. What were you saying about a letter threatening to shoot people on a city bus?"

"It's the Zodiac Killer, man," the chubby woman said. "Don't you read the papers?"

"I'm…" Walter's throat was so dry he could barely form words. "I'm from the east coast. I guess I don't really keep up on national news."

"Well," the chubby woman said, warming to the topic. "This psycho killer was running around murdering people about four or five years back. He sent letters to the paper and used this… what did they call it? Like a code."

"A cipher," the mannish woman said.

Nausea bloomed and twisted in Walter's gut.

"But the bus…?"

"He said he was gonna shoot senior citizens on a city bus, wrote it in one of his letters," the mannish woman replied. "What was that, '69?"

"October, '69," the chubby woman said, shivering slightly and wrapping her thick arms around her body. "I remember it like it was yesterday."

"But he never followed through," the mannish woman said. "Not yet anyway. Here, look."

She handed him the paper.

He looked down at the article, but the headline and the text below never registered. All he saw was a crude police sketch of the suspect. A sketch he recognized instantly.

It was the man at Reiden Lake.

A wave of dizziness swept over him, and he braced himself against the wall.

"Hey, are you okay?" the chubby woman asked, although her voice sounded as if it was at the far end of a long tunnel.

Walter nodded absently, then stumbled away from the two women, clutching the newspaper in sweating hands, a terrible memory seared into his reeling mind.

A Ridgid Tool calendar on a warehouse wall.

A girl in a bikini.

The date, September 21, 1974.

Today is September 20th.

Walter bulldozed his way through the crowd of female admirers around Bell and gripped his friend's arm.

"Hey, watch it," a tall brunette with glasses said.

"Jerk," spat another, shorter brunette.

"Belly," Walter hissed. "We need to talk."

"You're like a cold shower, Walt," Bell said. "You know that?"

Bell extracted his arm from his friend's desperate grip and dug in his heels, refusing to go any further.

"So what is it?" Bell demanded. "What the hell is so important that…"

"The man we saw at Reiden Lake," Walter said breathlessly, "the one who came through the gate. It wasn't a hallucination. He's real."

"Are you having some kind of flashback?" Bell gripped Walter's chin. "Let me see your pupils."

Walter shrugged him off and thrust the crumpled newspaper into Bell's hand.

"Look at this!"

Bell rolled his eyes and looked down at the paper with a skeptically arched brow.

When he saw the police sketch, all the color drained from his face.

"I guess you could say there are… similarities in certain features," he said.

"Similarities? It's him, Belly. You know it's him."

Bell looked up at Walter, his expression grave.

"If he is real," he said, "then what *is* he? He seemed… so human."

"Human, yes," Walter replied. "But… different in some way."

"In what way?" Bell asked.

"I remember that strange glow," Walter said. "Like sparks in the palms of his hands. Almost as if there was some kind of unknown process disrupting the very atoms of his flesh."

"Maybe he's a time traveler from a future that's been poisoned by atomic warfare," Bell suggested.

Without skipping a beat, Walter responded.

"Or perhaps some kind of pan-dimensional being who only adopts a human form in order to facilitate contact with the people of Earth," Walter said. "Maybe that glow is his true form showing through the artificial skin."

Bell tapped the article.

"But why would a pan-dimensional being want to shoot people with a normal gun?"

"It's so much worse than that," Walter replied. "This man publicly threatened to shoot senior citizens on a city bus. Just like in our vision. He hasn't made good on that threat yet, but in the vision, the bus shooting took place on September 21st, 1974." He paused, gripping Bell's sleeve. "Belly, that's tomorrow!"

"My God," Bell said, looking disoriented. "What are we going to do?"

"That's obvious," Walter replied. "We have to find a way to stop him."

2

The Doe library at U.C. Berkley was the kind of place where Walter could happily spend the rest of his life, under different, more peaceful circumstances. Built in the early nineteen hundreds, it was a large, stately building fronted by classic Doric columns and decorated with richly patinated copper trim. Several large rectangular skylights were embedded in the red tiled roof.

Walter took the stone steps two at a time, huffing and breathless as he pushed through the door. Bell was close behind.

Inside it was tranquil and beautiful. He was immediately attracted to a large, airy room with a curved, tiled ceiling and large arched windows. Leaded glass skylights filled the chamber with gentle natural light and each of the dozens of sturdy wooden tables had its own wrought-iron reading light. Tall shelves packed with colorful volumes lined the walls, beckoning Walter with their intriguing titles and vast cornucopia of knowledge. The smell of foxed paper and wood polish was seductive, and made him wish he was there for any other reason.

The librarian at the main desk was one of the tallest

women he had ever met, a little over six feet and standing eye to eye with Bell in her flat, sensible shoes. She was in her late fifties, with a stiffly lacquered poodle haircut that likely hadn't changed in twenty years. On the left lapel of her modestly cut blouse she wore a red Bakelite brooch in the shape of a key, and a name badge on the right that labeled her as Mrs. Alder.

Her face was wide and plain, but her green eyes sparkled with intelligence and wit.

"How can I help you gentlemen?" she asked.

"We're looking for information on the so-called Zodiac Killer," Walter told her.

"Ah, yes," she said with a knowing nod. "Popular topic these days." She indicated a stairwell off to the right. "Newspaper archive is in the basement, at the end of the hallway on the left."

"Thank you," Walter said.

"Do you think they'll ever catch him?" she asked.

Walter and Bell exchanged a look.

"Good God, I hope so," Walter replied.

The newspaper archive boasted a lot of carefully preserved newspapers, but it was primarily devoted to floor-to-ceiling shelves of microfilm. Where the upper areas of the library were quaint and old-fashioned, evoking images of turn of the century scholars in waistcoats and wire-rim glasses, the archive room was sleek and ultra modern, coldly illuminated by recessed fluorescent lights and outfitted with cutting-edge technology.

There were six brand-new microfilm readers, two of which already were taken by students. One was female, blond and wan with very pale skin and an underfed physique beneath her bulky striped sweater. The other was male, black and prematurely balding with glasses and a leather jacket. Both were so engrossed in their own research that they didn't even look up when Walter and Bell walked into the room.

The librarian in charge of the archives was a man, just a little bit older than Walter, with bushy sideburns and frizzy hair bullied into an ill-advised Afro. He wore a baggy green suit and a joke tie featuring monkeys with typewriters. His name badge read "Mr. Sternberg."

"How you doing?" he asked, revealing a hard New York accent. "What can I do for you?"

"Fine, thank you," Walter replied. "We are looking for information on the Zodiac murders."

"Man," he said. "You're lucky that Graysmith guy's not here today. He's in here all the time, pulling every single thing we have on the Zodiac and going over it with a fine-toothed comb." He turned around and grabbed a large cardboard box from a metal library cart behind his desk, setting it in front of Walter and Bell. "You're also lucky that I'm a lazy bastard and haven't re-shelved all his microfilms since his last visit. This is pretty much everything. Enjoy."

Walter couldn't imagine that he would "enjoy" reading up on the murders that had been committed by the man from Reiden Lake, but he made himself smile and thank the librarian. Bell grabbed the box and headed over to the closest available reader.

He set the box on a nearby table, sat down, and sorted through the microfilm reels to find the one labeled with the earliest date.

"December, 1968," Bell said, opening the cardboard box and holding up the reel. "Why, that's just two months after…"

His voice trailed off, and he looked around at the other people in the archives.

Walter nodded, understanding Bell's unfinished point. He held out his hand for the microfilm, and Bell handed it over. Walter pulled up an extra chair for himself.

He threaded the microfilm into the reader with a sense of dread, simultaneously wanting and not wanting to know the awful truth.

The two of them spent nearly three hours glued to the reader, studying article after horrifying article of the torture and mayhem caused by the man from Reiden Lake.

It began with a young couple at Lake Herman, in Vallejo. The boy was seventeen, the girl only sixteen, and the pair had been parked in the Lover's Lane area near the lake when they had been approached by a man with a 22. caliber semi-automatic pistol. According to the police report, their killer shot the boy first, point blank in the head, then shot his terrified girlfriend five times in the back.

Worse, Walter instantly recognized the pretty blue-eyed brunette from his vision at Reiden Lake. He'd seen her death, exactly as it happened two months before it occurred!

The next two unsuspecting teens were shot in a Lover's Lane area, as well, this time at Blue Rock Springs, also near Vallejo. Only this time, the boy actually survived the brutal attack, describing the killer exactly the way Walter remembered him.

The police had received a phone call from a man claiming responsibility for the shootings, describing details of the crime that could only have been known by the killer. That caller also took credit for the previous shootings, and the police knew they had a serial killer on their hands.

The third attack, at Lake Berryessa near Napa, was by far the most bizarre and frightening. A young couple were approached by a man wearing a black hood, with a white crossed circle painted on a flap of fabric that hung down over his chest. After some surreal conversation, the man tied the couple up and started stabbing them repeatedly. When he was finished, he just walked away, leaving them bound and bleeding. After being discovered by a local fisherman, both victims were rushed to the hospital. The young woman didn't make it, but her boyfriend survived the attack to relate all the horrifying details to the press.

Again the killer made another call to police, as well as leaving a written message on the victims' car door, listing the dates of previous murders. It was signed with the same crossed circle symbol.

Walter was appalled to find so many details that he remembered from his vision. The more he read, the more he started to feel punch drunk and overwhelmed.

The last case that was confirmed as a Zodiac murder was the shooting of a cab driver in the city, in an upscale neighborhood known as Presidio Heights. Another grimly familiar story. Walter was starting to wish he'd never found out about the killings.

Having gone through the details of all the murders, Walter and Bell began to examine the letters and ciphers that the killer had sent to various newspapers in the area, including the letter in which he threatened to shoot school children on a bus.

The more they read, the more a dull, drowning sense of hopelessness began to wash over Walter.

"What have we done?" he asked Bell.

"I think a more important question," Bell replied, "would be, what are we going to do about it?"

3

Walter paced up and down the length of the Howard Johnson hotel room he'd shared with Bell for the conference. They had spent nearly the entire day in the newspaper archive, digging up every single scrap of information they could find on the Zodiac Killer.

More and more, Walter was haunted by the faces of the victims. The teenage girl at Lake Herman. The cab driver with the mustache. But the one face he just couldn't get out of his mind was the face of that old black woman in the red coat.

LINDA'S GRANDMA.

On the scratchy bedcover beside him was a copy he'd had printed out of one of the Zodiac letters. His eye kept coming back again and again to the bottom of the page.

Senior citizens make great targets. Okay, I think I shall wipe out a city bus some morning, just shoot out the front tire + then pick off the grannies as they come bouncing out.

"We have to contact the authorities," Walter said. "I just don't see any other option."

"That's brilliant, Walt," Bell replied. "What are you going to do? Tell the police that you saw the future while you were on acid? That'll go over well—I'm sure they'll leap into action."

"I'm going to tell them the truth, Belly." He picked up the receiver of the bedside telephone. "I have a moral obligation, as a scientist."

"Would you just stop and think for a moment…" Bell began.

Walter ignored him, dialing the operator.

"Yes, hello," he said when she came on the line. "Give me the San Francisco police department."

"Just a moment," she replied.

"Come on, Walter…"

A gruff male voice answered on the first ring.

"SFPD," it said.

"I'd like to speak to someone in charge of the Zodiac case, please."

A long, weighty sigh on the other end, then, "Please hold."

Bell looked away, exasperated, and started studying a Xerox copy of one of the ciphers.

Walter waited patiently until a woman came on the line. She had a gentle voice, like someone's mother.

"Hello and thanks for calling the Zodiac tip line," she said. "Please state your information."

"Yes, I…" Walter looked over at Bell, who was deliberately ignoring him. "I need to speak to someone in charge of the case. It's extremely urgent."

"I'm sure it is, sir, and if you'd go ahead and let me know why you're calling, I'd be happy to pass your information on to the detectives, right away."

"But…" Bell was still ignoring him. "Well… This is probably going to sound pretty out there."

"Go ahead, honey," the woman said. "It can't be more out there that half the cranks I hear from every day."

"I'm a scientist," Walter said. "Specializing in biochemical processes within the human brain. I believe I may be responsible for bringing the man you've been calling the Zodiac into our world."

A moment of silence on the line, then, "I'm listening."

Walter told her everything about the trip, the gateway, and the vision he'd shared with the strange man. When he was done, he felt exhilarated—and a little bit sick to his stomach. He hadn't realized how it had been eating away at him, keeping that awful vision bottled up inside him for so many years. It felt like such a tremendous relief to let it all go, and put the burden of responsibility in the capable hands of trained law enforcement professionals.

"So what you're saying is that the Zodiac Killer is a radioactive alien from another dimension?" the woman said slowly.

"Well, not exactly…" Walter frowned and switched the receiver from his left ear to his right. "I mean, there's really no way of knowing precisely where he's from until he can be captured and questioned, but that's hardly the issue. I think it's infinitely more important that he be stopped from killing those people tomorrow. Naturally, I'm happy to work closely with the detectives in order to deduce the location of the shooting, but time is of the essence. It's imperative that investigation begin immediately."

"Thank you very much for your interest in this case," the woman said, her tone rote and dismissive now. "I've recorded your information exactly as given, and will pass it on to the detectives as soon as they come back on shift tomorrow night."

"Tomorrow night?" Walter said. "But that will be too late!"

"Hello?"

He was talking to a dead line.

"So," Bell said, without looking up from the cipher. "When does the cavalry arrive?"

Walter slammed the receiver back into the cradle.

4

Walter lay on his back, staring balefully at the ceiling. Several hours had passed, and they were no closer to devising a plan than they had been when Walter had first shown the article to Bell.

Clearly, there would be no help from the police.

"We did this, Belly, can't you see that?" Frustrated, he ran a hand over his eyes. "It's up to us to save that poor old woman."

"But how?" his friend replied. "We have no concrete data."

Any answer Walter might have come up with vanished with a sharp rapping on the hotel room door.

Walter got his bare feet under him and walked over to the door, leaning against it and opening it as much as the security chain would allow. Peering through the gap, he saw two men wearing identical suits and serious expressions. The man closest to the door was a grim, gray, older man. Gray hair, gray eyes, and gray skin. His companion was younger, with slick, black hair like patent leather, and pale blue eyes magnified by thick-lensed glasses.

"Walter Bishop?" the gray man said.

"Yes." Walter, looked back over his shoulder at Bell. "Can I help you?"

The gray man held up a photo ID inside a slim leather wallet.

"FBI," he said. "Please get dressed. We'll need you to come with us."

"Belly," Walter called back over his shoulder. "There are men here from the FBI."

"William Bell?" the gray man said, leaning into the crack in the door. "We need to talk to you, as well."

Bell was on his feet in a heartbeat, eyes wide with alarm.

"What the hell is going on?" he asked.

"I don't know," Walter said, struggling to get his sockless feet into his shoes without toppling over. "But we'd better do what they say."

"Let's go, gentlemen," the gray man said. "*Chop chop*."

"I don't like this," Bell said. "Why are they here?"

"This must be about the Zodiac," Walter stage whispered to Bell, slipping the chain off the door and opening it all the way. "Is that what this is? The Zodiac Killer?"

"Sir," the gray man replied, "I'm not currently at liberty to discuss the details of why we're here. Please come with us."

Walter looked back at Bell, suddenly anxious and unsure. Only minutes ago, he'd been longing for someone in a position of authority—someone who would step in and take this whole awful mess out of their hands. Now he was afraid.

It wasn't as if there was any other option, but for some reason he felt certain that going with these men was a terrible idea.

Bell stepped up beside him and slung his arm around Walter's shoulders.

"Don't tell them anything, Walt," he whispered between clenched teeth. "Not a goddamn thing."

The FBI men led them to an unmarked black car waiting in a no-parking zone. They were placed in the back seat, and it wasn't until the doors were closed that Walter noticed there were no handles on the inside.

"Not a goddamn thing," Bell repeated.

Walter nodded, hands twisting anxiously in his lap.

He wasn't familiar enough with the Bay Area to have any idea where they were being taken. Since they hadn't crossed a bridge, he assumed they were still on the Berkeley side of the bay. They drove along several different, unremarkable streets through forgettable neighborhoods, and then down into the underground garage of a bland, beige office building with no visible sign or company name.

Walter's anxiety ratcheted up a notch as they pulled up beside a bank of elevators. The man with the shiny black hair stayed in the car while the gray man got out to meet two more men—presumably agents—who were waiting by the elevator. Both of them looked like they had been grown in the same cloning vat as the gray man. Same conservative, dated haircuts, and same colorless, lifeless complexions.

They looked like men who spent way too much time under florescent lighting.

"Which one is Bishop?" one of the new agents asked the gray man, as if Walter wasn't standing right there. Like he was livestock, incapable of speech.

"I'm Walter Bishop," Walter said, indignant. "What

is this about? I know my rights!"

"You'll be fully briefed in due time, Mr. Bishop," the gray man said.

"Listen," Bell said, placing himself protectively between Walter and the stone-faced agents. "My friend, he's a little bit... eccentric." Bell touched his temple. "Reads too much science fiction. He gets... weird ideas sometimes, but it's nothing serious. Really, he's harmless."

"We'll be the judge of that, Mr. Bell," the gray man said.

"No, really," Bell persisted, gripping Walter's arm and looking into his eyes like he was trying to tell him something other than what he was actually saying. "He's crazy, get it? Crazy."

Walter got it.

The elevator door opened and the two new agents each took one of Walter's elbows, escorting him with gentle but implacable force. The gray man stepped in front of Bell, preventing him from entering the elevator with his friend.

"Hey, wait a minute—" Bell was saying, but it was too late.

The elevator doors closed, and Walter was alone with the two agents.

His mind was racing, wondering where he was being taken, and what was happening to Bell. He thought about what Belly had said, telling him to act like he was crazy. But why?

Bell harbored a powerful but understandable distrust of police and government agents. He had watched friends and fellow students being tear gassed and arrested for protesting the war in Vietnam. But perhaps these agents were the people in charge of the Zodiac case, and they wanted Walter's help.

Maybe they would be able to help stop the bus killing.

The elevator doors opened, revealing a long, institutional green hallway. A short, chubby man in a lab coat poked a Geiger counter at him before he was allowed to exit the elevator.

"What is the meaning of this?" Walter asked. "I'm not radioactive!"

"Just a precaution, sir," the man in the lab coat said. "Right this way, please."

He was led down a hallway, then another, through several turns and into a small, windowless room, empty except for a metal desk, two folding chairs, and a boxy camera bolted above the door. The agents withdrew, leaving him alone.

Walter sat in that room for what felt like an eternity, giving him plenty of time alone with his thoughts. Every second that passed brought September 21st closer and closer. He kept on seeing that old woman in the red coat, looking up at him with that terrible questioning look in the endless second before she was gunned down in the street.

He tried to distract himself with a mind game, in which he was working his way through the periodic table, seeing how many different words he could make by rearranging the letters that spelled each element. He was up to selenium, which was a great word with plenty of vowels and nice common consonants, but he couldn't stay focused. His mind kept returning to that awful vision over and over, like a scab he couldn't stop picking.

He checked his watch, then checked it again.

The passing minutes felt like a slow torture. Each minute gone left them less time to find and stop the killer.

Finally, after what he estimated to be nearly three hours, someone came in to talk to Walter.

Where the previous men had been grim, gray and serious, this guy was tan, hearty, and way too friendly, with twinkly blue eyes and a big, rubbery smile like a used car salesman.

"How you doing, Walt?" he said. "You don't mind if I call you Walt, do you?" He didn't wait for an answer. "My name is Special Agent Dick Latimer." He gripped Walter's hand and pumped it exactly three times, then took a seat in the empty chair. "I understand you have some information that you think will help us with the Zodiac murders. Is that right?"

"Um…" Walter pressed his lips together. "I… well…"

"Why don't you just start by telling me what you told Mrs. Berman on the tip line." Latimer leaned forward, predatory smile still at full volume.

Walter was torn, unsure. He still wanted desperately for someone in a position of authority to step in and take care of this terrible situation, but there was something about this guy Latimer that he just didn't trust. He wished that Bell was with him. Belly would know what to say. He always knew what to say.

And what not to say.

"I don't recall exactly," Walter said. He had hoped to sound confident, but his voice felt constricted in this throat.

Latimer's thousand-watt smile dimmed for a heartbeat, and his blue eyes went cold.

"Come on now, Walt," he said. "This is no time for games. You told Mrs. Berman that you had urgent information for us. Something to do with…" He leaned in even closer, so close Walter would have scooted his chair defensively back if it hadn't already been pressed against the wall. "Radioactivity?"

"I did, didn't I…" Walter paused, looking down. Then he looked up again. "Would you happen to have any grape Nehi?"

"I'm afraid not," Latimer replied. "But there's a soda

machine down the hall. I'd be happy to get you a 7 Up or something, as soon as you explain exactly what you meant by the suggestion that the suspect has been giving off an unknown type of radiation."

"I'm afraid it has to be grape Nehi," Walter answered. "Only grape Nehi contains the precise balance between citric and phosphoric acid to adequately protect us from the cosmic radiation from the future."

Latimer narrowed his eyes.

"I'm sorry," he said. "I'm afraid I don't follow you."

"Don't you watch *The Outer Limits*?" Walter asked. "It's just like 'Demon With a Glass Hand,' only this guy has a radioactive hand. He's a soldier from the future, like Robert Culp. I'm from the future, too. That's how I know." He reached into his jacket pocket and pulled out a roll of Necco wafers, offering one to the increasingly annoyed Latimer. "Candy?"

"Look, Walt, why don't you just take it easy and try to stay focused."

"I was hoping to get boysenberry pancakes at the Howard Johnson's, but they only had blueberry," he said earnestly. "Do you suppose that's some kind of regional thing? When I was a kid, my mother used to make the best boysenberry pancakes. The trick is to coat the berries in powdered sugar before you add them to the batter. Of course, you can substitute lingonberries, but I'd increase the amount of sugar to compensate for the radiation.

"Have you ever been to Vienna?"

Latimer stood up, metal chair scraping loudly against the linoleum floor.

"Enough," he said.

"Enough?" Walter asked, on a roll now. "That's a pretty subjective concept, enough. It's really relative to how much you already have, and how much more you imagine you might want. It's not a good solid concept like, for example, a number. Let's say, for the sake of argument, that you have three of something. Like three rolls of Necco wafers. You might think three is enough, while someone else could reasonably argue that three is too many. I, on the other hand, may believe that three is not anywhere near enough. And although we are each right in our own minds, none of us is right in the minds of the other two. Therefore, we are all both right and wrong at the same time.

"Are you familiar with quantum physics?"

"Jesus," Latimer said, reaching out to press a button Walter hadn't noticed on the underside of the table. The two stone-faced agents reappeared in the doorway. "Get this crackpot out of here, will you?" Latimer instructed.

"It was a pleasure meeting you, Dick," Walter said over his shoulder as the two agents hustled him out the door. "I hope you'll visit me in the future. I think you would really enjoy the year 1999."

His last glimpse of Latimer as the door closed behind him was of the big man wiping his hand over his face like an exasperated teacher. Walter really hoped he'd done the right thing.

5

The unmarked car dumped Walter and Bell on a nondescript street corner, just a few blocks from some kind of highway. It was getting dark, and few of the streetlights seemed to be operational. There was a damp chilliness in the air. The buildings all around them were a mix of industrial and office buildings, currently vacant or closed.

"You can't just leave us here…" Walter began.

But they did, pulling away the second the door was closed.

"Where the hell are we?" Bell asked.

Walter pointed out a disreputable looking gas station, barely visible on the other side of the street about five blocks down.

"Maybe we can get a map at that gas station."

"Is it even open?" Bell responded.

"Look, there's a phone booth."

Bell patted his pockets for change.

"I think I know someone who can come pick us up."

"Someone with two X chromosomes, I presume."

Bell didn't answer, but he didn't have to.

He pushed in the folding door on the phone booth, kicking aside a slew of crushed beer cans and urine-soaked newspaper in order to enter.

"Hold that door open, Walt," he said, lifting the grimy receiver as if it might bite him. "I don't want to asphyxiate from the ammonia fumes in this toilet."

Walter put his foot against the folding door while Bell held the receiver to his ear, joggling the cradle.

"Nothing," he said.

An olive green '69 Oldsmobile Cutlass pulled up alongside the phone booth. In the driver's seat was a man with unfashionable glasses and thinning light brown hair. His slim build and ill-fitting suit made him seem younger than Walter, like a kid playing dress-up in his dad's clothes, but there was something in his haggard face that aged him twenty years. Behind the magnifying lenses of those glasses, his watery blue eyes were sleepless and haunted.

"Get in," he said, reaching across the seat to open the passenger door.

"What?" Bell dropped the useless receiver and stepped out of the phone booth, hand protectively across Walter's chest. "Who the hell are you?"

"Special Agent Jack Iverson. You want to know what's really going on with the Zodiac Killer, you'd better come with me."

Bell looked over at his friend, brow arched. Walter could see he was skeptical, but Walter was dying for some answers. And there was something about this man's tortured gaze that drew him in. Where Latimer had seemed smarmy and insincere, this guy seemed to be raw and wide open.

He cast one more look back at Bell, then got into the passenger seat of the Cutlass.

"Come on, Belly," he said.

Exasperated, his friend got into the back seat.

"Just make room for yourself back there," Iverson said over his shoulder. "This car has become kind of like a second office, since I've been out on medical leave from the Bureau."

As soon as Bell closed the back door, Iverson peeled out, anxious gaze obsessively scanning the empty street.

"Medical leave?" Walter asked, peering into the back seat at all the crooked stacks of files and fast-food wrappers.

"You can't be too careful," he said. "I've been followed."

Walter was starting to wonder if getting into the car had been a bad idea. But if there was something more going on than what had been made available to the public, then Walter needed to know.

"We can't go back to my place," Iverson said, pulling into the empty parking lot of a closed carpet and flooring company. "So this will have to do for now." He eased the Cutlass into a slot under a jaundiced sodium light and killed the engine. The windows began to fog up almost immediately, the damp bay chill creeping into the interior of the car.

"Tell me what you told the woman on the tip line," Iverson said, turning to peer at Walter. "I couldn't get a straight answer out of Latimer."

"Well..." Walter said, pulling the worn lapels of his jacket tight around his throat, and wishing he'd taken time to put on a scarf.

"Look," Bell interrupted, leaning forward from the back seat. "Why should we trust you? Any of you?"

"You shouldn't trust Latimer," Iverson said. "I wouldn't. That weasel thinks he can capture the Zodiac Killer and figure out a way to use him as a weapon. He's got… ambitions." He said the word *ambitions* like he might have said *herpes*. "He was the bastard who hijacked my idea, for the formation of a special scientific division to handle cases that fall outside the boundaries of what would be considered normal criminal activities. Cases like this one." He shook his head, rueful and defeated. "When he took over the project, he told our superiors that I was cracking under pressure, and campaigned to get me sidelined on medical leave."

"Okay," Bell said. "So we agree that it's not a good idea to trust Latimer. But why should we trust *you*?"

"Because," Iverson said, "the Zodiac Killer has been writing to me. He still does, tells me everything. Things Latimer doesn't know. Even…" He reached into the back seat and grabbed a green folder off the top of a teetering stack, flipping it open and extracting the first sheet of paper inside. "About you two."

He held up a rumpled, repeatedly folded sheet of paper. At the top of the sheet, the words "Dear Special Agent Iverson" appeared, above a few lines of the familiar code Walter had seen in his vision and in the newspaper accounts. At the bottom there was a rough sketch. It pictured two floating heads, hovering above a double row of stylized waves like a child might draw. The heads were simplistically rendered, but the heavy, strongly arched brows on the left and the wild curly mop of hair on the right made it obvious who they were supposed to represent.

"He says he's from another world," Iverson continued. "And that you two opened a psychic gateway that allowed him to enter this one."

"Did he describe his own world?" Walter asked, excitement flaring magnesium hot in his belly and making him feel reckless. "Is it another planet? Or another dimension?"

"Hold on," Bell said. "Start at the beginning."

Iverson nodded, his look solemn.

"I don't know why the killer became fixated on me," he said, breath steaming in the chilled interior of the car. "It's not like I was in charge of the case, or in any kind of position of power. I was just one of several junior agents working under Latimer. But for some reason, the bastard singled me out. He's been writing to me, calling my house in the middle of the night, taunting me. I don't sleep. My wife left me. But in a strange way, I think Latimer is jealous." He shook his head. "Crazy, isn't it?

"Anyway," he continued, "the last confirmed and undisputed Zodiac murder on public record was the cab driver in Presidio Heights, back in '69. But the truth is, the killer was just getting warmed up. After two of his male victims survived his attacks, he gave up on messing with couples and started concentrating on single women." He flipped through the pages in the file on his lap, until he came to a photograph of a barely dressed dead blonde wearing the remains of a burnt polyester blouse. "Donna DeGarmo, age twenty-six, a dental hygienist from Alameda."

"I recognize this woman!" Walter said, nauseous but unable to look away. "I saw her blouse, burnt like this."

"There's something else that's different," Iverson said. "When her body was found, it was giving off highly concentrated gamma radiation. Especially in the throat and... um... " He cupped his hands over his pecs. "Chest area."

"My God," Walter said, remembering the vision, and the sparks dancing over the killer's hands.

"The landlady who discovered the body and two of the first responders on the scene were subsequently hospitalized with acute radiation sickness. The entire block was evacuated and the residents quarantined. Naturally it was kept out of the papers, to prevent widespread panic. 'Sewer leak.' That was the cover story. But here's the weird thing."

"What?" Bell said. "Weirder than a radioactive corpse?"

Iverson nodded.

"Much weirder. See, it took us several hours to mobilize all the equipment we needed to enter the location safely and dispose of the body. I mean, the levels of radiation we were dealing with, standard lead shielding would have been as useless as lingerie. We were actually talking about filling the whole apartment with quick-dry cement, demolishing the rest of the building around it and trucking the cement block out to the Nevada desert for disposal. But, less than three hours later, before we could get a conclusive reading on the type of gamma-emitting radioisotopes we were dealing with, the radiation was just *gone*."

"Gone?" Walter frowned. "What do you mean 'gone'?"

"That's impossible," Bell said. "Radiation doesn't just go away. It can take centuries to decay."

"Yeah, I know," Iverson said. "Impossible, but true. It was as if the unknown radioactive isotope somehow bonded with oxygen in the air and rendered down into harmless water."

"Astounding," Walter said. "Unprecedented."

"And worse, that was only the first time."

Iverson fanned out a handful of photos, each one featuring a different woman. All beautiful. All dead. Thirty-two total.

"The unusual gamma radiation was only found in six out of the thirty-two, but that's because the bodies of those women were discovered within three hours or less of their deaths. It seems to be getting stronger with each new victim, but after the three-hour mark, the radiation still dissipates without a trace, leaving behind nothing but garden variety water.

"Regardless, the killer has claimed responsibility for all of them, proving it with samples of their hair or clothing in the letters he mailed to me."

"This is horrible," Walter said. "It's so much worse than we ever could have imagined."

"But what exactly is going on here?" Bell asked. "Could this be some kind of unique, short-burst radiation that's as normal as sunshine in his world?"

"Or," Walter continued, "maybe the killer's very atoms have been somehow destabilized by passing through the gateway, resulting in a mirrored gamma-ray-like effect within the flesh of his victims."

"But why does he only seem to emit radiation when he's killing someone?" Iverson asked. "We've tried tracking him with Geiger counters, figuring that anyone as close as he was to so many repeated radioactive events must give off some trace radiation—something that would be detectable. But that hasn't been the case. It's as if he lets off this intense burst at the climax of each murder and then… nothing."

"Agent Iverson," Walter asked, dreading the answer. "In the letters he's sent you, has he mentioned anything more about a city bus?"

"It's a recurring theme," Iverson replied. "Repeated over and over again in almost every letter. He claims the women he's killed are all tramps—easy prey that nobody cares about, anyway—but that shooting senior citizens would be the ultimate thrill. Not so much for the sheer pleasure of killing, although that's clearly a factor. He claims that killing innocent grannies would provoke the maximum amount of outrage.

"He sees public outrage as a kind of ovation for his symphonies. Makes him feel powerful. Look at this." He handed Walter another handwritten letter. "In his most recent message to me, he expressed a lot of anger because details of his activities had been kept out of the media.

"The fact that he was able to get a few cards and letters through our net, and made it into the newspapers, has made him cocky. He claimed responsibility for several murders we know he had nothing to do with, just to mess with us. But that score at the bottom of his last public letter, '*Me = 37, SFPD = 0,*' that's the only hint the media ever got of what he's really been up to, over the past five years."

"Listen," Walter said, unsure if it was the right thing to do, but unable to stop himself. "I think we might know where the Zodiac Killer will be tomorrow…"

A pair of headlights pierced the gloom, refracting off the condensation on the rear windshield. A car pulled up behind them, and two ill-defined, fuzzy silhouettes got out and started walking toward Iverson's car.

The agent rolled down his window and peered back at the approaching men.

"Latimer!" he said, cranking the ignition and flooring the gas pedal.

Walter, who wasn't prepared for such sudden acceleration, bounced off the seatback, dropping the letter he was holding as he braced himself against the dashboard and the door with his palms.

Bell swore in the back seat as an avalanche of files slid into his lap, burying his feet.

It took Walter a second to realize that Iverson was headed straight for a chain-link fence, with no sign of slowing.

"Are you nuts?" Bell cried, voice constricted with fear.

Instead of answering, Iverson just crashed through the fence, dragging a large section of chain-link that had hooked onto the wipers as the Cutlass slalomed down a dirt embankment and cut across honking traffic. At that point, Walter covered his face with his hands, convinced he was about to die in a flaming wreck.

Bell's swearing in the back seat became louder and more creative, but Iverson was disturbingly silent. The pounding of Walter's heart seemed like the loudest sound in the car.

Then, just as suddenly as he'd taken off, Iverson screeched to a halt.

"Out!" he cried, reaching across Walter's body to open the passenger side door. "Go, *run*. I'll distract them."

He scooped up the file of letters off the floor and pressed it into Walter's hands.

"Find him!" he said, his haunted gaze locked on Walter. "You have to find him and stop him."

Walter took the file and scrambled out of the car. Looking back, he saw that another vehicle had pulled in behind them. Its lights were on, but it was just sitting there.

They were in a narrow alley, and there was an open loading dock on their right. The moment Walter and Bell got out of the Cutlass, Iverson threw it into reverse and drove backward until he slammed into the pursuing car, wedging it in tightly between two dumpsters and blocking it from proceeding down the alley.

"Come on," Bell said, climbing onto the high loading dock and giving Walter a hand up.

Walter looked back down the alley at the furious agents who were waving their arms and trying to climb out the windows of their trapped car. Then he stuffed Iverson's file down the front of his trousers and ran with Bell into the building attached to the loading dock.

It was a warehouse of some kind—stocking smoked and pickled fish, by the smell of it. But Walter barely had time to register his surroundings or the quavering protests of the ancient night watchman before the two of them burst out through the front door and onto a neighboring street.

"Belly," Walter said. "Maybe we should..." Before he could finish, Bell gripped his arm and dragged him across the street, into one end of a narrow greasy spoon café.

The place had its own oniony atmosphere so thick that it felt like walking into a lard sauna. It was nearly empty except for a thin, cadaverous fry cook doubling as a waiter and a single morose, genderless patron bundled up in multiple threadbare sweaters and an oversized tam-o'-shanter.

The fry cook's jaded, wordless greeting turned to baffled disbelief as Bell charged straight through the restaurant's narrow boxcar length, dragging Walter in tow like a reluctantly leashed cocker spaniel.

"Sorry..." Walter called back over his shoulder at the frowning fry cook, not even sure what exactly he was apologizing for.

They burst out of the back door of the restaurant, which led to yet another alley, this one redolent of old frying oil and slick rotting garbage. Walter was so turned around at that point that he had no idea where he was in relation to the FBI building, or the parking lot where they'd talked with Iverson, or even the other alley where they'd seen him last.

He had a vague notion that their current alley might be parallel to the previous one but he would not have sworn to it in a court of law. For all he knew it was perpendicular.

What he did know was that he was glad Bell was there to take the lead.

"Where the hell are we going, Belly?" he asked between gasps and huffs. "I'm afraid I can't possibly..."

"There!"

Bell pointed to a pickup truck parked near the mouth of the alley with its engine running. No driver in sight. When they reached it, he opened the driver's side door, then shoved Walter in and across the bench seat before getting in behind the wheel.

"We can't just..." Walter began, but he swallowed his protest as Bell punched the gas and peeled out of the alley.

"Listen," Bell said, blowing through a red light and making a squealing left turn. The plastic hula girl on the dashboard wobbled fetchingly, seeming to wink at Walter. "We need a safe harbor. Somewhere we can hunker down and formulate a plan. And we're going to need a native guide. Someone who knows this city and can help us find the location of the bus shooting before it happens."

"And then what?"

Bell didn't reply, but they both knew the answer already.

They had to find a way to stop the killer. Linda's grandma and the rest of the passengers were counting on them.

6

Walter was so deeply exhausted by the impossible events of the past six hours that he found himself dozing off to the hypnotic sound of their borrowed truck's tires humming as they crossed over a long bridge and into San Francisco.

He was awakened an unknown time later by Bell's gentle hand on his shoulder.

"We're here," he said.

"Where's 'here'?" Walter asked, suddenly alarmed when he realized the steep downward slant of the street on which the truck was precariously balanced.

"Nina's place," Bell replied with a little private smile. "Let's go."

Walter went to open the door and gravity pulled it out of his hand so that it bounced on its hinges, and then settled wide open. He cautiously put one foot on the impossibly steep ground, but was reluctant to let go of the frame of the truck.

"Are you sure it's safe to park on a hill like this?" Walter asked.

Bell chuckled.

"What do we care?" he said with a shrug. "It's not our truck."

Walter felt an irrational pang of sympathy for the now abandoned plastic hula girl on the dashboard. While Bell wasn't looking, he detached her from her magnetic base and put her into one of the deep pockets of his Norfolk jacket, before shouldering the heavy door closed and joining Bell on the sidewalk.

They were standing in front of a dilapidated group of identical Victorian row houses, distinguishable only by their peeling pastel paint jobs. The one on the far end of the block had been cheaply renovated, its delicate gingerbread details buried under bland aluminum siding. There was a faded "for sale" sign out front, but it didn't look as if there had been much interest. That one house reminded Walter of an older guy trying to impress women while his shabby, drunken buddies crowded around him.

That's when Walter noticed the tower.

Although he wasn't familiar with this city or its landmarks, he instantly recognized the looming gun-muzzle tower on the top of a nearby hill. It was just like his vision, only at night it was lit with a ghostly pale glow that made it seem even more sinister.

A bad omen.

He shivered, pulling his collar closer for protection against the chilly night air.

The house that Bell approached might once have been a delicate shade of lavender, but over the years the accumulated grime had rendered it more the color of an asphyxiated corpse. In contrast to the grim, faded exterior, the warmly glowing windows were all covered with colorful Indian scarves, tie-dyed flags, rock and roll posters, and whimsical hand-made stained glass. It seemed like a friendly house. A sanctuary.

Bell took the front steps two at a time and knocked decisively on the door. Walter was close behind when a man appeared in the long multi-paned window set into the door.

The guy wasn't exactly handsome, with a long dour face and large ears that protruded comically from long brown hair that had apparently never met a comb, but his dark, deeply shadowed eyes were intelligent, intense, and compelling. He was dressed in tight, brick-red corduroy pants that laced at the fly, a large, gaudy pendant, and nothing else.

"Is Nina home?" Bell asked, silently bristling at the sight of this unexpected shirtless person—although Walter couldn't imagine why. It seemed to him that Bell should feel some sense of kinship with the stranger, since the two of them had very similar eyebrows.

"Sure, man," the guy said, seemingly unfazed or unaware of Bell's unspoken hostility. He set to work unlocking what seemed to be a preposterous number of locks and chains. "Come on in."

Once the door was open, the man just turned and walked away without another word. Walter and Bell had no choice but to follow him in.

The stranger led them past a narrow staircase and down a musty hallway lined from floor to ceiling with taped-up psychedelic posters, and into a large common room shaped like a rectangle married to half an octagon. There were several mismatched sofas from various eras, all hiding their imperfections under colorful blankets, and clusters of mirror-studded pillows.

Every wall was covered by floor-to-ceiling bookshelves. Lamps were shrouded in sheer or metallic scarves. Candles burned in cracked teacups. Instrument cases were clustered against one wall, most of them approximately guitar shaped, but also for a banjo, an autoharp, and a fiddle.

A strong miasma of strawberry incense and marijuana overlaid a faint old-house mustiness and the distinct tang of a cat's litter box.

There were two other young men in the room already, one on a couch and one sitting cross-legged on the floor. They were sharing a joint and seemed to be in the midst of a spirited debate.

"I'm not saying that we should compromise who we are as artists," the one on the floor said. He was a tall, lanky guy with a mournful, horsey face and astounding blond mutton chops. "I'm just saying we gotta get with the times, man."

"No way," the guy who let them in said, as if he'd never left the conversation. "The minute you compromise to fit into the top-forty status quo, you lose the right to call yourself an artist."

The guy on the couch, a stocky Latin fellow with arms like a bricklayer and brambly black beard spoke up.

"Did you sleep through Altamont, or what?" He passed the joint to the shirtless guy. "The summer of love is over, Roscoe. Janis and Jimi are dead. Times, they are a-changing, whether you like it or not."

A fat Himalayan cat appeared suddenly, weaving in and out of Walter's legs, seemingly oblivious to the brewing argument among his human companions.

"So what," the shirtless guy replied, flushing a dangerous crimson. "You want to get a couple of Swedish bimbos with tambourines to take over the lead vocals? Or maybe I should start dressing up like a satanic wizard or a hooker from Mars." He gave the other men in the room a baleful glare. "In fact, why don't we just change our name to Violet Sedan *Starship*?"

"Please forgive the interruption," Walter said, unable to keep quiet for another second, and forgetting about everything else for a brief happy moment. "But you gentlemen wouldn't happen to be... Violet Sedan Chair?"

The shirtless guy took a deep toke off the joint and squinted at him.

"Yeah," he said, smoky voice hard and sarcastic. "Sure. Maybe you remember us from back when we used to be cool."

"And you..." He pointed right in the center of the shirtless guy's chest, ignoring the self-deprecating sarcasm. "You're Roscoe Joyce, aren't you?" Walter couldn't keep the big, enthusiastic smile off his face, and his words seemed to fall all over each other as they rushed to get out. "I loved 'Seven Suns'! Absolutely transcendent! 'Hovercraft Mother' is my personal favorite, not to take away from the rest of the tracks. But I have to know, is it true what they say about the eleventh song?

"I, myself, am very interested in the scientific study of the various methods by which one can induce hallucinatory effects to the human brain."

"William?" A new voice. A female voice. "William Bell?"

Walter turned toward the source and was treated to the sight of two young women. One was a waifish Keane-painting blonde in gingham granny dress whose delicate, slender limbs seemed barely up to the task of supporting her massively pregnant stomach. But that husky, arresting voice belonged to a stunning redhead with a thick spill of russet waves around her pale, serious face and sharp blue eyes that he would wager missed nothing. She wore green velvet flared trousers and a tight, cream-colored sweater. It was embarrassingly clear to Walter that she was not wearing a brassiere.

He made himself focus his eyes on her brown suede platform shoes, instead.

He needn't have bothered. She went right to Bell as if there was no one else in the room, and snaked her arms around him. She said something to him that was too soft to hear, even though the whole room had gone silent as soon as the women had appeared.

Bell smiled in response to whatever she was saying and hooked an arm possessively around her waist.

Meanwhile the pregnant blonde drifted over to Roscoe, who put a hand on her belly and passed her the joint.

"How's little Bobby?" Roscoe asked her.

"You're so sure it's going to be a boy, aren't you?" she asked, wrapping a dreamy smile around the moist end of the rapidly shrinking joint.

"Sure I'm sure," Roscoe said, tapping his temple. "Just like I'm sure he's going to be a rock star. Like his daddy." He spoke directly into her tummy. "Isn't that right, Bobby?"

"Nina," Bell said, waving a hand in Walter's direction. "I'd like you to meet my colleague Walter Bishop. Walter, this is Nina Sharp."

Walter wanted to say *oh, yes she is*, but he bit his tongue.

"Walter," Nina said with a knowing smile. "I've heard a lot about you. These are my housemates Roscoe Joyce and his lady Abby. The guy under the sideburns is Chick Spivy…"

"And you," Walter jumped in, gesturing at the guy with the black beard. "You're Iggy, right? Ruben 'Iggy' Ignacio. Drummer. But where are Alex and Oregon Dave?"

Roscoe shook his head, unable to suppress a smile.

"We don't all live in the same house, you know," he said. "We ain't the Partridge Family."

"Well, I suppose that's to be expected." Walter nodded, thoughtful. "But I can't tell you how pleased I am to meet you three."

"You're pleased now," Roscoe said, eyes going strange and unfocused. "But when we meet again, far, far in the future, we won't remember having met."

Walter cocked his head and touched his chin, curious.

"What makes you say that?"

"Sometimes I think Roscoe is psychic," Abby said, offering the joint to Walter. "He knows things."

"Is that true?" Walter asked.

"Yeah," Roscoe said with a self-deprecating shrug. "But I can never see the stuff that really matters."

"I'd love to perform some tests..." Walter began, reaching out.

"Walter," Bell said softly, shooting him a significant look and blocking him from taking the joint. "We need to have a private word with Nina."

Walter frowned, embarrassed and ashamed to think he could have gotten so swept up in meeting his favorite band that he'd forgotten all about Linda's grandma and the Zodiac Killer.

"Will you excuse us, gentleman?" Walter asked, ducking his head sheepishly.

"Hey, no problem, man," Roscoe said, hands spread magnanimously wide. "It's a pleasure to meet a true fan."

"The pleasure is mine," Walter replied as he let Bell and Nina led him up the stairs.

7

Nina's room took up the majority of the third floor, one end featuring four large windows that followed the same half-octagon shape as the living room below. To Walter's surprise, her private space was unexpectedly Spartan compared to the rock-and-roll Moroccan bordello look of the rest of the house. There were no candles or tchotchkes or figurines on her bookshelves, just precisely organized books, mostly non-fiction covering a wide range of intriguing subjects from physics to feminism to psychic phenomena.

The pristine white linens on her sleek, modern bed were neatly made with sharp hospital corners. Only one pillow. She had a small, well-organized desk centered in the windows with a brand new white Olympia typewriter and a matching telephone.

The only artwork on the clean white walls was a single black-and-white Japanese woodblock print of an owl. Walter imagined that her fashionable wardrobe and the various items that women require in their day-to-day beautification rituals—such as cold cream and hair brushes and lipstick and so on—must have been hidden somewhere in this mostly empty room, but he couldn't imagine where.

Walter himself preferred to be surrounded by soothing, friendly clutter, and rooms that were too empty like this made him uncomfortable, even antsy, like a little kid at the Guggenheim Museum.

The only places to sit were on her bed, on the desk chair, or on the floor. When Nina waved for them to take seats, Walter chose the desk chair, assuming—based on her previous amorous behavior toward Bell—that the two of them would be comfortable sitting together on her bed.

He was not wrong.

"William," she said, slipping off her big clunky shoes in such a way that they remained precisely together and aligned with the edge of the bed. Her small, perfect toenails were painted a pale, frosty coral. "Naturally I'm glad to see you, but I can tell it's not just my feminine charms that brought you here. Why don't you tell me what the hell is going on."

Walter didn't even know where to begin, so he let Bell speak for them.

When Bell was done, there was a long pregnant moment where Nina just silently sized the two of them up, like a casting agent evaluating a questionable Vaudeville act.

"So let me get this straight," she said. "You believe that this special blend of acid that you created allowed the two of you to link minds and open some kind of gateway, allowing the Zodiac Killer to enter our world?"

"That's right," Bell replied.

"And during this trip, back in 1968, you say you also linked minds with him and had a vision of him killing senior citizens on a bus here in San Francisco."

"I didn't realize it was San Francisco at the time," Walter said. "But that tower..." He gestured toward the windows, even though the tower wasn't visible from that angle. "I saw that tower on the top of the hill."

"The Coit Tower?" Nina's rusty red brows knitted. "That's where you think this shooting is supposed to take place tomorrow?"

Walter shook his head.

"No, no," he said. "I saw lots of different things, murders, ciphers, and letters. But the shooting, it was in this warehouse of some kind."

"Okay," Nina said. "I'm going to need a minute to process all this." She reached into a bedside drawer and extracted a pack of cigarettes, shaking one out and placing it between her lips. "You *do* realize how nuts your story sounds, don't you?"

She doesn't believe us, Walter realized with a jolt.

"Belly," Walter said, feeling a sudden panicky anxiety in his gut. "You said this girl would help us, but I fail to see any evidence to back up your hypothesis. I'm beginning to believe that you have allowed your libido to override your good sense."

"Hey," Nina said, pausing with a lit match halfway to her cigarette. "I'm right here, okay? Don't talk about me like I'm not in the room." She lit the cigarette and blew out the match with a stream of smoke. "And in case you haven't noticed, I'm not a little girl, I'm a woman."

"I'm sorry, I didn't mean..."

"And another thing," she continued, steamrolling right over Walter's meek apology. "I'm not some kind of decorative bunny who can't handle anything more complicated than putting toothpicks in cocktail weenies and mixing martinis. I just received a dual Masters degree in Chemistry and Business Administration from Stanford.

So how about getting down off your chauvinistic horse and treating me like a person?"

Chastened, Walter hung his head. He always tended to get flummoxed around women, and when they were angry even more so. He couldn't have thought of an appropriate reply if she'd put a gun to his head. Anything he said would be the wrong thing, so he just stayed quiet.

"Listen, Nina," Bell intervened, that warm, resonant voice of his pitched low and soothing. "We're just on edge because time is slipping away, and we still don't have a plan to stop this terrible thing from happening. I wouldn't have come to you if I didn't think you were smart, capable, and open-minded. We need you."

"I never said I wasn't going to help you," she said, turning her face away from Bell, even though it was obvious from her body language that she was softening up to him. "I just said I needed a minute to wrap my brain around what you're telling me."

"Fair enough," Bell said.

"Okay," she said, staring at the tip of her unsmoked cigarette for a drawn out moment. "For starters, do you remember the number or route of the bus?"

Walter looked up at the tin ceiling as if the answer might be found in its swirls and flourishes.

"It's been so long," he said. "Some details seem so vivid, and others have blurred and faded in the passing years."

"Was it 4?" Bell suggested.

Walter frowned, still focused on the ceiling.

"Yes, no... 44, maybe. And something starting with the letter P."

"You said the shooter was in a warehouse, right?" Nina asked.

"That's right," Walter replied.

"The 144 runs down Parkdale through an industrial neighborhood," Nina said.

"Yes!" Walter nearly leapt out of the chair, restraining himself at the last second. "Yes, that's it. 144 Parkdale!" He grabbed the telephone receiver, causing the base to tumble into his lap, cord tangling around his wrist. "We need to call the transit authority right away, tell them to suspend all bus service immediately!"

Nina stood and gently took the phone from his hands.

"It's 3:15 in the morning, Walter," she said. "There won't be anyone in the office."

"Right," he said, struggling to compose himself. "Right, of course." He paused, and then looked up at her. "So what do we do? Wait until morning to make the call?"

"Look how well things went the last time you tried to tell someone the truth about your vision," Nina said.

"But what *should* we do?" Walter asked. "We have to do something!"

"We could fake a threatening letter," Bell said. "We have enough of the Zodiac's letters in the file from Iverson, it shouldn't be hard to mimic his handwriting and syntactic style."

"Ah, right. The file!" Walter patted his stomach, then extracted the file from the waistband of his trousers. "I'd forgotten all about it. I was wondering why I've been feeling so uncomfortable when I sit down."

"Perfect," Bell said. "Even if our letter is eventually discovered to be a fake, they'd still cancel the bus service alone that line, wouldn't they? Just to be on the safe side?"

"But it's too late to post a letter," Nina said. "It wouldn't arrive in time."

"Maybe we should go in to the office first thing in the morning," Bell suggested. "Say that we received a threatening phone call."

"I think it would be best if you two stayed off the radar for a while." Nina smoked, thoughtful for a moment. "We don't want to tip off Latimer and his spooks."

Walter looked down at the file in his hand. One of the letters was poking out of the top, the Zodiac's handwritten salutation. *Dear Special Agent Iverson...*

"Do you think Special Agent Iverson is alright?" he asked, thinking of how the man had put himself at risk to allow Walter and Bell to get away.

"No way of knowing," Bell said. "But he would want us to stop this senseless tragedy before it occurs."

"Look," Nina said. "I think we should forget the transit office and trying to get authorities involved." She crushed her cigarette into a pristine glass ashtray on her bedside table. "We have to find the location where the shooting will occur, and intercept the bastard before he gets his chance."

"She's right," Bell said. "It's really our only option."

Walter found himself remembering that terrible glimpse into the Zodiac's mind and shuddered. They were dealing with a disturbed and dangerous person—if he could even be defined as a person at all, and not an unknown kind of being from some far-flung region of the universe. It was perfectly sensible to be afraid. After all, they were scientists, not Green Berets.

But just as vivid in Walter's memory was the questioning look in Linda's grandma's dark eyes, seconds before her life would be brought to a brutal, pointless end. Gunned down in the street by someone or some*thing* that wouldn't even be here in the first place if Walter and Bell didn't open up that mysterious door and invite him, Dracula-like, into this world.

"Okay," Walter said, not without trepidation, but willing to do whatever it took. "You're right."

"You said you saw a bar in your vision," Nina said. "Do you remember the name?"

Walter could see the woman and her red coat and her book so clearly, but the bar had faded to fragments.

"Night something?" Walter said.

"Eddie's," Bell said. "I thought it was Eddie's."

"But I'm sure the word night was in there."

"Hang on," Nina said.

She padded barefoot over to a small filing cabinet beside her desk and extracted a copy of the yellow pages. She laid it out on the desk, flipping to the listing for bars.

"Big Eddie's?" she asked, tracing the listings with a perfect oval fingernail.

"I don't think so," Walter said, feeling increasingly unsure. "I'm almost sure it was Night something."

She turned the page and there it was. Just a cheap, basic listing with no fancy extras. Telephone and address.

"Eddie's All-Niter?" Nina asked.

"That's it!" Walter said.

"Yes!" Bell said. "That's the one!"

"Okay," she said, tracing the address. "It's 1315 Parkdale, that's right on the 144 line. That's got to be it."

"We should go there right now!" Walter sprang up, file sliding off his lap and spilling the Zodiac's madness across the floor.

A photo of one of the dead women landed face up between Nina's feet. She bent to pick it up, and rather than looking girlishly squeamish or frightened, her blue eyes narrowed and hardened.

"Jesus," she said.

"Listen," Bell said, kneeling down and gathering up the scattered letters and ciphers, "we've been up and running all night. I don't know about you, Walter, but I need to rest, just for an hour or two. We can't be going off half-cocked or half-conscious."

"It's okay," Nina said, handing Walter a bus schedule. "The first bus on that route doesn't leave the garage until 7 am and will take at least forty minutes to reach that section of Parkdale. Never mind the fact that transit busses are almost always late. Meanwhile, William is right. We could all use some rest."

"If you insist," Walter said. "But I'm far too wound up to sleep." He took the gathered papers Bell offered him. "If it's all the same to you, I'll just look over these letters until it's time to leave."

"Fair enough," Bell said, handing the file folder to Walter but looking over at Nina. "But go look at them downstairs so we can get some rest."

Nina flashed Bell a challenging smile.

"There's blankets and pillows in the hall closet," she said, slinking over to her bedroom door and holding it open. "You boys are welcome to any couch that doesn't already have someone sleeping on it. I'll set an alarm and be down to wake you up at sunrise."

"Oh," Bell said, hesitating for a moment. "Well, alright then."

Although Walter couldn't decipher all of the complex subtext woven into that exchange, it seemed clear even to him that Nina had effectively taken the upper hand in the ongoing sexual negotiation. In all the years of their friendship, Walter had never seen anything like that happen. This was an extraordinary woman, this Nina Sharp.

Together, Walter and Bell headed down the stairs.

8

Nina turned her shiny green Volkswagen Beetle east on Glascock Avenue and started checking the street signs. They were searching for Eddie's All-Nighter.

It was 7:37 am.

"What was that street name again?" she asked.

Walter clutched her seat back, anxious and grinding his teeth. It seemed as if every passing second was absolutely crucial, and they were bleeding time at an alarming pace as the little car wove through the frustratingly illogical streets.

"Parkdale," he said. "It's Parkdale."

"You're supposed to be the one who knows this city," Bell said, his worry coming off as snappish hostility.

"Of course I do," Nina replied, utterly unflappable. "Only as far as I'm concerned, we're not really in San Francisco any more. Everything south of Army Street might as well be another planet."

"Please," Walter said. "Please drive faster! This terrible tragedy could be happening at any moment. In fact, he already could have started shooting!"

"Walter..." Bell turned in the passenger seat. "Do you

recall a particular time of day in the vision? I can't seem to remember anything specific. We might have hours, yet."

"Or no time at all," Walter replied. He frowned, struggling to recall, then shook his head. "The light was just like this. Gray, diffuse, no distinct shadows."

"That's all day, every day in San Francisco," Nina said.

"That bus runs until 10 pm," Bell said. "We may be in for a long—"

Walter cut him off as the sign at the next street came into focus.

"Parkdale!" he practically shouted. "There! Turn left! The address is north of here. Hurry!"

Nina rolled her eyes at him in the rearview mirror.

"One-way street, Walter. Have to take the next one and circle back."

His knuckles ached from clenching. It was all he could do not to bang his head on Nina's headrest.

"What a… uniquely aggravating city."

"Compared to say, Boston, for example?" Nina smirked and let out a short, sarcastic laugh. "I've never been lost in my life, but I got lost in Boston. I'd rather drive in Hong Kong."

Walter ignored her minor barb at his own beloved city and stared up Parkdale, looking for the bus as they passed through the intersection. He didn't see it, but that gave him no relief. Was he too late? Had the shooting already occurred? Surely there would be police. Or had he not looked far enough. Was the tragedy hidden behind a bend in the street?

Nina turned at the next corner, Flint Street, and bounced and jolted through a minefield of potholes between looming warehouses. That at least seemed right. It had been a warehouse in the vision. Three or four stories high. And now they were surrounded by them.

"Address?" asked Bell.

Walter consulted the page he had torn out of the yellow pages.

"1315 Parkdale," he replied

Bell looked out the window.

"Eleven hundreds," he said. "Two more blocks."

"Could you not possibly go *faster*?" Walter pleaded.

"Nitida's a good little bug." Nina patted the Beetle's tan dashboard. "But these streets are like Swiss cheese, and she's no hot rod."

"*Cotinis nitida*?" Walter asked, momentarily distracted by the familiar Latin name.

"I named her after the Common June Bug," Nina replied. "Naturally."

At last they traversed the thirteen-hundred block and Nina turned left onto Bentwood, then left again onto Parkdale. Walter desperately scanned the length of the street, searching for the dive bar he had seen in his violent vision. The east side of the street was a cliff of monolithic old industrial buildings, strata of bricks and dust-covered windows layered five stories high.

The shooter could be in any one of them, but which one?

The west side of the street was all businesses. One- and two-story storefronts and Quonset hut garages. Auto repair, metal work, tool-and-die. A big truck was being loaded with palettes full of roofing tile, but he didn't see the bar. Where was the goddamn bar?

There!

As Nina edged around the big truck, the sign appeared from behind its bulk. Walter yelped and stabbed his finger at it.

"There it is!" he cried. "The bar! Eddie's All-Nighter! Stop the car. Stop the car!"

"There's no parking," Nina said. "It's all loading zones. I'll have to go down a little."

Walter could feel his head getting hot, sweat under his collar. He was going to explode.

"But…" he stuttered. "But…"

"Relax, Walter," Bell said, looking through the back window and all around. "The bus isn't here. There are no signs that anything has happened yet. We still have time."

Walter forced himself to let out a long slow breath. Bell was right. They'd made it.

They had beat the killer to the site.

"Fine, fine," he said. "But please be as quick as possible."

"Here," she said, indicating a small empty parking spot between two trucks. "But it's tight, even for Nitida."

She tossed her long hair out of her eyes and looked over her right shoulder, backing the little car carefully into the slot. She had to cut in and back up again several times to work her way into the snug space. She was infuriatingly cautious, precise, and concerned about getting the car parallel to the curb.

"Look," Walter said, ready to smash the tiny rear window and jump out. "It doesn't have to be perfect. Would you just let me out?"

He looked back at the bar, then did a double take as he saw a flash of white through the back window.

A bus.

It was jouncing down Parkdale at the back of a line of traffic, only a block north of the truck. A block away from Eddie's. A block away from a massacre.

Walter spun, shoving at Bell's seat.

"Out!" he cried. "Get out NOW! The bus! It's coming! It's here!"

"Walter!" Bell shot him a glare as Walter's shoves

bumped him forward in his seat. "Keep your shirt on!"

Walter leaned forward and hissed in Bell's ear, pointing back through the rear window.

"Look!"

Bell looked back up the street and his glare disappeared. Suddenly he was clawing at his seat belt and pushing at his door. It flew open while the car was still rolling backward, and Bell was nearly knocked off his feet as he stepped out and the open door backed into his shin.

He hopped out, cursing, and turned to fumble with the seat release. Walter threw himself forward then squeezed out, breathlessly stuck for what felt like an endless moment until he popped out into Bell's arms.

Bell helped him steady himself.

Nina looked at them from the Beetle, still half-in, half-out of the space.

"What about the car?" she called. "I can't just leave her like this."

"You're welcome to finish parking, and then stay in the car where it's safe," Bell replied, taunting her. "Leave the dirty work to the menfolk."

"Not on your life, Neanderthal," she snapped, throwing open the driver's side door. "I wouldn't miss this for anything!"

Walter paid no attention. He was already running down the street. The bus was almost to the big truck now.

He could hear the clack of Nina's heels join the heavier thud of Bell's shoes as they followed close behind him down the sidewalk.

He looked up at the warehouses across the street as he ran, trying to figure out which was the one the killer would be shooting from. It had been clear in the vision, but he had only seen it from the inside. He had no idea what it looked like from the outside.

Walter tried to think. Tried to see it again. Had it been directly across from Eddie's All-Nighter? A little north? A little south?

Then he saw it. A dark square in the grid of dusty windows, three stories up. A missing pane. No gun was visible, but he was afraid that it was there, and that the killer was there behind it. Watching and waiting like a hawk in a tree, ready to strike at the hapless rabbits below.

He dropped his gaze to the bottom of the building and was confronted by a wall of blank brick. No doors.

They must all be in the parking lot in the back. They'd have to run all the way around the block. And by then, he was certain, they would be too late.

No, wait!

A narrow service alley, too small for cars, ran between the killer's warehouse and the one to the south. Walter tore across the street, heedless of traffic and the cacophony of horns from the vehicles that slammed on their brakes and swerved to avoid him.

"This way!" he cried.

Bell and Nina dodged cars and ran after him. Nina was cursing.

"Walter, keep it down, will you?" Bell shouted. "The killer will hear you!"

"You think he hasn't seen us already?" He gestured to the one missing window pane high above them, sucking in a gasping breath. When was the last time he had run for any reason? High school? Grammar school? "Maybe seeing us will shock him and..."

There was a flat crack, followed by an echoing bang, like a twig snap followed by a firecracker. Walter looked around as he reached the sidewalk and saw the bus swerving in the street, the pale and frightened driver wrestling with the wheel. The back end of the vehicle grazed the roofing tile truck and rocked them both.

Dozens of hands slapped against the windows as the passengers inside tried to brace themselves.

The driver hit the brakes and the bus shuddered to a stop, right in front of Eddie's. Right where it had been in the vision. Exactly. Walter felt light-headed, anxiety spiraling like barbed wire in his gut. It was one thing to be tripping out on acid, to imagine that something like this might happen. Quite another to see the bizarre vision playing out in real time, just like any other ordinary series of events. Seeing the future might have once seemed compelling and exciting, the kind of thing he thought he would be thrilled to experience. Now, as he watched the horrible scene unspooling before his eyes—just the way it had happened in his vision—it only made him feel ill.

He shook his head, forcing himself to snap out of it and carry on. There was no other option. He ran as fast as he could down the alley, still puffing and breathless, cursing his sedentary lifestyle.

There was a door up ahead, heavy, banded with steel straps, and caged with mesh across its tiny window. But amazingly, it was minutely ajar, a quarter inch of frame showing in the crack.

Impossible luck.

But no. It wasn't luck. It had been left open by the killer. This must have been the way he had entered, and the way he intended to leave. He had obviously left it open so that he could make a quick getaway.

"We have to go back to the bus," Bell called as Walter shouldered through it. "We have to tell the passengers to stay inside!"

"No, we'd be shot before we made it across the street," Walter replied. "We have to find a way to stop the killer from shooting them."

"And how do you propose we do that?" Bell asked as he caught up.

Walter ignored him and stepped into the space. It was nearly black, the only light filtering through the thick grime obscuring a row of narrow windows at the top of the back wall, far to their right. Where were the stairs? Walter peered around, frantic.

Strange angular shapes rose up in the gloom like the exo-skeletons of mechanical spiders, obstructing his view. He craned his neck, searching, but it was Nina who spotted them first.

"Straight across," she said. "There, behind the looms."

So that was what the hulking spiders were. Walter stumbled and wove around them, banging his shins and shoulders as he made his way toward the dark hole on the opposite wall. As he ran, his whole body cringed in anticipation of the terrible sound of another shot. A sound that would mean he'd been too late.

The hole became a doorway, with an all-steel stairway beyond it, and even less light. The three of them charged up the stairs as quickly as they could. Walter also made an effort to be as loud as he could, causing the metal treads to ring with every stomping step, then raising his voice to shout up the dark open well in the center of the stairs' square spiral.

"Police!" he said, trying not to let his gasping exertion show in his voice "Put down your gun! You are surrounded."

"Walter," Bell hissed. "Are you insane?"

There was no response from above—at least none he could hear over the ringing of their feet on the metal treads—but that was good. No response. No shot. No dead woman. Maybe they already had changed the future. Changed the vision. Maybe they had saved the day after all.

It wasn't until he got to the second landing that what they were actually doing sank in. They were running empty-handed to stop a man with a gun. There was a very good chance that they would be shot as soon as they ran through the door and into the third-floor space.

Walter found himself faltering on the stairs, icy fear suddenly crystallizing inside him, filling him with bitter black doubt.

Though he wanted to consider himself a rational man of science, Walter was at his core a passionate dreamer. He had followed his heart all his life, rarely if ever allowing practical considerations to get in the way.

Belly didn't push manfully past Walter to confront the killer either. He hung back several steps down. He had probably been aware of their situation all along.

He was a good man, and by no means a coward, but he had never once let his heart make decisions for him. Although he had occasionally been led astray by the functions of a more vulgar, southward organ, when the time came to make decisions that really mattered, Bell relied solely on cold, clear logic. Logic that would never allow him do something as foolish as running blind into a room with an armed killer, no matter how many innocent lives were at stake.

Yet he'd put that logic aside and followed Walter on this headlong fool's errand—one that might get them both killed. Nina, too. That knowledge weighed heavy on Walter in that moment, but he still couldn't shake that haunting image from his head. The image that had driven him here, and eliminated all other considerations.

The image of Linda's grandma in the fleeting moment before her death. Her red coat and her colorful scarf, her dark eyes silently asking why? Why did Walter let this happen?

To hell with practical considerations.
Walter threw himself through the third floor doorway without slowing, and charged the window, ready to do anything to save that woman.

9

Once he reached the window, he realized that there was nothing to do.

He skidded to a stop, confused. The space was exactly as he had seen it in his acid-induced vision, all those years ago. There was the Ridgid Tool calendar. There was the well-endowed pin-up with the feathered hair. There was the blacked out window grid with the single missing pane letting a square shaft of pale gray daylight into the far end of the room.

But the killer wasn't there. The gun wasn't there.

The only movement was the glittering swirl of dust that danced in the light from the open pane. He looked around the rest of the room. It was entirely empty, and entirely open. Bare concrete floors and rusting I-beam pillars all the way to the dusty back windows. There was no place for anyone to hide.

"He... he's not here." Walter looked back at Bell and Nina, hovering cautiously in the stairwell beyond the door. "He's gone."

They edged in, eyes scanning every inch of the space, then relaxed as they realized that he was right.

The killer was gone.

"We did it," Bell said, disbelieving smile spreading across his face. "We chased him away."

"Walter did it," Nina said. "Good thinking there, Walter. I thought you were insane with all that shouting, but it worked."

He hardly heard her. His eyes were drawn to the missing pane. He stepped to it. Looked through it, down at the street. The bus filled the frame as the harassed driver struggled to fix the flat. In front of it, a crowd of senior citizens, all chattering excitedly now that the big scare was behind them and no one had been hurt.

In the middle of the group, the old black woman in the red coat was laughing with the rest, gesturing at the flat tire with her cane.

Linda's grandma.

She was all right.

Walter's heart lurched as he watched her, and he had to fight back tears.

"She doesn't even know what almost happened," he said, half to himself. "None of them know."

Bell put his hand on his shoulder.

"And we certainly aren't going to tell them." He looked past Walter and out the window at the crippled bus. "We're going to leave it be, aren't we? Let them all have whatever lives they were meant to live before we..."

Before Bell could finish, Nina cut him off, speaking between clenched teeth.

"Boys."

Bell's head snapped around.

"What?" He frowned. "What is it?"

Nina was scanning the room again, shoulders tense and eyes gone hard and hyper-vigilant.

"If your gunman isn't here," she said, voice low and constricted, "And he couldn't have gotten out without passing us, then…"

"You're not police."

The new voice came from the doorway, flat and dull as the concrete floor. They turned. A man was standing there. Stocky, sturdily built, with an unremarkable yet familiar face.

He was aiming a rifle at them.

Walter blinked. The killer must have gone up to the fourth floor, then waited to see who they were. Clever, and frighteningly calm.

"What do you…"

He cut off abruptly, his bespectacled gaze flicking wide-eyed between Walter and Bell, Bell and Walter. His calm faltering for a critical second.

"It's you," he said, voice barely more than a breath.

As he hesitated, to Walter and Bell's stunned surprise, Nina pulled a small handgun from her fringed suede purse and drew a bead on the killer.

"Drop it," she hissed.

"Well," the man replied, flashing a thin reptilian smile like a cut throat. "This *is* an interesting development." He made no move to lower the rifle, aiming right between Walter's eyes. "I never would have guessed that the bitch would turn out to be the one with the balls. What do you say, Annie Oakley? Think you've got balls enough to shoot me in cold blood before I pull the trigger on your boyfriend?

"Or…" He shifted his aim to Bell. "Is *this* your boyfriend?"

Nina gaze shifted from the killer to Bell and back again. There was a gloss of sweat on her quivering upper lip. Walter was desperate to do something, say something, anything—but his whole body felt frozen, throat clenched tight as a fist.

"Eenie, meenie, miney, moe." The killer was chanting, shifting from Walter to Bell and back again. "Catch a hippie by his toe. If he hollers let him go. Eenie, meenie, miney…"

Instead of saying *moe*, he made a lightning fast lunge toward Nina, gracefully sidestepping her gun hand and whacking her above the ear with the butt of his rifle. Nina sagged bonelessly to the floor, gun skittering away across the concrete.

Anger swiftly overcame Walter's fear and natural disinclination to violence, and he launched himself forward, arms flailing. Bell followed him in, trying to pin the stranger's arms and prevent him from shooting Nina where she lay.

Their desperate and poorly coordinated attacks failed. The killer was as strong and precise as they were weak and uncertain. He kicked Bell in the chest, sending him crashing into the wall, then knocked Walter's strikes away with the gun butt and punched him in the face.

Walter had never been punched in the face in his life. He'd never even been slapped. The shocking impact of it jarred his skull, short-circuiting his thought process and filling his eyes with blinding tears. Then the hot wave of pain washed over him and his legs buckled, the world black and spinning.

Still he managed to grab at the killer's shirt, clawing at him, trying to drag him down.

"Walter!"

Bell lunged in again, and the killer shoved Walter away, spinning to face him. Walter hit the unforgiving concrete in a cloud of dust and something cracked him across the face, precisely where the stranger had hit him before.

The rifle. It was lying across his chest. Somehow he had managed to come away with it as the killer had turned.

Bell slammed down beside him, raising more dust, and the killer turned back to Walter, reaching for the rifle. Nina rolled and grabbed the killer, locking her fingers around one of his booted ankles.

"Shoot him, Walter!" she screamed. "Shoot him!"

Walter crabbed back toward the door and staggered up as the killer drove his heel into Nina's mouth.

He trained the rifle on the killer.

The killer held out his hand.

"Give it to me," he said.

Walter swallowed, dry throat clicking and clenching on nothing as he edged back, finger on the trigger. In that moment, even when confronting a ruthless killer, Walter was ashamed to find himself hesitating. He had never fired a gun, let alone had a reason to take a life, and he hoped to live out the rest of his natural days without ever doing so.

Even if he could find the courage to pull the trigger, and got lucky enough to hit his target, would the man go down? He looked so calm, so completely without fear, that Walter wondered if he might somehow be invulnerable. Or perhaps he could read Walter's mind.

Perhaps he knew.

Well, there's only one way to find out.

Walter sucked up a little half-swallowed sound he hoped wasn't really a whimper, and backpedaled into the stairwell. He turned to the rail, then dropped the rifle down the well in the center of the stairs.

A solid body smashed into him, pushing him against the handrail, crushing his ribs. Hard knuckles punched him in the back of the head. The world turned to blur and static, but a voice cut through it, hissing in his ear.

"Smart," it said. "I'll give you that. Too bad it won't be enough."

Then Walter slumped back onto the cold metal floor of the landing, wincing and wheezing as footsteps rang away down the stairs, fast and steady. A moment later—at least it might have been a moment, it was hard to tell—fuzzy black shapes filled the door to the third floor and he heard a gruff curse from a familiar voice.

"Walter. Are you alright?"

The fuzzy shapes came closer, and knelt beside him. It was Bell and Nina. Nina had retrieved her gun but she looked terrible, with a long gash on her forehead and a split lip that had bled down to her chin.

Bell was pretty bad off, too. He had a bruise forming on his left cheek, and was as white as Walter had ever seen him.

"Help me." Walter reached up to them. "We have to go after him."

Bell gave him a flat look.

"And when we catch him, then what?" he asked. "More of the same?"

"But he must..." Walter tried to sit up, stabbed by a vicious pain in his ribs that nearly stole his breath. "...be stopped!"

Bell and Nina took his arms and helped him up. Nina squeezed his arm.

"We stopped him from killing those people," she said. "That's something to be proud of, isn't it?"

Walter winced as his ribs twinged again, an echo of the earlier sharper pain. It still hurt to breathe.

"Of course," he said. "But it won't be enough. He said so. He's not going to stop. He's going to do something else. Kill someone else."

"Well, we can't be the ones to stop him." Bell spread his arms, and looked down at himself. "We tried, and look what he did to us with his bare hands. He knows what he's doing. We don't."

"So maybe we're still the same ineffectual wimps we were back in the schoolyard when we were kids," Walter said.

"Speak for yourself," Nina muttered under her breath.

"I'll be the first to admit that a life of reading and lab work does not a warrior make," Walter continued. "But that doesn't mean we just give up. We *can't* give up! We saved the people on this particular bus, but what about the next one? And the one after that?"

He started down the stairs, cringing with every step as his battered body protested.

"But... but he could be down there right now," Nina called after him. "Waiting. With his gun."

"And how long do you propose we wait to go down?" He looked up at her from the landing. "Will it be safe after an hour? Two hours? Five? And who else will he have killed while we were waiting?"

Nina sighed.

"Okay, okay," she said. "I see your point. But let's go slow and quiet this time, alright?" She raised the gun. "And let me go first."

"But..."

"Listen. If he's running, he's already gone. We'll never catch him. If he's down there, waiting, pounding down the steps like stampeding buffalo will only let him know we're coming. He'd pick us off one by one as we came through the door."

"Yes, that's true," Walter said. "Slow and quiet does make a good deal of sense." He grimaced and turned to start down the next flight. "Particularly since I don't think I could run if I…"

He stopped as he saw something small and rectangular on the next step. He bent, groaning, and picked it up. It was a pocket-sized notebook. There was too little light to make out anything more.

He turned to Bell and Nina.

"Did one of you drop this?"

Bell patted his own pockets, then pulled out a small, red, leather-bound notebook of his own.

"No," he said. "Mine's right here."

"Nina?"

She shook her head.

Walter flipped it open. The pages had writing on them, but more than that he could not tell.

"I can't…"

Nina's hand appeared and flicked her disposable lighter. The flame illuminated the page.

Walter stared.

Ciphers. Page after coded page of seemingly random letters and symbols. Even though it was illegible, there was a kind of toxic madness in the familiar, slanting handwriting that sent a cold chill through Walter's veins.

There was only one person who this notebook could belong to.

"If we can crack this code," Walter said, fingers tracing over the mysterious, jumbled letters, "not only could we gain the advantage over our opponent, we may learn more about who he really is, and where he came from."

"Well, we're not going to crack any codes by cowering in this stairwell," Bell said. "Let's get the hell out of here!"

Walter slid the notebook into an inner pocket of his jacket, and the three of them began their slow and cautious descent.

The killer was not in the warehouse. At least, he didn't choose to show himself or shoot them as they crept slowly down the stairs. And the rifle was gone, too. They searched the bottom of the stairwell carefully. It wasn't there.

Walter edged open the door they had come through and looked into the alley, still afraid of getting a bullet in the forehead. There was no one there. He beckoned to the others, and they all stepped out, squinting in the light, looking left and right.

"Should we check the lot behind?" Walter asked.

"No," Bell replied. "We should not. Come on."

He turned and started back toward the street. Nina followed him, but Walter hesitated, feeling guilty, and sick that they were giving up the chase. How could they just let the killer go? On the other hand, as Bell had said, how could they catch him? He had already lost them. And even if, by some miracle, they did manage to catch him, what would they do then?

They were like sheep trying to take down a wolf. Becoming his next victims wasn't the way to save the other sheep.

But perhaps there was another way. Walter patted the breast pocket of his coat where he had tucked the notebook, then started after them.

The VW had a parking ticket tucked under its windshield wiper when they returned to it. Walter was stunned at the breadth and vulgarity of Nina's vocabulary. It really was quite astonishing.

10

Allan was breaking down his rifle and packing it into a Ghirardelli shopping bag he'd scavenged from a trash can behind the warehouse. He'd been forced to abandon the duffle bag he normally used to carry the rifle, after that stupid scuffle with the kids from Reiden Lake. He couldn't just walk the streets with an assembled weapon in his hands, so he'd had to improvise.

But his hands were trembling as he removed the buttstock from the receiver legs, and wrapped it in crumpled newspaper. He'd tried so hard to stay cool, to stay in control, but the fear was back and raging inside him. The same fear that had nearly swallowed him alive on that strange night almost exactly seven years ago.

His destiny had been disrupted. The moment he'd dreamed of for years, the moment in which he would become the most hated and feared killer of all time, that sacred, perfect moment had been utterly ruined. Ruined by a couple of hippies Allan had thought were nothing more than figments of his tripping mind.

Worse, the hippies had brought with them a swarm of unanswered questions. And while he had easily evaded the bumbling idiots, the questions dogged him still. Questions about that strange and awful night. Questions about himself, and why he was here.

He was shaken to his core by this inexplicable encounter. The new life he'd established in this new world had been nearly perfect, and getting better with every new victim. His other life in that other world seemed like a fading dream.

But now, he suddenly felt unsure about everything again.

When he reached into the pocket of his navy blue windbreaker to touch the comforting, familiar shape of his notebook, he found that it was gone.

The fabric of the pocket had been torn during his struggle, and was hanging in a loose flap. Clearly, his precious notebook had tumbled out at some point during the whole fiasco.

An even greater panic dug its hooks into his chest, making it hard to breathe. His heart was beating way too fast, and he felt sure that he would vomit.

Everything was falling apart.

He was falling apart.

He was desperate to run back to the warehouse and look for it, but he was afraid those stupid kids might have called the cops. What he needed to do was run, get the hell out of there, but he was frozen.

"No," he whispered to himself. "No, no, *no*!"

"Hey, man," a male voice from behind him said. "You okay?"

Allan spun to face a young Chinese man with long, shaggy hair and a concerned expression. He was wearing a grease-stained mechanic's uniform.

Something let loose inside of Allan and he launched himself at the concerned stranger, tackling him and knocking him down. The young man was surprisingly strong, but his hard, angry punches and vigorous struggle inflamed and infuriated Allan more that they hurt him. The flare of sparks in his hands and forearms became hotter and brighter than ever, burning the flesh off the stranger's skull like a blowtorch as Allan smashed his face against the curb again and again. The unfortunate stranger stopped screaming and went limp in Allan's grasp, but he couldn't stop battering the lifeless body for several endless minutes.

Cracked and blackened teeth scattered down the alley like loaded dice.

His hands felt as if they were being attacked by angry hornets, deadly sparks flying with every blow like a blacksmith hammering hot metal. When he finally forced himself to stop and back away from the charred corpse, he felt spent, but calm.

He couldn't allow the idiot hippies to get the upper hand. He had to keep a clear head and think, to rely on the superior mental acumen that had gotten him this far.

He easily hefted the slender young man's body and tossed it into an open dumpster, covering it with damp, moldy cardboard and newspaper. He closed the lid, and then gathered up the scattered teeth, slipping them into the left front pocket of his fatigue pants. There was a rather substantial amount of blood around the edge of the curb, but it had turned dark brown and lumpy, flash-cooked on the concrete by Allan's furious heat. It looked more like the sludgy leakage from old rotten garbage than the evidence of a recent murder.

Allan had nothing to worry about.

He stuck the shopping bag under one arm and strolled casually back around to the door of the warehouse. No one was there. No authorities had been called. He slipped in unobserved.

He didn't find his notebook.

He scoured the stairwell and the whole of the third floor. It was gone. Which could mean only one thing.

They had it. The hippies from Reiden Lake had his notebook.

Well then, he thought. *Let the games begin.*

11

Back at Nina's thankfully empty house, the three of them sat on the soft, musty couches in the dim living room, trying to rethink their strategy, to brainstorm and see if they could make any headway with the coded notebook. But within minutes, the fear, anxiety, adrenaline, and stress—combined with the lack of sleep the night before—caught up to them with a vengeance.

Before long they were all out cold, as if they'd been sapped.

Walter woke to the soft, gentle clink of a teacup and saucer. When he peeled his sandpapery eyelids open, he saw that the fluffy Himalayan cat had curled up on his chest and Abby the pregnant blonde was sitting cross-legged on the floor, drinking a cup of tea and leafing through the pages of a large book featuring the art of Alphonse Mucha.

"Hi," she said with a sunny, childish smile when she saw that he was awake. "Would you like some tea? I just made a fresh pot."

"My dear," Walter said, knuckling the sleep from his eyes and gently moving the placid cat from his chest to the couch so he could sit up. "In this moment, I believe my body needs caffeine more than it needs oxygen."

"Did somebody say caffeine?" Bell asked from underneath a purple and red paisley throw pillow.

"Four hundred and fifty milligrams, administered intravenously, please," Nina said, sitting up, rotating her neck, and twisting her tangled hair into a topknot. "With cream and sugar."

Abby looked at Nina, then back at Walter with her big eyes even bigger than normal. Walter followed her gaze back to Nina and saw what Abby was seeing. The bruising, the spit lip, the signs of their ill-prepared hand-to-hand struggle with the killer. Walter's hands flew involuntarily to his own face, running his fingers over the damage there. Even the slightest contact made him wince.

His body hurt, too. Everything hurt.

Nina, noting the shocked look on Abby's sweet, simple face, shook her head, letting her red hair fall back down.

"You should see the other guy," she said.

"Wow," Abby said. It was all clearly more than she could wrap her pretty blond head around. "I mean... wow. I'd better... you know... go get that tea." She got to her feet with minimal struggle, considering her enormous belly, and then drifted away into the kitchen.

Walter took the killer's notebook from his pocket and was about to open it when Nina gave him a sternly arched eyebrow and a terse shake of her head.

So he slipped the notebook back into his pocket as Abby returned from the kitchen, balancing a tray of steaming mugs, a fancy silver Victorian creamer, a bouquet of mismatched spoons, and a whimsical ceramic sugar bowl shaped like an octopus. The minute she set the tray down, the three of them fell on the tea like animals. Walter drained more than half of the scalding hot liquid in one foolhardy gulp, utterly unmindful of his burnt tongue.

"Thank you, Abby," Nina said, getting to her feet with her mug in one hand and gesturing toward the stairs. "Now, will you excuse us? We're going to go on upstairs. We've got a few things to discuss."

"Oh…" Abby said. "That's cool." She picked up the lazy cat. "I'll just hang out down here with Cat-Mandu." She turned the feline over and cradled him like an infant, any shock or questions about their bruises long gone from her mayfly mind. Even if she realized that they didn't want her overhearing their conversation, she didn't seem to care at all.

She set the cat down and went back to her book without another word.

Walter and Bell followed Nina up the stairs, mugs in hand.

Back in Nina's large Spartan bedroom, the three of them plunked their sore, beat-up frames into the same seats they'd chosen before the madness. Nina and Bell together on her tightly made bed, and Walter at the desk by the windows.

"Okay," Nina said. "We're all thinking it, but I'm going to say it. That was really, really stupid. If I hadn't brought my gun, we'd all be dead."

"But we saved the passengers," Walter argued. "You said so yourself—isn't that what matters?"

"Nina's right," Bell said. "We didn't think things through, but we got lucky. Next time, we might not be so lucky. We need a plan."

Walter nodded, duly chastened.

"I suppose you're right," he said. "So from here on out, we need to find a way to fight the killer with brains, not brawn. Attack this problem like scientists, not… Dirty Harry."

"Right," Bell replied. "And what is the first thing a scientist does when confronted with surprising or atypical results?"

"Repeat the experiment."

"Repeat the experiment?" Nina echoed. "We almost got ourselves killed today. If you want to repeat that, you can count me out."

"I'm not talking about repeating the events of today," Bell began.

"Repeat the original experiment," Walter finished. He felt that old familiar flush of excitement—the one he got when he and Bell were perfectly synchronized in their thinking process, on the verge of a major scientific breakthrough. "Recreate the original *formula*. We need to see if we can reopen that gate."

"Because if we can do that," Bell said, pausing to let Walter finish.

"We can send him back."

Nina looked from Bell to Walter, a slight frown creasing her brow.

"Are you sure that's wise?" she asked. "I mean, the last time you opened this gate, you let a killer stroll right in to our world. What if it happens again?"

"She's right," Bell said. "What if we unleash a whole army of Zodiacs?"

"But I don't see any other way to stop him," Walter said. "We can't just let him keep killing."

"Okay," Nina said. "What if you two drop the special acid and concentrate on opening the gate again, and I'll stand by with Lulu." She pulled the handgun from her purse and gave it an affectionate pat. "Anyone or anything comes through that gate, I'll let 'em have it."

"I don't know if I can condone that plan of action," Walter said. "I mean, yes, clearly the last person or being that traveled through the gate has an unquestionably violent and unstable disposition. But that doesn't mean that every single individual from the other side of that psychic gateway can be condemned to death, based solely on the actions of one man.

"I wouldn't want to be summarily exterminated by aliens who judged the whole human race on the behavior of Charles Manson, for example," he continued. "The next being that passes through might be a scholar or a scientist or a grandmother not unlike the ones we saved today."

"Fair enough," Bell acknowledged. "But I still think having Nina standing by as ground control couldn't possibly be a bad idea. Not as an executioner—just as armed back-up, in case things get ugly."

"Also," Walter said, taking out the killer's notebook and laying it on the desk, "I think it would be wise to spend some time working on decoding this. It may contain information about the world on the other side of the gate. Information that might be useful—or at least good to know before we open the way again. Forewarned is forearmed."

"You see if you can get anywhere with that notebook, Walter," Bell said, pulling his own red notebook from an inner pocket. "And Nina and I will see about acquiring the chemicals and equipment required to recreate our original formula. Good thing I keep every single formula written down."

But Walter was barely listening. He opened the notebook to the last written page and stared at the groupings of letters, searching out double pairings and running a series of simple substitutions in his head. He reached for a pencil and a blank sheet of paper from a stack beside Nina's typewriter, and began to fill it with scribbled notes and test keys.

12

Some time later, although Walter couldn't have guessed how long if he'd been paid to do so, he became aware of a warm, spicy, almost ambrosial smell.

Chinese food.

Up until that moment he'd only been vaguely aware of a distant discomfort somewhere in his midsection, but when the smell hit him, he was suddenly voraciously hungry. In fact, he couldn't remember the last time he'd had anything to eat.

He lifted his blurring, exhausted eyes from the scattered pages of his notes and saw Nina and Bell. He hadn't noticed them leaving the room, but they clearly had gone somewhere and returned. Bell was carrying a large box of beakers and burners and heavy, brown glass bottles.

But Walter was only interested in what Nina was carrying. She was the one with the food. At that point, Walter was willing to trade his right arm for one of those wonderful little folded paper boxes.

"Nina," Walter said as she handed him one of the warm boxes. "You are my angel."

"And what am I?" Bell asked. "Chopped liver? Ergot seems to grow on trees in this town, but do you have any idea how hard it was to obtain monopropellant-grade anhydrous hydrazine?"

"Are there any forks?" Walter asked, peeling open his box of noodles and breathing in the fragrant steam.

"Just these," Nina replied, holding up a fist full of balsa wood chopsticks.

"That's okay," Walter said, tipping the box to his lips like a cup and slurping up the noodles.

"Lovely," Nina said, separating a pair of the chopsticks for herself and delicately dipping them into her own container. "Just try not to make a mess on my desk."

"No, no—of course not." Walter moved a page of his notes over to the right to cover a large splat of sauce. "Wouldn't dream of it."

"So Nina's got a small lab we can use, set up in the basement," Bell said. "Small, and nothing fancy, but it'll do. There's even a darkroom for Chick's photography." He peered over Walter's shoulder. "How are you getting on with the notebook?"

Walter slurped another mouthful of noodles, talking around them.

"I tried all the basic approaches," he said. "Including the one those teachers used to crack the cipher he sent to the papers. No dice. This is much more complicated, and far more secure. See, look here."

He poked at the notebook with a saucy finger.

"I started off with frequency analysis. Searching for pairs, right?" He flipped the pages and pointed first to a double Q and then a double F. "Hoping to lock down my L. The most common double-letter pairing in the English language being the double L, of course, challenged only by the double T. But here's the thing. It's rarely the same."

Another massive mouthful of noodles. "There are only one or two repeats in the whole book. So that got me thinking polyalphabetic substitution."

"Vigenère?" Bell asked, putting down his box of chemicals and grabbing some food of his own.

"Could be," Walter said. "But that seems like such a pain. Plus we have a few symbols mixed in here and there, though not on the last ten pages."

"What's Vigenère?" Nina asked.

Walter sorted through his notes until he came up with the Vigenère's square he'd laid out.

"It uses twenty-six substitution ciphers," he told her. "One for each letter of the alphabet. But the problem is that it requires a keyword to solve." He pulled out a list he'd made of logical guesses that he'd already tried. Words like *Zodiac* and the names of several known victims. But none had panned out. "We could spend the rest of our lives trying to randomly guess his keyword. And worse, I'm fairly certain he's using multiple keywords, maybe even more than one on every page. I wouldn't say it's crack-proof, but I believe it may be beyond my own personal abilities."

Bell had stopped eating with his chopsticks frozen halfway to his mouth. He put the box of noodles down and came over to the desk, eyes zooming in on the last written page of the notebook.

"Try *Reiden*," he said.

"My God," Walter said, putting his own food aside and grabbing the pencil.

Less than an hour later, Walter had most of the last page of the notebook deciphered. He held the handwritten translation up and read it out loud to Nina and Bell.

After I take down the bus I shall kill another teenage whore. A pretty brunette, like the first one on this side. I've been watching one girl who I think will fit the bill perfectly. Her name is Miranda.

My last girlfriend was older, a sad drunken waste of a person, and I found myself abruptly distracted at what should have been my most beautiful moment by the loose skin on her neck and the baggy, worn-out shape of her breasts. Yet the sparks in my hands were brighter and burned longer than ever before.

Not that I regret my previous choice. It's only that the anticipation of killing has me feeling particularly appreciative of youth. That young teenage whore will be the perfect reward for what is sure to be my most acclaimed performance to date.

I'd like to see that sad sack Iverson and his FBI cronies try to keep this one out of the press.

I think I shall make myself wait a few days to claim my reward. The sparks are getting hungrier every day, but controlling appetites is what separates man from beast. I shall wait until

"Until when?" Bell asked. "Wait until when?"

"That's it," Walter said. "The key shifts at this point, leaving these last few lines unreadable. Except for this."

He turned the notebook around for Bell to see. At the very bottom of the coded page were two words in plain English, scratched so hard into the page that they were imprinted deep into the paper.

BY KNIFE

"Son of a bitch," Bell said.

"A few days," Nina repeated. "That has to be at least two, if not more. At least we can be fairly certain this won't happen tomorrow."

"As long as his failure with the bus doesn't cause him to change his plans," Walter said. "But we have to proceed based on that assumption. It's not nearly enough time, but better than nothing," he added. "We should get to work immediately on recreating the exact pharmacological launchpad we used that day at Reiden Lake."

"Come on," Nina said. "I'll show you boys the setup."

13

"Do you feel anything?" Nina asked.

"Not yet," Walter replied. "Belly?"

"Nope," Bell said. "Nothing." He looked at his watch. "But it's been only fifty minutes. According to my notes, it was fifty-four minutes before the onset of hallucinogenic effect on the night of the original experiment."

"Four minutes," Walter said, "seems like four hours."

They'd already waited for what felt like ages for Roscoe and Abby to split for some kind of gallery opening. Chick and Iggy had never come home the night before, but according to Nina this was a fairly regular occurrence, usually attributable to drugs, women, or both. While Walter was glad everyone was gone, he had been particularly adamant that the pregnant Abby be as far away from their experiment as possible. He would feel horrible if anything happened to her and her baby, all because of him.

Thinking about Abby and her baby set his mind back to Roscoe's strange claim that he and Walter would meet again in the far future, but wouldn't remember having met. Although Walter was the first to admit that his own memory wasn't the best—that he forgot people's names all the time even when he'd been introduced more than once—he found it hard to believe that meeting one of his musical idols could vanish from his memory, just like that.

He found himself struck by a sudden fear that something might happen to him in the future that would destroy his memory. Some kind of disease or mental breakdown. He became instantly sure that, if he could just remove the top of his own skull and peer inside, he would see that future synaptic disaster spelled out in the whorls and convolutions of his brain.

Walter suddenly became aware of a strange chill seeping into his lower body. When he looked down, he saw that he'd sunk nearly to his nipples into the glossy hardwood floor. Alarmed, he stood up and found that he wasn't trapped, as if in cement or quicksand. The surface had simply become liquid beneath him—a thin, water-like liquid, approximately knee-deep now that he was standing. He reached down to scoop up some of the liquid floor with his cupped palms.

"Remarkable," he said, allowing the floor to trickle out between his fingers. "Belly, do you see this, too?"

He turned to his friend and was stunned to realize that Bell was gone.

So was Nina.

Walter was all alone in a huge, empty room with no windows. The room was so enormous that its distant walls were hazy and indistinct. There was no furniture. No detail. Just miles and miles of this strange liquid floor.

Walter had never thought that solitary confinement sounded like particularly bad punishment. He enjoyed his own company, had plenty of mental games he liked to play, and a wide variety of intriguing theories to contemplate. In fact, the idea of being locked in a small room seemed kind of comforting. Almost womblike in a strange way.

As a child, Walter had always sought out small hiding places as temporary refuges from bullies.

But this vast empty room was the loneliest, most awful place he had ever been. Its dimensions were soul-crushing, making him feel as small and irrelevant as an ant in the middle of a salt flat. An ant without a colony, banished to die alone.

His mind immediately seized on this metaphor and when he looked down at his wet hands he saw that they had taken on the elongated, dual clawed form of an ant's bristly pretarsus. It should have been terrifying, but the very spook-show scariness of this newest twist had an opposite, pacifying effect on Walter.

It's not real.

The image of his creepy ant-hands was nothing more than a standard, slightly silly hallucination. A day-glo carnival, haunted house kind of fear, rather than the all too real fear of loss and loneliness evoked by the huge empty room.

Ant hands, he could handle. Pun intended.

Walter was a scientist. A veteran user of consciousness expanding substances of all sorts. He wasn't about to let himself be distracted by irrelevant mental trickery. He needed to focus.

And just like that, the huge room was gone, and Walter found himself standing up to his knees in Reiden Lake.

Only it was more like a soundstage dressed to look like Reiden Lake. The trees looked flat, like they'd been painted onto the walls in a harsh, stylized manner meant to read well on black and white film. The reeds and brush around the edge of the water seemed monochromatic and papery, and there were only three different groupings, repeated over and over all along the shore.

The red Coleman lantern was there, too—the one they had been using the night of their first encounter with the Zodiac Killer. But instead of a flame, it was just a lick of flapping orange-and-yellow fabric. The water around his legs was the only thing that seemed real.

But what was still really bothering him was the fact that Bell and Nina were nowhere to be seen.

"Belly?" he called. "Belly, are you here?"

Nothing. No reply. He was still alone.

This seemed wrong somehow. It seemed impossible that their first use of that particular blend had evoked such a power empathic connection, and yet this time, Walter was off on his own disconnected trip, unable to even see his friend. Could they have gotten the mixture wrong somehow? Could one of the ingredients have been tainted, or of questionable quality?

It was an annoying and frustrating setback, but there was nothing Walter could do but ride it out, record every aspect in detail, and then go back to the lab and try again.

That's when the gate started to open.

At first, it just looked like the kind of subtle bubbling under the paint that might be seen when there was water leaking behind a wall, only it was the air itself that was bubbling and peeling away. Rather than being directly in front of Walter, the way it had been that first night, the budding gate was slightly to the left and lower down, tilted at a tipsy angle. As it started to split and gape open, Walter took an involuntary step back, green lake water sloshing around his shins.

Where the hell is Nina?

Nina and her gun were supposed to be watching over Walter and Belly, waiting for the appearance of the gate and any new, potentially dangerous visitors that might come through. But she wasn't there, leaving the unarmed Walter alone and unprotected.

Then it occurred to him that it was possible Nina could hear him, even if he couldn't hear or see her.

"Nina," he said. "Nina, I hope that you can hear me. I'm going to do my best to verbalize what I'm experiencing."

He paused for a moment, wishing desperately for a reply, even though he was sure he wouldn't get one. Unsurprisingly, he didn't.

"Alright," he continued, determined to articulate as much information as possible. "I seem to be inside a kind of artificial environment. Almost like a... a simulacrum of Reiden Lake."

When he said the word simulacrum, the lake, trees and sky around him suddenly fluttered, like a painted curtain rustled by a passing breeze. He ignored the disturbing ripple and tried to focus on the gateway.

"The gateway has opened," he said, "but it seems smaller. Crooked, almost unstable. If I were to try and pass through it, I would have to do so on my hands and knees."

That's when he was struck with a notion so compelling, he felt physically staggered by it. A notion so simple and obvious that he couldn't believe it had never occurred to him until that moment.

What if he did just that? What if he went through the gate?

Of course, it was a terrible idea. He could almost see the raised eyebrow on Bell's disapproving face at the very thought of it. After all, they had absolutely no idea what lay on the other side. Would the atmosphere be breathable? Would there even be an atmosphere at all, or would he find himself in some purely theoretical dimension? One of pure thought and energy, where mundane functions of the human body—such as breathing—would be rendered meaningless and irrelevant.

But, could he truly call himself a scientist if he were to pass up such a unique opportunity? What about all the potential knowledge that might be gained on the other side?

What about the danger? What if, in passing through, he was transformed into a radioactive monster like the Zodiac Killer?

Walter stared, mesmerized and silent, at the glistening gate. He was locked in a profound inner war with himself. He knew he would be crazy to take that kind of risk, but he'd also be crazy not to.

He reached a hand slowly toward the gate.

Gracile, reaching tendrils started forming around the edges as the gate pulsed, widening, then narrowing, then widening again. It would be a tight fit, and Walter would need to time himself precisely to push through when the gate was at its widest.

He took a sloshing step closer, fingers less than in inch from the undulating opening.

That's when he heard a terrified scream.

He jerked his fingers back—convinced that the gate itself had screamed—and stood, unmoving and silent, for several heartbeats, waiting for something to happen. The only sound was the gentle lapping of the water against his legs.

Then a thud, followed by the sound of breaking glass. As if reacting to the sound, the gate shrank and curled in on itself like a salted slug, and then it was gone.

Another scream, this one even more drawn out and intense. Walter spun toward the sound...

...and found himself standing in the middle of Nina's bedroom. Disoriented and swirling with vertigo, he sat straight down on the suddenly normal, solid wood floor, pushing a shaking hand through his hair and struggling to pull himself together.

He looked around and spotted Bell and Nina together on the other side of the room. They were kneeling, facing each other, holding hands and staring, enraptured, into each other's eyes. Nina's gun was on the floor beside her, forgotten.

Walter jumped, startled when he heard another reverberating crash, this time coming from behind the left-hand wall, from the house next door. It sounded as if someone had knocked a television set off its stand. The floor actually shook with the impact.

It was followed by a shattering of glass. Bell and Nina didn't seem to notice.

"Belly," Walter said. Excited agitation obliterated any tactful desire to leave the two of them alone in their clearly intimate moment. "*Belly!*" He reached out and shook Bell's shoulder. "I saw the gate! Just for a fleeting moment. But now the majority of the hallucinogenic effects have dissipated, other than a lingering audio component that sounds like screams and crashes."

"Crashes?" Bell shook his head, as if he'd just been woken up from a deep sleep. "I hear that, too." This puzzled Walter, for he felt none of the empathic link.

Nina also shook her head, looking down and quickly letting go of Bell's hands, flushing crimson with embarrassment.

"How peculiar," Walter said. "Our minds failed to sync up telepathically this time, and yet we are sharing this minor auditory…"

Another resounding howl of human misery. Nina leapt to her feet, gun in hand.

"Jesus," she said. "That sounds like Mrs.

Baumgartner! She and her husband live in the basement flat next door!"

The howl came again from the neighboring house. Actually it was more like crying now, ongoing sobs that ebbed and flowed like a tide.

"You hear it, too?" Walter asked.

"Of course I do," she snapped. "It's real!"

"It sounds as if someone has been hurt," Bell said. "We'd better see what's happened."

14

Once they were outside, they realized that night had fallen while they were tripping. Nina led them down the stairs, through the kitchen and out the back door onto a wooden porch that looked out over a wild, overgrown yard. There was a locked and rusty gate between Nina's yard and the one next door, and she unlocked it with a small key.

The yard next door was nicer, better kept, and full of robust rhododendrons and camellias, as well as a small leggy patch of pumpkin vines with only a single, softball sized pumpkin. There was a large mossy birdbath guarded by several stone bunnies in various poses.

A set of concrete steps led down to the door of the basement apartment. As they stood there, anguished wails continued to come from within.

The phosphorescent lushness of the bougainvillea that crowded the doorway and the way Nina's knock caused light to flash in the corners of Walter's eyes let him know that he had not yet fully come down from the trip. The cries from within the apartment were also unnaturally intensified, seeming to bore their way into the soft tissue of his hypersensitive brain, like hungry maggots.

He shook his head to escape the image.

"Mrs. Baumgartner!" Nina called. "What happened? Are you okay?"

The wailing stopped, replaced by a faint, papery voice with an old country accent.

"Help me. Please, God help me…"

Nina tried the door. It was unlocked. She pushed through it into a neat little kitchen that smelled like a jarring combination of onions and cloying rose-scented air-freshener. Walter wrinkled his nose at the warring odors.

The room was decorated in porcelain kitsch. Milkmaids and bakers and sad-eyed praying children. Cows with strangely human smiles on their bovine faces, and dapper pigs in waistcoats. The sound of canned television laughter came from further into the apartment.

"Mrs. Baumgartner?" Nina called. "Where are you?"

Another sob instead of a reply, and Walter and Bell tiptoed behind Nina as she crept through the dim kitchen and then into a narrow, cluttered dining room that lay beyond.

They all had to turn sideways to inch past the massive antique table that filled the entire room. There was one single place setting at the far end, with a small, neatly folded pile of papers and clipped coupons beside it. The rest of the table was covered with another platoon of ceramic figurines, all rallying around a giant gaudy centerpiece of plastic fruit and candles that had never been lit.

At the open archway to the living room, Nina stopped and gasped, then stepped back involuntarily into Bell. He took her shoulders and looked around her into the room.

"What…" Bell whispered. "What happened?"

Walter came forward and peered around them.

"My God." He winced and turned his head.

The living room was as clean but cluttered as the kitchen and dining room had been, with too many doily-covered end tables, overstuffed velvet chairs, and a coffee table crowded with glass dishes full of ribbon candy and butter mints. There was a brown floral couch with a single pillow and a crocheted afghan, as if someone had made their bed there. A black-and-white TV was nattering away, some kind of a game show.

Here the scent of fake roses was underscored with the bright iron reek of blood.

In the center of the room sat an old man in a wheelchair. He was as scrawny and helpless as a baby bird, his frail, wrinkled neck barely up to the job of supporting his large, bald head. He wore oversized blue pajamas, a threadbare plaid bathrobe, and a bulky, hand-knitted scarf. His skinny, coat-hanger shoulders were stooped, his hands tucked under a faded yellow blanket on his lap.

The old man was staring with wild, jittery eyes at a small, plump woman in a floral dress and pink cardigan, who lay cowering against the baseboard near a birdcage. She looked as if she had been mauled by a tiger. Her face, her hands, her forearms, and shoulders all had deep, ragged gashes in them, some nearly to the bone, all seeping blood into her already crimson-soaked clothes.

She looked up at Nina with terrified eyes.

"Help me," she whispered. "Please."

"Mrs. Baumgartner!" Nina crossed the living room and knelt by the old woman, calling orders over her shoulder like a field medic. "Walter, Bell, make sure Mr. Baumgartner is okay and then check the rest of the apartment. Whoever did this may still be here. Then call an ambulance and bring me any first aid stuff you can find."

Walter and Bell glanced at each other, neither one relishing the idea of being the brave hero who found the escaped tiger in the bedroom. Finally Bell pulled a sturdy walking stick from a stand near the front door and started for the archway that led to the bathroom and bedroom. Walter went over to the wheelchair and put a gentle hand on the old man's knife-blade shoulder.

"Are you okay, Mr. Baumgartner?" he asked. "Are you hurt?"

"It's me," the old man hollered, his voice shrill and cracking. The suddenness of it caused Walter to pull his hand back involuntarily. "Me! It's me! It's me! It's me!"

Clearly the poor old fellow was suffering from some kind of dementia, but he seemed to be more or less unharmed. Walter left him and went to check the front door. It was locked, chained from the inside. He grabbed a pink, floral print umbrella as a sorry excuse for a weapon and followed Bell into the bedroom.

There was nothing. The room contained a single hospital-style bed with metal rails on each side, a motley assortment of outdated medical equipment, an army of pill bottles, and a bulky stainless steel bedpan.

The bathroom had a shower with a yellowing plastic stool and a thick, blue rubber mat stuck to the tile floor by suction cups. On the toilet tank was a copy of *Reader's Digest* and a doll with a crocheted pink-and-white dress that hid an extra roll of toilet paper. There was no tiger. No intruder. No signs of a break-in.

Walter found a well-stocked first-aid box in a bedside drawer and brought it to back to Nina. Bell appeared seconds later with a stack of clean towels. He handed the towels to Nina, and then followed the cord to the tipped over telephone.

As he dialed 911, Walter brought a pot of hot water

from the kitchen, then squatted alongside Nina and tried to help her dress and bind Mrs. Baumgartner's wounds. The old woman moaned and flinched at their touch. Walter took her cold hand and squeezed it.

"Please try to calm down, Mrs. Baumgartner," he said. "I realize that you have experienced an awful shock, but it's vitally important that you tell us what happened. Who attacked you?"

Mrs. Baumgartner started sobbing again.

"I..." She clutched at Walter's shirtfront. "I don't know! There was no one! No one!" The tone of her voice was swiftly ratcheting up into hysteria. Walter squeezed her hand again, firmly but gently.

"Please, Mrs. Baumgartner. Slow down and start from the beginning. Think it through. Do you mean you were attacked from behind?"

The old woman stifled another sob and shook her head.

"No," she said. "I mean there was no one. I was sitting on the couch, watching *The Match Game*, you know? And then... then I got dizzy. Like maybe I was going to faint. Then something... something hit me! In my face! This thing, it kept on hitting me! Cutting me! But I couldn't see it! There was no one there! No one!" She looked up at Walter as if it was all his fault. "Who was hitting me? Who?"

A sob came from behind them. Walter looked up. There were tears running down the old man's face. He was staring at Walter.

"It's me," he said again. "It's my dream. Don't you see. My dream, it got out!"

Walter turned to him as Nina continued to work.

"What dream?" Walter asked. "Did you see what happened?"

"Try to think," Bell said, hanging up the phone and sitting on the arm of the couch beside the man. "Did you see who did this?"

"It's me," the old man said again. "Me! I did it. It's me!"

"He's obviously not in his right mind," Nina snapped. "Can't you see that?"

The old man pulled his hands out from under the blanket. Only there were no hands. Just old, long-healed stumps.

One stump was slightly longer than the other, and seemed to contain a functioning wrist joint so that its tapered tip curled and straightened as he held them out to Walter.

"It's me!" he shouted. "ME!"

Nina let out a derisive snort.

"See," she said. "He couldn't have done this."

The old man squinted at Nina, suddenly canny.

"In my dream I can," he said. "In my dream, I have hands. With claws."

Walter stared at the old man, a flock of terrifying thoughts suddenly crowding into his head unbidden. Sweat prickled his brow.

He turned to Bell.

"Belly?" he said. "Do you think…?"

"I don't know a goddamn thing." Bell turned to the door, showy anger like a stripper's feather fan not quite covering his underlying fear. "Anyway, it's not our job to figure out what happened. That's for the police. I'm going to go outside and wait for the ambulance."

Walter watched as he went out the front entryway and up the shadowed stone stairs to the street, leaving the door wide open. Walter turned back to Nina. She looked up from binding a wound on Mrs. Baumgartner's arm.

"What?" she asked. "What are you thinking?"

"I'm not sure I'm ready to say it out loud. I…" Walter shook his head. "I want to be wrong. I want this all to have a reasonable…"

Footsteps brought his head up again. Bell was coming back down the stairs, his pace slow and measured. He stopped in the door. His face was a cold mask.

"Walter," he said. "You'd better come up and have a look at this."

15

Walter rose from the old woman's side, frowning.

"What is it?" he asked.

"You'd better come and look," Bell repeated.

Walter looked down at Nina. She waved him on.

"Go ahead," she said. "I've got it here. There isn't much more to do for her at this point anyway."

He nodded, then crossed to the door and followed Bell up the stone steps. At the top, Bell stood aside and spread his hands at a scene of chaos and destruction.

"I believe this is the source of the smashing sounds we were hearing earlier."

Walter stared, stunned. All around in the glow of the street lamps lay scattered and smashed pieces of furniture, kitchen appliances, record albums, books, shoes, clothes. A broken TV had caved in the roof of a white Mustang. An upright piano lay on its back in the middle of the street, split open like a dead whale and blocking traffic in both directions. A painting in a gilded frame was impaled on the spikes of the iron fence of the building next to Nina's place. And in the midst of it all stood a middle-aged man and woman in their bedclothes, arguing violently.

He was a large, portly man with a thick crown of blond curls and a meaty, square-jawed face that had probably been handsome twenty years and way too many three-martini lunches ago. A high-school quarterback gone to seed. His cheap, gaudy robe had been haphazardly tied and was gaping open to show his bare chest and hairy belly.

She was an aging model type, strawberry blond with a rail-thin, cocaine physique under a floaty sheer tangerine baby-doll negligee. She wore heeled gold mules with marabou on the toes and her long, horsey face was shiny with night-cream.

"No problem," he was saying. "We're gonna be okay. We're insured."

"We are *not* okay!" the woman screeched at him. "What exactly are you planning to put on the claim? Act of God?"

"Would you *shut up* for one second and let me think?"

Just then a young man in blue jeans and a western shirt ran out of a building across the street and jolted to a stop beside the caved-in Mustang, his jaw hanging open.

"Who did this?" he shouted. "Who the hell did this to my car?" He looked up at the man in the pajamas, who was pointlessly trying to match up jagged fragments of shattered records. "Is this your stuff? Is this your TV? Did you drop your goddamn TV on my brand new car?"

The older man backed up as the car owner advanced menacingly toward him.

"I didn't do anything!" the older man said, empty hands held out like a peace offering. "It just happened! My wife and I were just getting ready for bed, and all of a sudden, everything in the room starts shaking and flying around, smashing through the windows and dropping to the street. It must have been some kind of an earthquake."

"There was no earthquake!" The angry young car owner looked around at the gathering crowd. "Did anybody feel an earthquake? No. Did you?" He shook his head. "You're talking out of your ass, pal!"

"So what are you suggesting?" the wife said, getting fearlessly in the young man's face, stabbing his chest with a pointy red fingernail. "Do I look like I could have thrown a goddamn piano out a window?" She waved her hand. "Does *he*?"

Walter turned away as the argument continued, and looked up at the building. On the third floor, the floor directly adjacent to the room in which Bell and he had just taken their trip, all of the tall, elegant Victorian bay windows had been smashed out, casements splintered, sills shattered, revealing the insides of an apartment that now looked as if it had been hit by a tornado.

Furniture was upended, draperies sagged off broken curtain rods and flapped in the wind, pictures hung crooked on the walls. And standing in the middle of it, his hands in tight fists at his sides, was a staring, teenaged boy, sharp-featured, mop-haired, dark-eyed, and utterly and absolutely terrified.

"In my dream, I have hands," Walter repeated softly under his breath.

"What did you say?" Bell looked around at him, frowning.

For a long moment, Walter didn't reply, just pursed his lips, thinking.

"Belly," he finally said, "I know that you're familiar with the latest theories of poltergeist activity."

"I was afraid you were going to come to that conclusion," Bell replied. "Yes, of course I'm familiar with those theories. The repression of rage, of frustration, building up in the hormonally charged cortexes of pubescent adolescents, is thought to manifest itself in telekinetic storms that are often mistaken for the work of malicious ghosts."

Walter nodded.

"And perhaps in demented old men, as well."

"What are you saying?" Bell asked. "You believe the two events were different occurrences of the same phenomenon?"

"I'm afraid I believe more than that," Walter replied.

"We can't know that," Bell countered. "There's no reason to cast blame on…"

"Oh, come now. It can't be a coincidence." Walter waved a hand at the wreckage that surrounded them. "This kind of event is so rare as to be the stuff of myth. Modern science has never managed to verify that it has ever truly occurred. Ever! And yet we have just witnessed not just one instance, but two. Two! And both happening at the exact moment when we were in the middle of…"

"Keep your voice down, Walter," Bell hissed. "We don't want to add to the already considerable panic."

He took Walter's arm and led him back down the steps into Mrs. Baumgartner's apartment, and then out through the kitchen into the back yard, where things were quiet and calm and green, and the world didn't seem quite so crazy. The cement bunnies remained serene and unaffected by the chaos.

"What the hell is going on out there?" Nina called from inside the apartment.

Walter hardly heard her. He was still trying to make his point.

"There must be some correlation," he said. "There has to be!" Then he remembered what he'd seen when he first came out of the trip. Bell and Nina kneeling face-to-face, staring into each other's eyes.

"Belly," Walter said. "You linked minds with Nina, didn't you?"

"Well," Bell began, unable to meet Walter's gaze.

"Embarrassment has no place in scientific method!" Walter said brusquely. "Anyway, never mind all that, tell me—did you or did you not link minds with Nina, instead of me?"

"Yes," Bell admitted. "I have no idea how it could have happened, when she wasn't even tripping."

"Clearly she was the one who was foremost in your thoughts in that moment," Walter said. "Not that I blame you, given her apparent aversion to brassieres, but that's something for us to analyze later. What's far more important to consider is the fact that both times we used this particular blend, a powerful psychic link was created. The first time it was you and me, then later on, with the killer as well. This time it was you and Nina. Am I correct?"

"Yes, you are correct," Bell said. "Okay, so...?"

"So, she wasn't tripping with us, but somehow our own heightened psychic abilities caused any latent power in her to be activated, as well."

"What are you saying?"

"What I'm saying is this—what if our special blend not only enhances our own abilities, but also causes some kind of psychic pulse that radiates outward. We become, for lack of a better word, amplifiers, like the ones in a radio set. Perhaps, in our heightened state, we pick up weak psychic energy around us, such as the angst of a teenager, for instance, or the unfocused rage of a demented old man, and amplify it a hundredfold."

"Or maybe it was the gate itself that activated and amplified the phenomenon," Bell countered.

"Could be," Walter said. "But either way, this amplification of latent psychic power occurred, and all of a sudden the repressed frustration hidden inside the affected individuals explodes outward in a storm of psychic fury and… and…" Walter paled as something occurred to him. "My God, Belly. We are very fortunate that no one was killed."

Bell gave him a cold look.

"You're acting as if you believe this is our fault."

"Of *course* it's our fault!" Walter was almost shouting now. "Maybe it was a side effect of the way our minds were enhanced, or maybe it was caused by the gate that we opened by using the special blend, but ask yourself this: Would any of this have occurred if we hadn't done our experiment?" Before Bell could reply, Walter continued. "It would not! We are directly responsible for that poor woman's wounds, and for all that property damage on the street."

"I told you to keep your voice down, dammit."

"But…"

Bell grabbed his arm.

"Listen to me," he hissed into Walter's ear. "We can analyze what went wrong and discuss our own responsibility or lack thereof in private, but shouting that we are responsible out here, where that angry mob out front can hear us? That's a very bad idea."

Nina came out through the back door of Mrs. Baumgartner's apartment.

"The paramedics have arrived," she said. "Want to fill me in on what the hell happened out there?"

Walter looked from Bell to Nina and back again. He nodded.

"Right," he said. "Let's go back inside."

As they stepped in through the back door of Nina's house, Roscoe and Abby were coming in through the front door.

"Man," Roscoe said. "Looks like somebody bombed the building next door!"

"I don't think anybody was hurt," Abby said, looking back over her shoulder. "But, oh, that poor piano!"

"Crazy, huh?" Nina said, hustling Walter and Bell up the stairs. "We'll see you later."

Walter heard Roscoe's voice echo up after them.

"What's with them anyway?"

Then Abby's faint response.

"Are there any more Ding Dongs? Little Bobby is starving."

Nina shut her bedroom room door and then ran over to the windows, peering out into the street below.

"This formula we've created is obviously extremely dangerous, and unpredictable," Walter said. "I can't help but wonder if we will be causing more harm than good by continuing to experiment with it."

"But how else can we hope to send that monster back where he came from?" Bell asked. "I just don't see any other way."

"We could just shoot him," Nina suggested.

"Maybe so," Walter replied. "But putting aside the moral ambiguities of vigilantism, do we even know that he's human? Maybe he can't be killed, in the conventional sense of the word."

"He definitely seemed human," Nina said.

"I still think we need to stick to our original plan," Bell said. "We brought him into this world, it's up to us to send him away."

"Walter," Nina said. "Before all of the craziness, you said you saw the gate, didn't you."

"Yes," he said. "But it was smaller than the first time, and seemed kind of... I don't know... unstable. I'm fairly certain that, because Belly was distracted and wound up linked with you instead of me, my own chemically enhanced ability wasn't strong enough to keep it open single-handedly. Or, should I say, single-mindedly?"

"So," Bell said. "We need to figure out a way to link our minds together deliberately, rather than leaving it to chance."

"What about some kind of biofeedback?" Nina said. They looked at her, and she continued. "I know a guy doing cutting-edge research on the use of biofeedback to regulate organ function. We should be able to borrow equipment from him."

"Biofeedback?" Bell grinned. "Yes, yes, a portable biofeedback setup might work as a basis for the type of machine that we would need. We'd need to find a way to synchronize our alpha waves and link our minds together during the trip, so that we can concentrate on holding the gate open long enough to force the killer through."

"We'll need to make some slight modifications to the standard rig," Walter said, grabbing a piece of paper from Nina's desk and swiftly sketching out a schematic. "See here, if we can eliminate the need for wiring each person in individually, through the use of multi-wave broadcasters like this…"

Nina turned away and began to leaf through the newspaper as Walter and Bell brainstormed ideas. But without warning, she leapt up with a gasp of excitement.

"Guys," she said. "You need to see this."

16

With a feeling of apprehension, Walter accepted the paper Nina thrust under his nose.

"Here," she said, pointing out a classified advertisement about a third of the way down the page. "Look at this!"

"Regarding incident at Reiden Lake," Walter read out loud, pausing to exchange a significant glance with Bell. "Meet me at the northwest corner of Alamo Square Park at midnight 10/23. Crucial new information has come to light. A friend in the Bureau."

"A friend in the bureau?" Nina said.

"Iverson," Walter said.

"Who else could it be?" Bell replied. He looked down at his watch. "But it's nearly 11:45 now!"

"Right," Nina said. "Come on!"

They dropped everything and went thundering down the stairs.

"Hey," Abby said as they barreled past her, holding a large wooden spoon slick with some kind of sauce. "Do you want some…"

Whatever she was offering, they were out the door before she could finish her sentence.

The small park was bordered by colorful Queen Anne houses and seemed nearly deserted at that hour, except for a single older man in a trench coat and long, bright green plaid scarf, walking a large slobbery sheepdog.

The northwest corner featured a break in the low wall that surrounded the park, marked by a pair of rounded stone posts like silent sentinels. A sloping path, bordered by whispering pine trees and willows, led up into the dark interior.

There was no sign of Iverson.

Walter nervously toed a crushed bottle cap while Bell alternated between scanning the street and looking at his watch. Since Iverson didn't know Nina, and might be spooked by the presence of a stranger, she had decided to keep an eye on them from her Beetle, parked across the street. Walter couldn't see her face, just the glowing tip of her cigarette.

"Where is he?" Bell asked.

"Do you think something might have happened to him?" Walter asked anxiously. "Latimer? Or maybe…"

He didn't finish that sentence, but didn't need to. He could see that Bell was thinking the same thing.

Had the killer gotten to Iverson somehow? Was yet another person dead because of them?

Still, they waited. A young couple passed them, holding hands, all oblivious dreamy smiles and leaving behind a trail of pheromones. An old Chinese woman passed, going the other way, bundled up against the night like an Arctic explorer on a grim race to the North Pole.

Still no Iverson.

They waited nearly two hours, but it was becoming increasingly clear that, for whatever reason, he wasn't going to show.

"Now what?" Walter asked.

Bell shrugged.

"It's not like we don't have work to do," he said. "We still have the deadline from the killer's notebook. Even though we don't know the exact date and time of his next murder, we *do* know that it will be sooner, rather than later."

"Very well," Walter said. "Right. So we continue our experiments on getting the gate open and stabilized. But in the meanwhile, we should watch the classifieds, in case Iverson tries to contact us again."

Walter looked up and down the intersecting streets one last time.

Nothing.

No one.

He couldn't help but speculate what it was that Iverson wanted to tell them. Some new breakthrough regarding the gamma radiation? Or maybe something to do with the true nature of the killer? Or the nature of the gateway.

Of course, this kind of speculation was a waste of mental energy, and he knew it. All they could do at that point was watch and wait.

The two of them returned to Nina's Beetle with slumped shoulders and glum expressions.

"What the hell happened?" she asked, flicking the butt of her latest cigarette out the widow to join its slain brothers in a pile on the sidewalk. "Why didn't he show up?"

"No idea," Bell answered. "He just didn't."

"All we can do right now is go back to your place and get some rest," Walter said.

"Yeah," Bell agreed. "I think we're all feeling a little punchy."

"All right," she responded, cranking the ignition and putting the Beetle in gear. "But I don't like this. It seems, I don't know. Weird."

Walter climbed into the back seat, hoping again that Iverson was okay.

From the safety of a stolen Volvo station wagon, parked down the block, Allan lifted his binoculars and watched the two hippies and the red-headed bitch get out of her car and cross over to enter a Victorian row house that had seen better days. The bitch's house, presumably, but he jotted down the address so he could check up on that.

He'd had a dark, angry moment when he thought they might not have fallen for the ad he'd placed in the classified section. So angry, in fact, that he'd almost driven away and headed directly to Miranda's house to execute her parents and take her that very night, rather than waiting for the perfect moment, like he'd planned.

But lucky for pretty little Miranda, the hippies from Reiden Lake had showed up at the very last minute, all out of breath and wild-eyed and tumbling out of a brand new green Volkswagen Beetle. Allan wrote down the license plate number and then settled in to watch.

They never once even looked at the Volvo, let alone at him, but he pulled the wool cap down over his forehead and slouched low in the seat, just to be on the safe side.

He found it tremendously exciting to be so close

to them without them knowing he was there. He only wished the redhead had gotten out of the car to wait with them. He felt no boredom, nor desire for time to pass more quickly as they waited, together but not together.

In fact, he felt perfectly calm and content, studying every detail of the pair while composing taunting letters in his head, which he would send to them later. It was going to be extremely difficult to make himself wait for the right moment to let them know he was watching. Almost as difficult as waiting to be with Miranda. He was dying to see the fear in their faces as they realized he'd been watching.

Eventually the pair gave up waiting in the park and led Allan back to their home base, just like he knew they would. And now he would be able to start stalking them in earnest. Getting to know them. Learning their routines. Connecting with them the way he'd connected with Iverson. Because although he could easily take them out from a distance, like hunted deer, it would be so much more fun to torment them. To terrorize them and watch them squirm.

This was the best part.

17

Back at the house, Nina watched Walter stagger into the living room and plop down on one of the sofas beside the purring fur throw pillow that was Cat-Mandu. But Bell lingered in the hallway, hands stuffed in his pockets and that charming little half-smile on his face. The same smile that had caught her attention when they first met back in March, at the annual meeting of the American Society for Neurochemistry in New Orleans.

They'd both been involved with other people at the time, but the neurochemistry between them had been difficult to ignore. It was a wild weekend, full of all kinds of drunken misadventures in the French Quarter, but somehow the two of them had never found a way to be alone together. On the last day, she'd given him her card and told him to stay in touch. She had figured she'd never see him again. Until he showed up on her doorstep with this wild tale of psychic gateways and atomic murder.

When she looked over at him, his smile faltered slightly and he looked away. Things felt so strange between the two of them now, ever since the strange psychic link that they'd formed during the ill-fated acid trip.

The thing that had been so astounding about that link was that, while it was the most profoundly intimate connection she'd ever experienced with another human being, it was neither romantic nor sexual in nature. It was this powerful sense of commonality. Something not unlike the discovery of a spiritual twin, of intertwined destinies and an unshakable life-long connection.

All her life, Nina had found that nearly everyone she met was put off by her naked ambition. Men tended to feel threatened, and women were intimidated, but looking into Bell's mind that night was like looking into a mirror, and Nina had seen her own voracious ambition reflected back at her with flawless synchronicity.

But it wasn't just some kind of hippy-dippy soul mate "spiritual bonding" thing. Because, underneath it all, there had been something very dark and ominous about their connection. A connection that seemed to propel them both into some terrible unknowable future in which the fabric of their universe would be torn asunder by their twin ambition.

Yet that shared ambition felt stronger than ever in the face of such awful knowledge. And it was that understanding—that they were both willing to pursue their ambitions without regard for consequences—that had cemented the inexplicable bond between them.

Nina had experimented with a wide variety of hallucinogenic substances before, and many of the trips she'd experienced had presented her with images or ideas that seemed immensely weighty and significant at the time, only to be revealed as trivial and silly in the sober light of day.

In a way, she wanted desperately to believe that the dark bond she thought she had shared with Bell was just like that. An amusing figment of her chemically enhanced mind, like the time she became convinced that the paisley pattern of a friend's shirt revealed the secret formula for a new clean-burning fuel that would revolutionize global transportation and make her a millionaire.

But every time she locked eyes with him, she could feel herself resonating inside like a tuning fork, hungry for the success that she knew she wouldn't be able to achieve without him. The success that he would not be able to achieve without her.

And in the midst of all this impossibly weird mayhem, that small sliver of weirdness was the one that preyed on her, making her feel vulnerable and off kilter.

Standing there with Bell in her darkened hallway, she knew that he felt it, too.

"Crazy day," she said softly, stepping deliberately forward into his personal space.

"Yeah," he replied. He didn't step back. "Listen, about last night…"

She reached up and pressed the first two fingers of her right hand against his lips. His breath was warm against her skin.

She hadn't planned to sleep with him yet, even though she'd wanted to. Now, it seemed so much safer—and simpler than facing the true nature of the connection between them.

"Let's go upstairs," she said.

He just looked down at her for a long, weighty moment, some kind of private war going on behind his dark eyes. She turned away and headed silently upward.

There was a moment where she thought maybe he wasn't going to follow her, and she paused halfway up, heart beating too fast. Then she heard the sound of his footsteps on the stairs behind her. She smiled and continued to her room.

In her bedroom, she didn't bother to turn the light on. She just walked over to the pool of yellow streetlight pouring in through her sheer curtains and, without turning around, pulled her sweater off over her head. Her hair crackled with static as she tossed it aside.

She was very aware of Bell standing close behind her for a silent minute. Then she felt his big hands on the curve of her waist, tentative at first, then pulling her back against him and sliding over her belly and braless breasts. She leaned into him, feeling as if she was melting. All the madness, all the mayhem, all the strange and heavy events of the past twenty-four hours were melting, too, washed away in warm, dopamine oblivion.

She turned to face him and pulled his mouth down to hers, kissing him just like she'd wanted to so badly, back in March. Pretending they were in the French Quarter, happy and buzzed and laughing like nothing mattered. Holding on tight to the solid physicality of his long, lanky body. To the simple biological imperative of their desire. The smell of his skin, the taste of his mouth, the feel of his hands on her body.

All these things were so simple and so real.

It was exactly what she needed.

They tumbled together onto her bed, wrestling with buckles and buttons. Still half-dressed, but unable to hold back another second, they made love like over-eager teenagers. Graceless and hungry, as if it was the end of the world. Which didn't seem all that far from the truth.

Afterward, Nina lay with her cheek against the black fur on Bell's chest, listening to the slow, even rhythm of his heartbeat and dozing breath. She felt warm and satisfied, but all the questions and uncertainty about the true nature of their connection still lurked there in the background, like wind rattling the windows of a cozy room.

It was a long time before she slept.

18

When it became clear that the hippies were tucked in for the night, Allan decided he needed a little recreation. Something light hearted and non-committal.

A quickie.

One of the inexplicable side effects of having passed through the gate and into this strange and wonderful mirror world was that he rarely slept. His body and mind seemed fueled by the arcane energy burning inside his flesh, and the only time he ever felt tired was when he had gone too long between killings. As a result, he found that he got twice as much done, and became intimately acquainted with the fascinating, ever-changing rhythms of the twenty-four-hour city.

The graveyard shift was his favorite time of night. The feeling of passing between building after building packed full of sleeping, vulnerable citizens made him feel like a kid in a candy shop. And those who were awake and walking the streets were a fascinating blend of the wild, the lost, and the forgotten. Very few of whom would be missed if they were to meet Allan in a dark alley.

Still wanting to be thoughtful and pragmatic about

his spur-of-the-moment plan, he figured it would be wise to head down into the Tenderloin, and not leave a dead mouse on the redhead's doorstep. He didn't want to spook his real prey.

He took a long, roundabout stroll down the hill, zigzagging along random streets and occasionally doubling back when the mood struck him. He wasn't in any rush, just open for suggestion. Polk to Myrtle to Larkin, then Olive back to Polk again and up to the tawdry circus of O'Farrell Street.

The seedy single-room-occupancy hotels and low-rent apartment buildings in that neighborhood were like vending machines filled with victims. An embarrassment of riches. It was almost too easy.

A young couple leaving the O'Farrell Theater caught his eye, making him feel a warm, gentle nostalgia for his lover's lane phase. She was bleached blond and fat-bottomed in gold-lamé hot pants and cheap boots. He was a male model type on the skids, still handsome but a little too thin inside his barely buttoned eye-searingly tacky shirt.

Following them for a few blocks, Allan started to get the feeling they were more likely just co-stars in the live sex show on offer at the theater, rather than a genuine couple. Which didn't bode well for any kind of added emotional torment when he made one watch the other die. He was about to give up on the pair and start looking for inspiration elsewhere, when a female voice called out to him from a shadowy doorway.

"Hey, man."

He turned toward the voice, which belonged to a skinny brunette with a pixie haircut and a silver raincoat. Her bony shoulders were slumped and defeated. Her eyes were already dead. She wouldn't meet his gaze.

"Hey," he replied.

"Got a light?" she asked, raising an unlit cigarette to her chapped lips.

He pulled a disposable lighter from his hip pocket, cupping his hand over the flame, and lit her cigarette. She inhaled deeply, gaze flicking up to him for a fleeting second, then away again.

"So," she said. "You wanna…?"

She tipped her chin back toward the door behind her. He nodded.

She led him past a row of warped, pried open and broken brass mailboxes, then into the dim and stinking lobby. She paused for a second, her back to him, then toed a crumpled Chinese takeout menu on the octagonal tiled floor. He thought maybe she was having second thoughts. Rightly so, considering what he planned to do to her. But then she plunged her cigarette into the dirty sand that filled the tall steel ashtray and motioned that he should follow her up the cracked marble stairs.

Her single room was on the third floor, at the end of a long, crooked hallway that smelled like urine, roach-spray, and despair. From behind one of the doors there came a vociferous argument going on between two drunks of indeterminate gender. This might be a good thing for Allan, because it would mask any sounds the girl might make during their encounter. Or it could be problematic if it became too violent and attracted the police.

Allan smiled to himself at his overly cautious thinking. After all, how often did the police get called by the denizens of a place like this? Not unless someone was dead, Allan surmised. And by that time, he would be long gone.

Inside the girl's room it was dank and shabby. The kind of room that was destined to be immortalized in a crime scene photo. The only decoration was a torn and peeling black light poster of a topless woman with an afro and a pet panther. The bed was a spavined, overworked wreck that sagged in the center. The colorful Navajo blanket thrown over the worn-out mattress didn't do a very good job at hiding the stains.

The girl's name was Desiree, or that's what she said it was anyway. Allan honestly could not have cared less. What he did care about was the impression that she was a woman who had completely and utterly given up on life. Under her raincoat, she wore only a bra and panties, both of them cheap and mismatched with worn-out, sagging elastic.

Her emaciated arms and legs were peppered with weeping, infected track marks. She moved as if hypnotized, face mask-like and eyes far away. Going through the motions, like a person who was already dead and just didn't know it yet.

Like a Casanova who sees a frigid woman as a challenge, Allan found himself profoundly aroused by her indifference. How sweet it would be to torture her and make her want to live again, only to see that fresh, rekindled hope die in her eyes as she realized that wasn't going to happen.

"Why don't you lie on the bed," he told her. "On your stomach."

She did what she was told.

He took out his knife and smiled.

19

"Institute for the Advancement of Bio-Spiritual Awarness," Walter read off the small, unassuming sign above the buzzer in a urine-scented Berkley doorway, between a delicatessen and a head shop. "Sounds intriguing."

"Sounds like some kind of cult," Bell said. "You know, like est, or the Moonies, or something."

"Doctor Raley's not a guru," Nina said, pressing the buzzer. "He's a scientist. You'll like him." A muffled buzz and a click, and Nina pushed the door open. Walter and Bell followed her through.

Inside was a clean, modern waiting area with several groupings of orange and white plastic chairs and low Lucite tables strewn with a variety of interesting scientific journals and magazines. It looked not unlike an ordinary doctor's office. A slender young Asian woman in a lavender pantsuit was sitting behind a desk and reading a dog-eared copy of Erving Goffman's *The Presentation of the Self in Everyday Life*.

She stood when they entered and greeted Nina warmly.

"Hi, May," Nina said. "These are my friends William Bell and Walter Bishop. They're in town for the ABS Conference."

"Nice to meet you both," she said, reaching out a delicate hand to shake first Walter's, then Bell's. "I have a background in biochemistry myself." She smiled, revealing gapped teeth. "I did my thesis on the circular dichroism of helical polypeptides, but more recently I've become interested in the use of biofeedback technology to regulate what up until now has been considered involuntary organ function."

"Fascinating," Walter said, utterly charmed by this lovely and studious young lady. "My colleague and I just presented a very well-received paper on hepatic microsomal drug-binding sites. Have you had any success using biofeedback to regulate other kinds of liver function? Perhaps we could compare notes sometime." He reached into his pocket. "Necco wafer?"

"Walter…" Bell warned.

"Is the good doctor in?" Nina asked, suppressing a grin.

May reached out and selected a clove-flavored purple wafer from the roll. That was his favorite.

"Thank you," she said, popping the candy into her mouth with what Walter swore was a flirtatious expression. Though he was the first to admit he was often wrong about such things. "Doctor Rayley is in the lab working on a new experiment. You can wait for him in the observation room, if you'd like. This way please."

At that point, Walter was prepared to follow May anywhere, but he was disappointed to find that she had no intention of joining them. She just showed them to a door at the end of a long hallway, and then returned to her desk.

"I think I'm in love," Walter stage-whispered to Bell, taking a lime Necco wafer off the roll for himself, before putting the package back in his pocket.

"I hardly think this is the time for sexual liaisons, Walter," Bell said.

Nina said nothing, but her subtle smile and arched brow made Bell stammer and blush.

"Well," he said. "I mean…"

"Come on," she said, opening the door and ushering the two men inside.

The long narrow room reminded Walter of the viewing area adjacent to an old-fashioned operating theater, where medical students would observe various procedures, back before sterilization and the invention of closed circuit television cameras. There were three rows of stadium-like riser seats facing a large one-way pane the size of a movie screen. And, like an old-fashioned operating theater, there was a small group of enraptured young people with notebooks—students, presumably—observing the procedure occurring on the other side of the glass.

Walter stepped up to the glass to see what was going on in the adjacent room.

There were two subjects, both male and Caucasian, but that's where the similarities ended. The man on the left was young and gangly, with an unfortunate beaky profile and long, sandy hair. The man on the right was older and pudgy, with a gleaming bald head and a weak chin hidden beneath a steely gray goatee. Each man was hooked up to a heart rate monitor that displayed the function of that organ for the students to observe.

The two were laid out on the sort of low-profile, bed-shaped couches you might see in an analyst's office, heads toward the middle of the room. In the center, sandwiched in the narrow space between two folding rice paper screens, was a third man.

He was in his mid-forties, with a thick shock of unruly white hair, large square glasses, and a jovial, slightly mischievous manner that reminded Walter of Willy Wonka in that film that had come out a few years back. He was dressed in a lab coat and was fiddling with a toaster-sized machine that sat on a spidery steel table. This, he assumed, was Doctor Rayley.

"What is he working on today?" Nina asked a young, redheaded man with a spare mustache and a Dr Pepper T-shirt.

"He's synchronized the subjects heartbeats," the young man said, "and is now seeing if one is able to control the frequency of the other."

"Any success?" Walter asked.

"More luck with slowing than raising," the Dr Pepper kid replied. "They tend to go out of sync once they go above a hundred beats per minute."

"Well," Walter said, "that's still quite impressive, and potentially relevant for our own study. I'm particularly interested in the fact that he is able to achieve synchronization of subjects without the use of wires or electrodes to connect them either to the biofeedback machine or to each other." He turned. "We must speak with him at once, Belly!"

"We can't just barge in on an experiment in progress," Bell replied.

"I suppose you're right," Walter admitted, chastened.

"It's been an hour and forty-five minutes already," the Dr Pepper kid said. "Shouldn't be much longer now."

Walter sat down on the far end of one of the risers, studying the machine in the center of the room and trying to work out its various components and functions.

Trying to think of ways it might be adapted to serve their purpose. He unfolded the schematic he'd sketched out for Bell, and started making a few modifications.

Before he knew it, the experiment was over and the two subjects were attended to by nurses who checked them over thoroughly and helped them sit up. They both seemed upbeat, excited by their accomplishments and impatient with the nurses' poking and prodding. Doctor Rayley embraced each of his subjects as if they were family, before allowing them to leave the lab.

He then disappeared through a hidden door and reappeared in the observation area, greeting each of his students by name and taking time to thoughtfully answer all of their questions. Bell had to grab Walter by the back of his collar to prevent him from barging over to accost Doctor Rayley with a hundred questions of his own.

But Nina had more subtle ways of attracting Doctor Rayley's attention and within minutes, she'd drawn him into her gravitational field without even trying.

"Miss Sharp," he said, arms wide. "To what do I owe this unexpected pleasure?"

"I have some friends from out of town who are very interested in your biofeedback studies," she said, allowing herself to be embraced and yet somehow not fully participating in it, like a cat tolerating a hug while waiting for food. "Walter Bishop, William Bell, this is Doctor Jeremey Rayley."

"Yes, yes," Rayley said extending his hand to both Bell and Walter. "A pleasure, indeed."

"We are currently conducting a series of experiments not unlike your own recent work, involving the synchronization of multiple minds," Walter blurted out. "We were hoping that you might allow us to borrow one of your devices, to test their use under very specific field conditions."

"If it were anyone but Miss Sharp," Rayley said. "I wouldn't even consider letting one of my patented machines out of the building. But what you say intrigues me—I don't mind telling you that I've been very interested in the use of biofeedback to control various brain functions. Particularly the more esoteric ones, such as…" He paused for dramatic effect, waggling his considerable eyebrows. "Telepathy and telekinesis. I know for a fact that those are specific topics of Nina's personal studies." He cast a glance in her direction.

"We will gladly share the results of our research," Walter said, ignoring Bell's warning glare. "As scientists, we are all in this together, aren't we?"

"Ah, yes, quite right," Rayley said. "Science, like love, should be free for all."

20

They left the Institute for the Advancement of Bio-Spiritual Awareness with two large cardboard boxes filled with equipment and supplemental parts. There was barely enough room in the back seat of Nina's Beetle to fit everything so Walter ended up having to hold one of the boxes in his lap for the drive back in to San Francisco.

He didn't complain, though, and when Nina looked up at his reflection in the rearview mirror, she could practically see the wheels turning behind his eyes. He almost looked happy. She wished that she could share his enthusiasm, and sincerely hoped that this crazy plan of theirs would work, but all she could see were flaws and weaknesses.

They returned to the house, and Walter and Bell immediately went to work on modifying the biofeedback rig to Walter's specifications. Nina tried very hard not to be bothered by the mess of wires and solder they made in her pristine bedroom, which offered a much more effective working space than the crowded basement.

After a time, she decided to go out for cigarettes.

Outside, the mess had been cleared out of the street, but the neighbors' house was still in chaotic disarray, the missing wall along the front of the top floor covered by a flapping tarp. The place looked deserted, no sign of the family—the McBrides, she thought their name was. They must have gone to stay with relatives or friends.

She felt a slight twinge of guilt over what had happened to them, and to Mrs. Baumgartner, too, but quickly sloughed it off, focusing instead on planning ahead, running scenarios in her mind and picking them apart.

As she turned and headed down the block toward the liquor store, she lit the last cigarette left in the pack. The street seemed weirdly empty for midday. An occasional car trundled up the hill and past her. The only person in sight was a colorful bum that she saw almost every day, an eccentric local character nicknamed "Circles" by the people in the neighborhood.

He had a dozen colorful ribbons braided into his dirty beard and had earned his nickname because of his strange way of walking. Instead of moving in a straight line, he got from place to place by walking in a chain of tight circles. Sometimes it took him two or three hours just to travel the length of one block.

When he saw Nina, he executed a couple of agitated circles in her direction, waving his skinny arms.

"The man wants you!" he shouted. "You watch out! He'll do it to you! I know!"

"How you doing, Circles?" she said with an indulgent smile, wrinkling her nose against the scent he emitted. She held up her cigarette. "I'd give you a smoke, but this is my last one. How about I give you one on the way back from the store, okay?"

"The man!" he said again. "He doesn't think I know, but I know." He tapped his temple with a black fingernail.

"Nobody's gonna tell me what I know!"

Clearly she wasn't going to get through to him.

"See you later, Circles," Nina said, waving with her cigarette hand and walking away, smoke trailing behind her.

Even though the streets were relatively empty, there was a small line at the liquor store, including an elderly woman who wanted to get input from everyone about which lottery numbers "felt most lucky." Nina was about ready use a bottle of Tab to conk the old biddy on the back of her bouffanted head. But she wasn't confident that the bottle would make a dent in that blue Aqua Net helmet.

The woman finally got her lucky numbers sorted out, and Nina finally got her two packs of Virginia Slims and her diet soda.

On her way out the jingling door, she stuffed the soda and one of the two packs of cigarettes into her purse, and then started to peel the cellophane off the second pack. She was planning to give one of the cigarettes to Circles, like she'd said she would, but as she turned to walk back to her house, she didn't see him anywhere.

Strange, she thought.

Circles was so slow that it took him ages to get anywhere, and he had been in the middle of the block when Nina had talked to him. Yes, it had been a longer wait then she'd expected at the liquor store, but not more than ten or fifteen minutes. It would usually take Circles at least an hour to cycle his way from the middle of the block to one of the cross streets.

No one on the block would have invited him into their house or car, smelling the way he did. The only place he could have gone was up the driveway on the left side of the shabby apartment building across the street from her place.

Curious, she waited for a car to pass, then headed over, open pack of cigarettes in her hand. But when she reached the mouth of the driveway in question, she paused.

It was broad daylight, and while her neighborhood certainly wasn't the safest in the world, it was hardly a crime-infested war zone. There was no reason why she should hesitate about entering the alley.

But she did.

It just didn't feel right.

Circles wasn't visible from where Nina was standing, but that didn't mean he wasn't in there. There were a large dumpster, some stray trash bags, and a stained, discarded twin mattress down at the far end. He easily could have been behind the debris. Probably just taking a piss. Or worse. And that was nothing she needed to see.

Nina looked down at the pack of cigarettes, then turned on her heel, tucking the smokes into her purse and heading back home.

"Aw, don't go," Allan whispered. "Come back and join us, Miss Nina Sharp."

But she didn't, and with conflicting emotion, he watched her walk away. On the one hand, he knew that the time wasn't yet right for him to have her, and any deviation from the plan made him anxious, as if it might spiral wildly out of control. But there was another part of him that yearned for her without regard for all his cautious preparation.

He still knew next to nothing about the two hippies from Reiden Lake, but Nina Sharp, she had been easy to research. Starting with her registration for the cute little green Volkswagen Beetle, Allan had leapfrogged through her paper trail, eager to learn everything he could about her.

Nina Louise Sharp was twenty-eight, never married. Middle child of three daughters, born here in San Francisco to Sullivan and Marie Sharp. Abandoned by her philandering father and ignored by her overworked mother, Nina seemed to have thrown herself into achieving academic excellence. Her school records showed that she was a straight-A student and the valedictorian of her graduating class at Balboa High School.

From there she went on to be accepted at Stanford with full academic scholarship.

Allan had been surprised to find that Nina owned not only the ugly lavender house she lived in with those insufferable musicians, but also a second rental property that was bringing in a tidy little income. She had substantial resources, as well, from a variety of shrewd investments. Miss Nina Sharp was not only ambitious, she was extremely good with money and while she was far from wealthy now, he could see that she would be in the future.

Too bad she wouldn't have a future.

Beneath Allan's boot, the bum with the stupid ribbons in his beard writhed and choked, blood bubbling from the necklace of stab wounds around his filthy throat. He clutched weakly at Allan's pant leg, and Allan kicked his shaking fingers away. Torturing the human vermin had seemed mildly amusing for a few moments, but now the bum's agony just seemed pathetic and irritating.

He knelt down beside the useless bum and stared into his contorted, uncomprehending face. So much of the joy of killing was watching his victims come to the understanding that they would not survive. Torturing a mentally incompetent person like this man was never satisfying on that deeper level, because they had no idea what was happening to them.

Allan looked down at his hands. They were completely normal, not even the faintest hint of the sparks below the skin. The bum's suffering had failed to invoke any reaction whatsoever.

With a weary sigh, he slid the blade of his knife into the creature's right eye. He held it there for a moment, until the body stopped moving. When he was sure that the bum was dead, he pulled the knife out, wiped both sides of the blade on the man's filthy purple shirt, and put it back in his jacket pocket.

Time to go see what Miss Nina Sharp and her two boyfriends were up to.

21

"Everything okay?" Bell asked when Nina walked back in to her room.

"Sure," she replied, shrugging. "Just went for cigarettes." She peered over his shoulder. "How's it going?"

"Excellent," Walter said, patting the newly assembled machine sitting on greasy newspaper in the center of her bedroom floor. "I could probably continue to play around with a variety of optional modifications, if time were not a factor, but I feel that the prototype is ready for its first trial run."

"Here's the thing," Bell said. "I don't think it's a good idea to try to open the gate again in this house. This neighborhood, it's just too densely populated."

"I agree wholeheartedly," Walter said. "We should try to find a different location, a place that is both secure and relatively isolated."

The two of them looked over at Nina.

"Right," she said. "I'm thinking..."

"Think faster," Bell said. "We mustn't forget that the longer it takes us to figure out how to reliably open that gateway, and keep it open long enough to put the Zodiac back where he belongs, the more time he has to act on his murderous impulses."

"Yes, of course," Walter said. "But that doesn't justify risking the lives of innocent bystanders."

"I've already said as much, Walter," Bell responded brusquely. "There's no need to belabor the point."

"I've got it," Nina said. "Roscoe and his band have a rehearsal space over in India Basin. It's big, secure, and was specifically chosen because there are no neighbors to complain about the noise. The few neighboring buildings that have active businesses all close down before 6 p.m. and that block isn't zoned for residences. It's perfect."

"The place where Violet Sedan Chair rehearses," Walter intoned. "I would love to see it."

The three of them packed up their equipment, piled into the Beetle and headed down to India Basin.

The Violet Sedan Chair rehearsal space really was perfect. It was inside an unmarked and unremarkable brick building on Spear Avenue, across the street from an abandoned shipyard. There wasn't a single vehicle parked on the street, no sign of a living soul. Unless one wanted to include the fat brown wharf rats Walter spotted trundling over the piles of scrap.

They entered the building through a smaller door cut into a huge metal rolling door the size of a drive-in movie screen. Nina flipped a huge switch that wouldn't have looked out of place in Doctor Frankenstein's laboratory. For such an impressive switch, the resulting illumination was somewhat disappointing. Just a few motley antique floor lamps with red and blue bulbs, a single black light that made their teeth and eyes glow, and a small lamp illuminating the keyboard of a majestic old grand piano.

There was a giant Persian rug that made the rough shape of a stage in the center of the concrete floor. The piano and a garish, fluorescent green and orange drum kit were situated on it, as if the door were the audience. Along the back edge of the rug stood a wall of amplifiers that made Walter's ears hurt just looking at them.

There were also several battered couches and chairs situated as if to observe performances on the rug-stage. A streamlined, 1950s refrigerator was off to one side, and a portable heater plugged into a long, snaking extension cord on the other. When Walter peeked into the fridge, he discovered that it was empty except for a single lonely can of beer and a package of Ho Hos.

Directly above the rug-stage was a large, grimy skylight.

"Yes," Walter said. "Yes, I think this will be ideal."

"It's a bit chilly," Bell noted, waving his fingers through the pale steam formed by his breath. He set down the canvas messenger bag that he had used to carry the alpha wave generator.

"Clearly that's what this is for," Nina said, cranking the knob on the heater and releasing a dusty hot electric train smell.

"I wish we'd opted for hot coffee instead of cola for the mixer," Bell said, setting down the small cooler at Walter's feet.

"Absolutely," Walter agreed, opening the cooler and taking out a bottle. "But we want to keep as many variables consistent as possible."

Bell took a bottle for himself, and then pulled out the tiny vial of their special blend. He dosed both of their beverages with the exact same amount as the previous experiments, then placed the vial and syringe on top of the cooler.

"Okay, boys," Nina said, pulling her gun and a stopwatch from her purse. "Where do you want me to be?"

"I think it would be best if we lay down here, on this rug beneath the skylight," Walter said, taking a swig of his medicated cola. "We can place the biofeedback machine in the center and Nina, you wait there by the piano."

"We don't know exactly where the gate will open," Bell said. "But I can't imagine it would be more than a few feet away."

"What if I can't see it?" Nina asked. "What if only altered minds are able to perceive the gateway?"

"Well, we have no prior data to assess," Walter said, casting a meaningful glance in their direction. "So we won't know until we try. That's why we have to experiment like this, in a controlled area, so that when it comes time to confront the killer, we'll be ready to put him back where he belongs."

"But for now," Bell said. "We'll do our best to articulate what we're seeing. That way, even if you don't see it, you'll know exactly when it opens and where it's located in relation to us."

Walter and Bell clinked their bottles together and drained their dosed colas, then went to work setting up the small, battery-operated biofeedback rig they'd modified to sync their alpha waves during the trip.

When everything was set, they lay down on the faded carpet and waited.

Walter concentrated on the soothing hum of the wireless machine, working on staying as calm and open-minded as possible, then focusing on the rhythm of Bell's breath and trying to slow his own to match.

▲

He was just starting to experience the first hints of hallucinogenic onset, simple geometric shapes hunching along the edges of perception like bulky, glowing inch worms, when the band showed up.

"Hey, Nina!" Roscoe said, a big inebriated smile on his usually dour face. "Great to see you, babe." He paused, a comical look of surprise supplanting the grin. "Is that a gun?"

Nina plunged her gun hand into the suede purse.

"Um... no." She took her now empty right hand from the purse, and ran it over her hair. "What are you guys doing here? I thought you usually rehearsed on Thursdays."

"You know how it is," Chick said, the sticker-covered guitar case in one hand. "Some times you just get bit by the inspiration bug."

Two other men whom Walter hadn't met yet came in behind Chick, both with guitar cases of their own. He didn't need to be introduced to the other two members of Violet Sedan Chair. He instantly recognized Alex Chambers and Oregon Dave Ormond from the photo on their album cover, and his tripping mind painted their skin with the appropriate psychedelic colors and organic paisley shapes.

From an experimental standpoint, this was a disaster, but he couldn't suppress his childlike excitement over the appearance of the whole band. He wanted to jump up and greet them, but he was surprised to find that his body had melded with the weave of the dusty rug beneath him, making it impossible to get up.

He watched Chick hug Nina, lifting her off her feet and spinning her in a circle. Her shimmering red hair and green suede heels left spiral trails in the air, distracting him until Roscoe found the vial of their special acid blend on top of the cooler, and held it up for the rest of the band to see.

"Check this, man," he said. "This looks like some pharmaceutical grade shit right here."

"You put that down," Nina said, lunging at him.

Roscoe tossed the vial to Chick, like big kids playing keep away from a smaller child in a schoolyard.

"Look at these two," Iggy, the drummer said, gesturing to Walter and Bell splayed out on the carpet. "They're tripping balls!"

"Far out," Roscoe said. "We need to knock off a piece of that action."

Chick grabbed the syringe and started to fill it from the vial while the other laughing musicians kept Nina back.

"Chick, don't..." she began, but it was too late. He squirted the dose directly into his mouth.

Nina threw up her hands, disgusted, as Chick passed the vial to Roscoe.

"Don't be so uptight, Nina," Roscoe said, dosing himself. "You need to loosen up. Live a little. Share the wealth." He went from person to person, dosing the rest of the band like a mama bird feeding her chicks.

"Okay, look," Nina said. "We're conducting a scientific experiment here."

"My kinda science," Alex said, opening his mouth wide to receive the chemical sacrament.

"Just shut up and *listen*," she snapped.

The band members settled down, like unruly kids brought to heel by a feared teacher.

"Since you've already helped yourselves," she continued. "The least you can do is help us in return. Right?"

"Help you how?" Iggy asked.

"The experiment," she said, "is in telepathy and

shared experience. My two colleges are attempting to sync minds using a combination of the hallucinogenic compound you just ingested, and enhanced biofeedback technology."

"Far out, man," Dave said. "What do you need from us?"

"Why don't you guys lie down in the circle here," she suggested. "And see if any of you are able connect your minds with them. The image that I want you to picture in your minds is a gateway, like a portal in the air. Okay?"

Brilliant, Walter thought from within the depths of his trip.

She's brilliant, Bell's mind echoed inside Walter's head. *Brilliant and ruthless.*

If the musicians were on the trip with them, linked in and working in synch, would it not naturally strengthen and enhance the gate? It might even allow the gate to stay stable, and open even longer. And while Walter had never even considered involving anyone else in their experiment, due to the risks involved, Nina didn't bat an eye. She just saw an opportunity to take advantage of an unexpected situation, and took it.

Walter could feel Bell's mind reaching out to her again, drawn to her like a moth to a flame. A flame like her red hair, falling coquettishly around her face like shimmering waves of liquid autumn.

Walter shook his head, feeling himself drawn to Nina, as well. But they needed her on the *outside*, now more than ever. They needed to stay focused, and so did she. Especially with this sudden and unexpected influx of unknown individuals.

Belly, he said, or thought, or just imagined that he thought. *Focus!* He reached out to Bell with his mind, calling him back into the loop of their own intimate connection. Reluctantly, Bell allowed his attention to be turned away from Nina and back to the task at hand.

The band members settled into a rough ring around the biofeedback machine, heads toward the center. At first they were snickering and goofing around, but as the acid started to kick in, they all settled down and grew quiet.

Roscoe's mind opened itself to Walter first, revealing an intricate, endless Fibonacci spiral, like a transparent nautilus, each tiny chamber haunted by a treasured fragment of music. Then Chick and Alex joined the psychic orchestra, light and dark twins blown like autumn leaves on the wind of Roscoe's music. Then Dave, a quiet, soulful presence defined by simple pleasures like sunshine and a girl's laughter and pancakes and memories of a childhood dog. Then Iggy, his strong, comforting thoughts as regular and steady as his drum beats, creating order out of the tripping chaos.

And Walter, feeling like a conductor, poised with baton held high above the orchestra pit.

"Now," he said. Or maybe he just thought it.

And the gate opened.

Allan peered down through the skylight of the warehouse at the tremulous shimmer that had boiled to life like steam from a kettle in the middle of the circle of musicians. He had seen that light before, on the same night he had first seen the two hippies from Reiden Lake. The same night the pigs and their dogs had chased him into the water. The same night he had tumbled through the strange gateway and found himself in another world that was so like, and yet so *unlike*, his own.

He had always wondered what had opened the gate

that brought him to this world, but he had never been able to formulate any kind of concrete theory. It had all happened too quickly, and in the middle of such chaos, that he hadn't been able to objectively observe the phenomenon.

He'd turned the mystery over in his mind during his idle hours, and had even considered the possibility that it might have been his own desperate desire to escape that had somehow opened up a hole between worlds, and granted him his wish.

But here was a much more convincing explanation. He had just seen the entire assemblage take acid and arrange themselves in a circle around this weird machine, to participate in some sort of communal trip. And out of that trip had risen the shimmer.

It must have been the same at Reiden Lake. He was tripping, and those kids must have been tripping, too, linking the three of them into a mutual experience that had opened a hole in the fabric between their worlds, and allowed him to fall through.

Allan's heart clenched like a fist in his chest as it all became clear. Those two seemingly harmless, bumbling idiots had come to San Francisco not just to stop him, but to send him back to the world of his birth.

He stood and stepped back from the skylight. This could not happen. He could not *allow* it to happen.

As he drew his gun and turned back to the edge of the roof, he paused. There was smoke in the air. And the sound of screaming.

22

The trip was breaking up, fading fast. Above them, the shimmering gate was dissipating as well, its long, reaching tendrils breaking into watery fragments that spun away into misty nothingness.

Roscoe sat up beside Walter on the Persian carpet and looked up at the skylight.

"Oh... wow, man," he said. "That thing, it was... wow... I think I got enough material out of that trip for an entire concept album. We need to jam. Right now, while the juices are still flowing!"

Roscoe leapt to his feet and staggered over to the piano. Walter blinked and looked up—he had been completely focused on Bell, trying to hold open the connection for as long as possible.

In the background, he registered sounds from outside, but they were too far away for him to identify their nature.

"B-flat," Roscoe said, fingers playing over the keys with a funky little riff.

Walter ignored the ecstatic singer and looked over at Nina, who still stood by with her handgun and stopwatch, just outside of the circle.

"How long?" he asked. "How long was it open."

She checked the watch.

"Thirty-seven seconds," she said. "Maybe thirty-eight."

Iggy the drummer sat up, scratching his beard and wearing a dreamy expression. Beside him Chick Spivy was suddenly reanimated by the sound of Roscoe's playing, and responded by rolling over and unlatching his guitar case.

"That's it, man," he said, unwrapping a length of cord and plugging into the wall of amps. He prodded the prone base player with the toe of a battered Frye boot. "Come on, Davey! Get in on this."

A blast of wailing sound hit Walter like a tidal wave as Chick strummed out a set of heavy power chords.

"Alone I was only able to open the gate for a few seconds," Walter hollered, gesturing wildly at Bell and shouting at the top of his lungs to be heard over the music. "And together, you and I kept it open for what, ten seconds? Fifteen?"

"It's so obvious, I can't believe we didn't think of it sooner." Bell rolled away from the drum kit as Iggy mounted up and started banging out a back beat. "More people. Longer time. And having the alpha wave generator helped us all synchronize minds and stay connected. It allowed us to link minds and share the same trip. We opened the portal together, wider and longer than ever before."

Bell scooped up the alpha wave generator and slipped it into the canvas messenger bag he'd used to bring it in.

"But this is excellent." Walter grabbed one of Bell's arms with his right hand and one of Nina's with the left, and dragged them toward the door, away from the wall of throbbing sound emanating from the happy and oblivious musicians. "Thirty-eight seconds, even twenty-eight, would surely be enough time to goad our quarry through the rift. All we have to do is gather another similarly sized test group." He shouldered open the door and shoved Nina and Bell through. "Then lure the killer to the spot as the trip reaches its—" he slammed the door "—peak."

The shouted word *peak* echoed down the street, way too loud now that the music was muffled by the closed door.

"Is *that* all?" Nina said, raising a sarcastic eyebrow. "And how do you propose that we set it up? Who do you suggest we…"

Walter frowned, held up a finger, and looked around.

"Does anyone else smell smoke?" he asked.

They scanned the length of the block, and spotted flickering orange light playing over the brick and corrugated metal skins of the buildings at the far end of the block. The night was suddenly thick with the stink of burning plastic, and filled with frightened shouts. From the shipyard across the street came a sound like bridge cables twisting in a high wind.

"Oh, dear." Walter closed his eyes. "Not again."

"I thought there weren't any people in this neighborhood?" Bell said.

"There weren't supposed to be," Nina said. "Not on this block, anyway. But if more trippers equaled a longer duration for the gate, maybe it also equaled a wider psychic blast radius."

"Did you notice the tendrils spreading out from the edges of the gateway?" Walter asked.

"Yes!" Bell replied. "Clearly that's the moment when the psychic bleed through begins. Nina, do you remember how long the gate was open before the tendrils became visible?"

A scream from an alley three buildings to the left cut off her reply.

"Get 'em off me!" A high, tremulous voice echoed through the alley. "Get 'em off!"

Walter and Bell exchanged a look and ran to the mouth of the narrow passageway. A few yards in, a homeless man was crabbing backward out of his bedroll as if there was a snake in it, and pressing against the dumpster that had been serving as a shelter.

"Get 'em off!" he screeched.

"The DTs?" Bell suggested, brow arched. "Not uncommon in alcoholics."

Walter took a few cautious steps closer to the squirming man.

"No," he said. "Look!"

Under the harsh glare of a security light, he could see the man's naked, grime-caked torso was covered in what looked like rat bites. He was bleeding from more than a dozen crescent-shaped punctures.

Walter ran and grabbed the bottom of the roll and pulled, helping the man shuck clear of the bedding, then threw it away and knelt beside the man.

"Are you alright?" Walter asked. "What was biting you? Was it rats?"

But the man was still twisting and swatting at nothing.

"Get 'em off me!" he cried. "Get 'em *off* me!"

As Walter watched in horror, more bites appeared in the man's flesh, bloody holes torn in his arms, belly, and neck, though there was nothing visible attacking him. It was as if he were being savaged by an invisible swarm of some sort.

"Maybe it really is the DTs," Bell murmured. "Only

they've been psychically amplified by our experiment."

"Dreams made flesh," Walter whispered, half to himself. "But what can we do?"

"I..." Bell shook his head. "I don't know."

"But this is our fault, Belly," Walter said. "You can't deny it this time. It's our fault, and our responsibility."

Walter buried his head in his hands.

"This is terrible," he said. "Terrible."

From the shadows of the alley across the street, Allan peered through his rifle sight, and watched the agitated group. He had several clear and easy shots, including the lovely redhead, Miss Nina Sharp, but he didn't take them. After all, it would be completely pointless to kill them now. They would die like slaughterhouse cows, too stupid to understand what that big bolt gun was for.

No, he wanted time to taunt them, time to play with them and show them who had the upper hand. But Nina and his two special friends were alone now. No witnesses, except for the crazed bum.

Allan was a man who liked to stick to the plan no matter what. Yet here was such a tempting opportunity. He could kill the tall one first, to show the other two he meant business, then threaten Nina and make the curly haired one beg him to spare her life. It would be interesting to see how far the kid would debase himself to save her, and then whether or not he would plead for his own life once she was dead.

He moved toward the mouth of the alley and was about to raise the rifle to his shoulder when running steps to his left checked his stride. A policeman, young and red-faced, with a sad attempt at a mustache like a smudge of ash on his sweaty upper lip. He was running down the sidewalk, gun drawn and staring ahead at the glow at the end of the block.

Allan stepped back into the shadows. The cop glanced into the alley after him, then ran on. Allan let out a long, slow, relieved breath.

Too soon.

The cop skidded to a stop and looked back, then raised his gun and started edging back toward the alley, raising his high-pitched and strident voice.

"You in the alley," the young cop called. "Put your weapon on the ground and kick it out where I can see it, then step out."

The glowing sparks had already begun their gleeful dance under the skin of his hands and forearms. The stupid little piggy was ruining his perfect moment, and now he would have to be taken care of, too. But not out on the street.

Allan took a step back. And then another.

A voice rose above the moans of the bleeding homeless man, and pulled Walter's attention back down toward the street. A young cop with a mustache was aiming his gun at the mouth of the alley on the far side, and calling for someone to come out. Walter looked into the alley and stiffened in shock. There was a man in the shadows.

A man with a gun, backing away.

Although the retreating man's body was shrouded in darkness, his arms and his hands glowed as if lit from within, the mesmerizing dance of sparks reflecting in the squared lenses of familiar glasses. Walter's heart kicked into double-time at the sight. He knew those sparks. He knew that face.

"The killer." Walter took a step back and stumbled into Bell. He pointed. "The Zodiac Killer. He's there!"

"But how?" Bell frowned, disbelieving.

"He must have followed us!"

Nina grabbed them both and shoved them behind the dumpster.

"Let the cop deal with it," she hissed. "There's nothing we can do."

Walter and Bell ducked down behind the metal bulk and peeked over the lip.

"Is this it?" Bell asked, incredulous. "Is this how it ends?"

"I hope so," Walter replied. "Lord, I hope so."

"Come on," Nina whispered. "Be a good little piggy and shoot that bastard."

Allan took another step back, his teeth clenched in annoyance. Why wasn't the cop coming into the alley? He couldn't shoot him if he was standing out in the street.

Why wasn't he following?

Then he understood. He needed to put himself into the unevolved animal mindset of the cop brain. Prey that faced him required caution. Prey that fled triggered the instinct of the chase. If Allan ran, the cop would come after him. The primitive protocols of his hindbrain would give the dumb animal no choice.

So Allan ran, and was instantly rewarded by the sound of shouts and footsteps entering the alley and echoing after him. Predictably, the cop had taken the bait and was following him to his doom. Allan scanned ahead of him, looking for the place to turn and fire. He couldn't keep on luring the little piggy forever.

"Stop," the young pig cried. "Stop, or I'll shoot."

There was a mountain of garbage bags, piled up around an overflowing dumpster. They were already primed for an avalanche. Pull one down as he went by, and the cop would be stumbling through a landslide of trash. It would be simple then to shoot him before he recovered, then finish him before anyone came to investigate.

Suddenly Allan's foot slipped in some foul slime dripping from the dumpster, and instead of grabbing at the mountain of garbage bags, he crashed into them. He came up again, in an instant, flailing for balance, and turned toward the office, rifle in hand.

Blam!

Pain flared hot in Allan's left shoulder, and he staggered back, grunting as fear and rage melded with the pain, and transmogrified into something more than the sum of their parts. The unnatural sparks of his strange sickness melded together and blossomed out like a miniature mushroom cloud, enveloping the cop, the alley, and the buildings to either side in an eerie glittering light.

And then, just as quickly as it had appeared, the glowing cloud was gone—and so was the cop, reduced to atoms by the radiation exploding from Allan's body. Half the trash bags were gone, too, vaporized. The other half were on fire. The metal of the dumpster had melted like candle wax. The bricks in the walls of the buildings to either side were charred and smoking.

Allan knelt in the center of it all, hissing through his teeth and clutching his shoulder. The pain was overwhelming, blurring his vision, numbing his mind. He forced himself to focus. He'd never been shot before. It was… illuminating. Interesting to be on the other side of things, for once.

Now, however, was not the time to dwell on it. He

had to get to safety. See to his wound. Regroup.

"I seen you!"

Allan looked around. There was a woman, coming out of the darkness at the far end of the alley, wearing the filthy clothes of a vagrant. The glare from a parking lot security light showed him the side of her face as she passed. It was bright red, as if she had stuck half of her head in boiling water. Her hair was smoking.

"I seen what you done," she shrieked. "Blew that cop up. Blew my goddamn hair right off my head. *I seen you!*"

Allan ground his teeth. Another witness. This situation was becoming untenable. He had to extricate himself.

He raised his gun.

The woman squealed and ran. Allan pulled the trigger.

It didn't fire. He looked at it. All the moving parts had fused into a single gun-shaped lump of metal. He cursed and started after the woman, wincing as his shoulder wound jolted him with every step.

The far end of the alley was blocked off by a fence, and the vagrant woman was flailing against the fence like a trapped insect, too stupid to realize that she could climb.

Coming up behind, Allan grabbed her around her waist. She was rail thin, light as a box kite, but panic made her strong. She tried to bite Allan's arm, but her loose, wobbly teeth fell out of her burnt and bleeding gums. The skin on her birdy little ribcage sloughed off in Allan's grip like the skin of a boiled tomato.

Disgusted, he threw her down on the ground and knelt on her chest, crushing her throat with one shin. She scrabbled and kicked furiously for what felt like forever, but eventually the life ran out of her and she went still beneath him.

There was no joy for Allan in this kill. No thrill, no sparks, just a grim sense of duty, underscored by the same annoyance and resentment he'd felt when putting down that stinking bum with the ribbons in his beard.

He had no idea how the hell things had gotten so far out of hand.

23

Walter rose cautiously from behind the dumpster where he and Bell and Nina had ducked when the eerie flash had happened. He looked down the alley across the street. It was dark again. There was no more unnatural light. There were no more sparks. In the murk, he couldn't tell if the killer was still there, or if he was gone, or dead.

He couldn't see the cop, either.

"Did you see it?" he asked. "Did you see what happened?"

Beside him, Bell nodded, but didn't seem able to speak. Nina answered for him.

"The cop, he just vanished. He fired his gun, and the guy screamed, and that light came out of his body, and…"

"Gamma radiation." Bell finally found his voice. "When Iverson told us about that, I found it very hard to believe. But I have no choice but to believe the proof of my own eyes. Incredible!"

"Maybe it was the shock of being shot," Walter said. "Or perhaps the pain of it. Either way, his reaction caused the radiation to spike, and… my God!"

A third of Nina's face was as pink as rare roast beef, from her left ear to a little less than halfway across her left eye. The line of demarcation between the pale, unaffected skin and the burnt skin was mathematically perfect. He took Nina's chin and turned the inflamed portion of her face toward Bell.

"It's like... like a sunburn," he said to Bell. "And you, too. The left side of your face."

Bell looked back at him.

"And you too, Walt," Bell said. "You got it the worst out of all of us."

Walter reached up to touch his own face. More than three quarters of the skin felt hot and tight, sore to the touch.

"A sunburn in the middle of the night," Walter said, shaking his head.

"If we had been any closer..." Nina swallowed, pale but for the pink flush of her left side. "We wouldn't be making sunburn jokes, we'd be gathering our teeth up off the pavement."

Walter flinched, picturing the cop's silhouette, vanishing like sand blown away by the wind. It was so much worse than he'd ever imagined.

"And we may have still been too close," Bell said. "The long-term effects of such a blast, we might not know for years. It could affect our health, our children."

Nina cut him off.

"Let's not worry about our future offspring just yet," she said. "We don't know if that bastard died in his own blast, or not, but we'd better make sure."

Bell caught her as she started toward the street.

"If we go into that alley right now," Bell said, "those theoretical long-term effects will happen to us in the short term. Any residual radiation would kill us in a matter of days. Skin loss, organ failure, blindness, cancer."

Walter nodded.

"Iverson said the radiation remained for several hours before dissipating," he added.

"Yet another thing that seemed so hard to believe, at the time," Bell said. "But now…"

Walter looked behind him. The alley they were in ended in a cul-de-sac. He started toward the street, motioning the others to follow.

"Come on," he said. "We should get out of this area as quickly as possible, then warn the authorities about the radiation."

It took courage to walk toward the area where the blast had occurred. Even though he was reasonably certain that the radius of the lingering radiation wouldn't extend out to the street, his skin still tingled with psychosomatic itching at the very thought of the invisible poison in the air.

As they turned right and started for Nina's car, shouts from down the block cut him off. He saw a young blond man in bell-bottom jeans and a bright yellow shirt turn the corner, running right down the middle of the street. He was maybe twenty-one, tops, with a sensual, girlish mouth that didn't look like it belonged on the same face as his big shapeless nose and close-set eyes, half hidden under feathered hair.

He had a wild panicked expression that made a lot more sense when a shouting gang of men in workman's overalls rounded the corner behind him and started chasing after him. The young man was faster than the bigger men, but he was tottering on a pair of precarious platform shoes, and as Walter watched, the inevitable occurred.

The blond man twisted his ankle in a pothole, and nearly fell. The front runner of the gang of work men, a huge, beefy but disturbingly baby-faced man with thinning black hair, caught up to the blond man, grabbing him by the collar of his shirt, spinning him around and then hauling back a meaty fist.

"You set my goddamn car on fire!" he bellowed.

The young blond man cowered and covered up.

"I didn't!" he screamed. "I was just trying to get away. It's your fault. You pushed me!"

"Oh, so it's *my* fault?" The man sneered at his cohorts "He says it's my fault." He turned back. "You want to know what's *your* fault? *This*." He laid a fist into the young man's gut that doubled him up and sent him retching to the ground. "Don't got much to say about that, do you?"

"Leave him alone!" Nina called.

She was striding toward the men, fearless, while Walter and Bell were hanging back. But before she had taken two steps, the young blond man screeched like a bird of prey and every parked car on the street exploded, as if a dozen bombs had been set off in perfect synchronization.

Walter, Bell, and Nina fell back, crashing into the warehouse wall and shielding their faces with their arms as great billows of flame erupted from the gas tanks of the cars, and bits of shrapnel pinged off the bricks around them.

The eruptions sent the workmen running back the way they came, swearing or praying—or maybe both. The young man in the bell-bottoms ran the other way, crying and covering his wavy blond hair as the cars blazed all around him.

"It wasn't me!" he wailed. "I swear it wasn't me!"

Bell sat up and stared after him, shaking his head.

"Amazing," he said. "Poltergeist activity, pyrokinesis, phantom wounding, gamma bursts. All that potential power locked inside ordinary human beings, just waiting to be harnessed or released. We haven't even begun to reach our full potential as a race."

"Or our full potential as mass murderers." Walter turned on Bell, furious. "We have unleashed *monsters*. Turned people's own minds against them. Allowed frightened innocents to lash out at the pain of the world with the strength of gods! This is a nightmare!"

"Yes," Bell said, "but imagine if one could harness these powers of the mind, at the same time as we were amplifying them. If the formula could be perfected and used in a more controlled setting, perhaps with younger subjects whose minds are still open. Think how powerful the human race could become."

"Too powerful," Walter said. "There would be a psychic apocalypse that would tear apart the very fabric our universe."

Nina stood close by.

"Oh, my God," she said. "What about the band? What's happening to them?"

Bell laid a hand on her shoulder.

"Don't worry," he said. "They're as safe as they can be, in the warehouse. It's built to withstand tons of damage. And the way they were playing, I doubt they have any idea what's happening out here."

She nodded. In the distance, police sirens were wailing. Someone had called in the fires. She looked down the street in the direction the blond man had run.

"Come on," she said. "We'd better try to calm that poor guy down before he blows up any more…"

Crash!

She stopped as a section of the wooden fence that surrounded the shipyard smashed flat to the sidewalk. They looked up to see what might follow.

An old boat, rusted and wrecked, with its engine missing and its hull smashed full of jagged holes, was hovering a few feet above the ground and slowly drifting as if caught in a lazy current. It had knocked down a section of the fence, and was now drifting into the next section, splintering the boards and snapping them off at ground level.

Bell swore.

"What now?" Walter asked.

Walter and Nina stared as they saw that the boat was not alone. Behind it, in the dark of the shipyard, other huge shapes floated and spun, all caught in the same inexorable current—propellers, anchors, heavy chains, rusted boilers, engines. It looked like a slow motion cyclone, with all the junk circling the center of the yard.

An army of terrified rats was fleeing down the street like a squirming brown river. Walter watched in horror as several straggler rodents were swept up into the whirlpool, squeaking and defecating in fear as they sailed through the air end over thrashing end.

"Oh, God," said Nina. "It's expanding."

Just as she said it, the rusted out hull of a fishing trawler mashed into the wall of the welding shop next door. It glanced off again just as slowly as it had hit, and only dislodged a few bricks, but Walter saw that Nina was right. The entire whirlpool was getting wider, and more and more junk was going to start smashing into the surrounding buildings.

Walter started across the street.

"Someone's in there, doing this," he said. "We have to stop them. We have to bring them down."

Bell caught his arm and tried to pull him back.

"Are you crazy?" he asked. "We could be crushed! We have to get out of here."

Walter turned on him.

"You remember last time?" he asked. "You said it wasn't our fault because we didn't know what would happen. This time we did know what would happen, and we did it anyway. It's our fault, Belly! The radiation. The fires. We have to do what we can!" He turned to face Nina. "Wait around the corner and warn the firefighters about the radiation in the alley. Say you saw a man with a weird kind of bomb, or a mushroom cloud, or something like that."

"A weird bomb?" Nina rolled her eyes. "Yeah, *that* sounds believable."

"Look I don't care what you tell them," Walter responded, "as long as you make them understand that the area must be cordoned off. I am going into that yard."

Walter wrenched his arm out of Bell's grip and hurried across the street. Nina gave Bell a hard look.

"Alright, Walter," Bell groaned, then he raised his voice. "Alright. I'm *coming*." He backed away from Nina. "Go home as soon as you talk to the firemen. We'll meet back at your place."

"Let's just hope that my car isn't on fire," she said with a look.

24

Allan breathed a sigh of relief as he stepped out of an underground parking garage. The woman had been dealt with, and already the sparks were subsiding.

This had not been a Zodiac killing. It had been another act of necessity. Not that he minded taking the extra lives, but he felt as if his talents were ultimately being wasted. The bum. The Chinese man at the warehouse. They just weren't up to his usual standards. They would be reported as a simple street crime, nothing more. Not even his good friend Special Agent Iverson would know it had been him.

At least he had been able to share Desiree with Iverson. He'd written a long, detailed letter describing all the special moments, and speculating how many other human cockroaches had been taken out by the after-effects of his little one-night stand. And when the time was right, he would write a letter to Iverson about Miss Nina Sharp and her little friends.

From that moment on, there would be no one in this world who would be able to stop him.

He jogged back to the street where the rehearsal studio it was located, hoping he would have a chance to reconnect with the Reiden Lake boys and Miss Sharp. He was suddenly desperate to see them.

He felt like a man in love.

There were sirens on the wind, but still far away. He needed to find the hippies before they fled the scene.

He stopped as he came around the corner. Only a moment earlier, when he had run from the cop, the street had been dark, lit only by the glow of a minor fire down the block. Now the whole street was ablaze with light and thick with black smoke. At least eight cars were burning like torches along both sides. What had happened? Had the boys done this? How could they? No, they wouldn't have had the time.

What the hell was going on?

Then he saw them through the flames—two of them at least, the two boys, their silhouettes entering the shipyard across the street from the rehearsal studio. He increased his pace, then slowed again as a portion of the shipyard fence splintered and toppled onto the sidewalk. Something in the smoke had pushed through. Something large and dark. Was there someone in there operating some kind of wrecking equipment?

The smoke cleared for a moment, and he saw an old shell of a boat, spinning in a lazy circle, like a leaf in a river, as it floated five feet off the ground, flattening the fence as it went. More psychic disturbance. These fools were causing more chaos than he ever had.

That thought should have made him feel jealous or competitive, but instead it increased his desire to play with them. Finally, he had worthy opponents. Not equals, of course, but prey worth chasing. Prolonging the game, until they could share the exquisite moments of their own inevitable deaths.

He went on, more cautious now, and peered through

a broken gap in the fence. The entire contents of the shipyard seemed to have lifted up into a slow swirl, like a cloud of rattle-trap asteroids circling some invisible sun.

No. Not invisible, just hidden. Whatever the gravitational center of this solar system of junk, it looked like it was inside a rusty airstream trailer that appeared to serve the yard as an office. And just as Allan suspected, his quarry were making their way toward it, picking fearfully through the moving maze of floating constellations of rubbish.

Allan slipped inside the fence and started after them.

Walter edged ahead and to the left as a bathtub started to float over his head, then he slipped between a chain fall hoist and a fork lift that looked as if they were dancing together. Bell tiptoed after him, holding his breath as if the slightest sound or movement would bring the whole impossible whirlpool crashing down around them.

There were smaller objects in the air, as well—batteries, springs, gas tanks, a coil of rope undulating like a snake. It was surreal and beautiful and terrifying all at once. A defiance of gravity and logic and science.

Walter wished that they might be experiencing these events under different circumstances, fascinated as he was by the hidden secrets of the mind that this amazing phenomenon suggested. Secrets that had to be explored, and he could imagine spending the rest of his life digging deeper into those mysteries. If only the risks weren't so dire. If only the potential for destruction and death wasn't so terrifyingly clear.

The rounded, silver airstream trailer stood just ahead, alone in a circle of empty air like the eye of a hurricane. Walter stepped up to the door with Bell at his side, each man letting out a relieved breath as they left the floating maze behind.

There were sounds coming from inside the trailer as Walter reached for the handle. An odd, arrhythmic thumping, and tortured grunting. Walter pulled open the door and peered inside. It was dim, but not black. The blue light of a TV flickered from the far end of the trailer, revealing that things were floating in there, too. Papers, books, lamps, pens, pots and pans, a pack of cigarettes. The calendars and posters of bikini girls on the walls rippled and flapped as if they were in a high wind, though the air was dead and still.

The thumping grew louder.

Walter stepped up into the trailer, pushing a floating stapler out of the way, and looked toward the back, toward the light and the noise. He stopped. The TV was on its side pointing at the left wall, a table overturned beside it. On the floor, bathed in the cathode glow, was a man.

He was an older black man with a round jowly face, dressed in coveralls and a knit cap. His back was arched and rigid, and he was twitching as if he'd touched a live wire, with froth bubbling between rigid lips and his eyes wide and staring. The thumping was his right heel kicking spasmodically against the linoleum, as his other limbs twitched and jerked.

"He appears to be in the midst of a grand mal seizure," Walter told Bell over his shoulder. One of the man's flailing hands was encircled by an engraved medical alert bracelet featuring the Hippocratic snake and staff, and the word *EPILEPTIC* in large red letters.

Bell squeezed in on his left.

"Do you think his epilepsy might have been triggered by our… event?"

"Undoubtedly," Walter said, nodding. "And the

electrical storm going on in his head is manifesting in the physical world as that psychic cyclone outside." He started through the debris, ducking through flocks of flapping paper and slowly spinning pens. "But a seizure usually lasts less than a minute. No more than two. We saw that car flatten the fence at least four minutes ago."

"A feedback loop," Bell offered. "The psychic pulse triggered the fit which triggered a larger psychic burst which in turn…"

Walter knelt by the man.

"What can we do for him?" he asked.

Bell knelt beside Walter.

"Nothing," Bell said. "Except maybe turn him on his side so he doesn't choke on all that drool, and make sure he's not going to bang his head on anything."

"Ah, yes. We can do that. Although…" Walter looked up at Bell, uneasy. "I'm concerned about what happens when he comes out of it. Do the things in the air settle gently to the ground, or do they drop all at once? There could be a lot of damage. Someone could get hurt."

"Not much we can do about that, either," Bell replied.

Allan stepped under a floating boat hull and into the clearer air around the trailer. Only a few smaller things—wrenches, pipe fittings, and beer cans—drifted there. He glanced behind as the sound of sirens grew louder. It seemed so unfair that capricious circumstance would force his hand like this, but it was becoming increasingly clear that it would be best to take out the Reiden Lake boys right now.

They were too dangerous and could not be allowed to live. All the other connections to his old life, his old world, had been severed, all except these two. With them gone, the final tie would be cut, and he would be free.

But all the arbitrary killings were wearing on him, making him feel like a butcher, rather than an artist. This was not his destiny, not who he was meant to be.

Should he kill them? Or not?

He crept closer to the trailer door.

Walter put his hands on the man's shoulder and hip, and pushed to rock him over onto his side. His body was so rigid that it was easier than he expected, and the man nearly flopped face first onto the floor. Walter grabbed awkwardly at him to save his teeth, and touched his hand—flesh to flesh.

All at once every floating object in the trailer dropped straight to the ground.

Bell gasped, and began to speak.

He was drowned out by a thunderous crash that shook the trailer. Walter thought he heard someone outside let out a stifled cry, but he couldn't be sure. A bookshelf full of ring binders tipped forward and dumped its load on him, and the battering he received made every other sensation take a back seat.

After a few seconds of coughing and brushing off and sitting up, Bell squinted around, waving at the clouds of dust.

"So much for gently lowering anything to the ground."

Walter looked toward the door.

"I thought I heard someone outside," he said. "We should check. They might be…"

He cut off as the sirens they had been hearing in the background suddenly pushed to the foreground. They could see flashing red and blue lights through the windows of the trailer, and heard the slamming of doors.

"Or perhaps…"

"Wha… what the hell was that?"

They both looked down. The confused watchman was looking up at them, an expression on his face that was equal parts fear and embarrassment.

"I had another one of my fits again," he said. "Didn't I?"

Bell nodded, then shot another glance at the window.

"Er, yes, sir," Walter said. "I'm afraid so. But you're fine now, and there is an ambulance here to help you. We'll just go let them know where you are."

"Yes," Bell said, edging toward the door. "We'll send them your way." He turned. "Come on, Walter."

Walter didn't want to leave the man alone. In fact, he wanted to question him, ask him about the experience. But trying to give the police a rational sounding explanation for what had happened here would be an exercise in futility. So he gave a guilty salute to the befuddled watchman, then edged around him.

"Right behind you," he called after his friend.

Allan hurried away down the street, police sirens bouncing off the surrounding walls and painting the night in a wash of blue and red. He had been less than three feet from the trailer door and about to reach for the knob when all of the mysteriously suspended objects around him had suddenly lost their animation and dropped to the ground.

A large jagged chunk of rusty metal the size of a washing machine had dropped down an inch from his toes. So close that he could feel the wind of its passage. If he'd been reaching for the knob, his right arm would have been crushed, broken, or perhaps even severed.

He got the message. He was being impulsive, over-eager. He had been thinking of deviating from the plan. And look where that kind of thinking got him.

He would still have his special moment with those two, and with Miss Nina Sharp, as long as he stuck to the plan. He just needed to be patient. Let them make plans of their own. Watch it all play out, and act accordingly.

25

They got back to Nina's house just as the sun was coming up. Pregnant Abby was curled up on a couch, dozing with Cat-Mandu. Looking down at her, Walter felt a pang of guilt for involving the father of her child in all this madness.

The three of them dragged themselves up the stairs to Nina's room, mentally and physically exhausted.

"So what's our next move?" Nina asked.

"Next move?" Walter ran his hand through his hair. "I don't know about you, but my next move is to collapse from exhaustion."

"But what I want to know," Bell said, "is how did he find us?"

Walter shuddered. He'd been thinking the same thing, and wasn't happy with the conclusions he'd come to.

"There's been something bothering me since last night," Walter said. "But you know how bad my memory is, so I just told myself I was wrong."

"What?" Bell asked.

"Well," Walter said, "I'm pretty sure we never told Iverson about Reiden Lake."

Bell got it. His eyes went wide.

"The classified ad," he said.

"It said 'regarding events at Reiden Lake,' right?" Walter asked. "But we never told Iverson, or any other authorities about where the initial trip took place. There's only one other person who knows that."

"The killer," Bell said.

"How could we have been so stupid?" Walter said.

"You know what this means," Bell said. "This means he's probably following us. He may be watching us right now!"

"But if he's been watching us all this time, why doesn't he just kill us?"

"Look," Nina said. "It's obvious that he wants to toy with you—with us. That's his thing, right? Psychological torture, mind games, taunting letters."

"Okay," Walter said. "I see your point."

"But what do we do now?" Bell asked.

"We beat him at his own game," Nina said.

"Beat him how?" Bell asked.

"We're no good at hand-to-hand combat," she said. "We know that. But mind-to-mind combat, that's a whole different ball game. *Our* ball game."

"In theory, yes," Walter said. "That's likely to be a superior strategy."

"But how…" Bell said again.

"Will you let me finish?" Nina asked.

"Right, sorry," they both said simultaneously.

"We talked about needing to get him through the gate, right?" Nina continued. "But clearly, even the rehearsal space isn't remote enough. We need some place even more remote. I have a good location in mind, but then the problem becomes how to get him to that remote location."

"Kidnapping seems a little more physically

demanding than any of us are capable of," Walter said. "Plus, we don't know where he is."

"Yet he knows where we are," Nina said. "If he's following us, we need to use that to our advantage."

"You've lost me again," Bell said.

Nina sighed like a teacher dealing with a recalcitrant student. She went over to her desk and slipped a blank sheet into the typewriter.

"Dear Special Agent Iverson," Nina read aloud as she typed. "We want to warn you that the Zodiac has been imitating you in order to trick us, so be suspicious of any communication that is delivered by any method other than this, our previously arranged drop spot."

"Excellent," Bell said, catching on immediately.

"Brilliant," Walter said. "The bit about him tricking us adds an extra element of credibility."

"At this point in time," Nina continued, "the danger has become too great, and for our own safety, we feel that we have no other choice but to return to the east coast. However, we have an encrypted notebook in our possession which we feel would be invaluable to your case.

"We will hide the notebook under the third flagstone from the left in the fireplace of a cabin up in Fairfax, CA. There is no address, but it's the second building on a private, unmarked, and unpaved driveway off Iron Springs Road about 100 yards east of the junction with Timber Canyon Road.

"Please see included map."

"Map?" Walter said.

"Yes," Nina said, opening a desk drawer and pulling out a neatly folded map. She opened it and drew a neat red X to mark the location. "We can't take chances that he might not find the cabin."

"You are amazing," Bell said. "Will you marry me?"

"Marriage is an outdated relic of patriarchal oppression," Nina replied, arching a russet brow. "But if you ever need someone to run your business affairs, you just let me know."

"Not to spoil your special moment," Walter said, "but what are we going to do with our friend the Zodiac once he arrives? Chase him through the gate with harsh language?"

Nina reached into the box of chemicals that Bell had scored to mix the acid blend, and pulled out a large brown glass bottle.

"Chloroform," she said. "As soon as he comes through the cabin door, we chloroform him and then toss him through the gate."

"We'd need to seriously sedate him," Bell said. "I mean, chloroform is fine for the initial knockout, but we'll need to keep him under while we open the gate, and that will take time. It's not like we can just flick a switch."

"Definitely," Walter said. "It's been made terrifyingly clear that there's a direct link between pain or heightened emotion and his strange radioactivity. We don't want him going off like an atom bomb while we're trying to put him through."

"Agreed," Bell said. "You go and drop off the trick letter and I'll work on formulating an appropriate anesthesia blend for our friend. Meanwhile, Nina, we need you to talk to the band, and see if you can get them to join us at the cabin for another epic acid trip."

"Free acid in a beautiful pastoral setting?" Nina smiled. "Won't be that hard to convince them."

"But…" Walter stood, pacing. He pictured dumb, sweet Abby sleeping on the couch downstairs. "I mean… well, it's not exactly ethical to experiment on human subjects without making them aware of the potential dangers inherent to their participation."

"It's even less ethical to let this monster continue to kill without restraint, just because we got squeamish about ethics," Bell countered. "This isn't just an ordinary experiment, Walter.

"Besides," he continued, "you were the one who always used to say that free acid for everyone would make the world a better place."

"Nevertheless," Nina said, "we don't want to plant the note for the killer to find until we're absolutely sure the band will be willing to participate in setting up our chemical trap. They have a gig tonight night at a club called the Downward Dog. We can talk to them when they get off."

"Yes," Bell said. "Meeting them after the show would be the best way to gather them all in one place and, more than likely, in an inebriated and agreeable mood."

Walter remained silent. In spite of everything, he couldn't help but feel a twinge of excitement at the prospect of seeing his favorite band live. While it was true that it would have been ideal to see them at the height of their fame, back in '66, and that their psychedelic folk style was considered by many to be passé, his own inner teenage self was doing a little happy dance.

He hoped that they would play "Hovercraft Mother."

Yet that excitement was tinged with guilt. He still felt that it was wrong to involve the band members in something so dangerous, and he would feel absolutely awful if something were to happen to one of his musical idols.

It was like mentally weighing the value of the band members' lives against the lives of Miranda and all the other Zodiac victims yet to come. Could there really be a lesser of these two evils?

Unfortunately there was.

There was every chance that the band would come out of the experiment unharmed. But there was no question what would happen to Miranda if they didn't send the Zodiac back to his own world.

"I suppose we don't have a choice, do we?" Walter said.

"No," Nina said. "We don't."

26

Having come to that decision about what had to be done, they still had a whole day to kill before the show at the Downward Dog. They were getting more than a little bit ragged around the edges, and Nina didn't have to ask Walter to leave her bedroom so she could get some rest.

He staggered down the stairs and found Abby awake and bustling in the kitchen. He waved to her in a haze and collapsed on the couch that she had recently vacated. It was still warm from her body. Cat-Mandu snuggled up to him, seeming unfazed by this personnel change.

Within seconds, he fell soundly asleep.

He didn't budge until Nina shook him gently awake several hours later.

"Come on," she said, "let's get some lunch. A little fuel to stimulate proper brain function. What do you say?"

Walter stood slowly, brushing an avalanche of cat hair off his sweater and pants. His brain felt as fuzzy as his clothes. He realized that he had slept in his shoes.

Nina took them to a restaurant called the Swan

Oyster Bar. It was a narrow, almost claustrophobic place with a long marble counter and some of the smallest stools Walter had ever seen. He perched reluctantly on the tiny round wooden seat, not entirely confident that it would hold his weight.

The guy behind the counter was a jovial and burly fellow whose massive hands were surprisingly deft and delicate with the oysters. He shucked them from their rough shells with a practiced twist of the wrist, smiling and joking with the customers while he worked.

Walter himself was not a big fan of raw oysters, but he loved clam chowder and was pleased to see that they made it there just like they made it back home. He ordered a bowl, along with a large plate of Crab Louie. He tried to remember the last time he'd had a nice bowl of clam chowder, and couldn't. It was as if his life had not existed before this whole Zodiac thing.

Nina and Bell shared a huge plate of oysters, and while Walter was tempted to make some kind of joke about the supposed aphrodisiac properties of the legendary bivalves, he just didn't have the heart. In a strange way, this food felt almost like a last meal.

"I'll tell you one other thing that is bothering me about all of this," Bell said, pausing to slurp an oyster out of its shell.

One thing? Walter thought. *More like everything.*

"What's that?" Nina asked, adding a dollop of horseradish to her cocktail sauce.

"Let's say it works," Bell said. "Let's say, for the sake of argument, that the band agrees to help us and the whole plan goes off without a hitch, and we send that bastard back where he came from. We will have saved an unknown number of lives, no doubt about that, but..." He downed another oyster. "We may never know exactly what he was or where he came from."

"So what?" Walter said. "You're saying we should be trying to capture him and study him? Try to turn him into some kind of profitable commodity? Or a weapon? Are we no better than Latimer?"

"I'm not saying that studying him is a feasible possibility," Bell replied. "But aren't you even the slightest bit curious about him?"

Walter looked down at the pink mess that remained of his Crab Louie, thinking of that heady moment where he'd actually considered going through the gate himself.

"Of course I'm curious!" he replied. "I couldn't call myself a scientist if I wasn't. I wonder about him constantly. Is he human? If not, what is he? What sort of world is he from? Another planet? Another universe? So many intriguing questions."

"So what *are* you suggesting?" Nina asked, giving Bell an intense but wary look.

"I'm not suggesting anything," Bell said. "I realize that it would be impossibly dangerous to capture and study him. But I'm curious. That's all I'm saying. I feel as if we've stumbled on something really astounding here. Something historic, on the order of splitting the atom. Something that I suspect might alter the course of all our lives, forever."

He and Nina exchanged a complex look that Walter couldn't even begin to interpret. He poked at a shred of crab on his plate, but he seemed to have lost his appetite.

He was afraid that Bell was probably right.

What was more, he wondered what would happen to that world on the other side, if they succeeded. Had he been radioactive before he came through the gate? Or were they saving their world by sending a killer to prey on victims in another?

He shook his head, but couldn't dislodge the doubts.

They paid their bill at the oyster bar and headed back toward Nina's house.

"Do you suppose he's following us right now?" Walter asked, looking back over his shoulder.

"He must be," Nina replied. "But stop looking around like that. We don't want him to know that we're on to him. If we tip our hand, he may go to ground or execute a preemptive strike against us. Possibly even kill us. The key here is to make him think that we are totally naive. Lull him into a false sense of security."

"Yeah," Bell said, elbowing Walter in the ribs. "Smile. Laugh. Act like you don't have a care in the world."

Walter cringed away from Bell's prodding and then tried on a tentative smile for size. It seemed way too small, and tight in the corners.

"I just…" He started to look back over his shoulder again, but stopped himself. "It just feels creepy to know that someone is watching me."

"Remember," Nina said. "We *want* him to watch us."

"If he's not watching us," Bell said, "then our whole plan goes right down the crapper."

"Of course," Walter said. "I understand. I just…"

They were passing an open-air newsstand, when all of a sudden, there was a loud rumble that shook the magazine racks. A spill of lurid men's adventure and nudie magazines tumbled down and scattered across Walter's path. He nearly jumped out of his skin, clinging to Bell's arm like a scared little boy.

"My God!" he cried. "Is this some kind of residual telekinetic manifestation from the opening of the gate?"

Nina smiled and put a calming hand on Walter's back.

"No, silly," she said. "That's just a garden variety earthquake. Nice one, probably about a four-point-oh. Welcome to California, boys."

A pair of tall, broad-shouldered women in extremely high heels had been teetering toward Walter arm in arm when the tremor had hit. They'd paused for a moment, steadying each other against the concrete shimmy. When it was over, they exchanged knowing glances with Nina and the news vendor, an unspoken understanding shared between native San Franciscans and earthquake veterans, and then sashayed away down the street.

Nina and Bell both bent down to help the news vendor clean up his spilled inventory, but Walter had his hands full trying to slow his own panicked heartbeat. He'd never experienced an earthquake before, and couldn't imagine that it was the kind of thing that he could ever get used to.

He looked up and down the block at the other denizens of the city. They all seemed utterly blasé about the whole thing. It was as if he was the only one who'd been the slightest bit scared.

He couldn't help but wonder how the Zodiac felt about the quake.

Back at Nina's place, Walter was playing with Cat-Mandu, dangling a piece of red and green yarn, when Nina came over to him carrying a shirt on a hanger and a pair of pants folded over one arm. The shirt had brown and purple stripes, big blousy sleeves and a large pointy collar. The pants were brown corduroy with a wale so wide he could have played with Matchbox cars in the grooves.

"You and Roscoe are about the same size," Nina said.

"He won't mind if you borrow some of his threads for the concert tonight."

"Oh," Walter said, frowning at the flamboyant shirt. "Gee, thanks, but I'm okay like this."

Bell appeared behind her in an entirely new outfit, a western-style shirt with red floral stripes and jeans that were a little too loose in the waist and a little too short in the leg.

"Walter," Bell said, "she's just too polite to tell you that you stink. Take the clean clothes and go have a shower, will you? And wash that hair of yours while you're in there."

Walter frowned, pulled a pinch of his sweater up to his face and sniffed it. It smelled fine to him, but he figured he'd better humor their hostess.

"I'm still going to wear my own jacket," Walter warned, accepting the clothes. "It's lucky."

Bell rolled his eyes dramatically.

"Trust me," he said to Nina. "I've been trying to get Walter out of that jacket for ten years. It's a lost cause."

27

The Downward Dog was a tiny hole-in-the-wall that was barely visible from the street, and made even less visible by the massive throng of brightly clad men and women waiting to get into the crowded disco next door.

Nina led Walter and Bell down a long, narrow stairway and into the basement club where Violet Sedan Chair would be playing. The powerful funk of old beer and smoke—both legal and otherwise—was as thick as the San Francisco fog in the low-ceilinged venue. A long bar ran the length of the right-hand side, a rococo, turn-of-the-century relic that might have been billed as "antique" if it wasn't in such sorry condition. Its once sleek wooden hide was now scarred and patchy, disfigured with cigarette burns and scratched-in initials.

Behind it, the bartender looked just as old and just as badly treated.

All four walls and even the tin ceiling were covered by layer after layer of old posters advertising bands like Country Joe and the Fish, Captain Beefheart, Moby Grape, Big Brother and the Holding Company, and the Mothers of Invention. The posters were nicotine stained and curling at the edges, and the most recent of them was dated five years earlier.

There was something sad about the place, as if it had been shoved aside by its gaudy, more popular neighbor. The disco music from next door thumped through the walls, rubbing it in.

There was a small but devoted crowd waiting for Violet Sedan Chair to go on stage. Primarily single men, but a few couples and one large group of boisterous women who seemed to have come together. The men all had beards and granny glasses and colorful headbands. The women all had ironed hair, handmade patchwork dresses, and blissed-out expressions. This crowd was clearly immune to disco fever.

Walter fit right in.

Nina spotted Abby sitting on the corner of the stage at the far end of the room, smoking a joint and talking to another pregnant woman, a plump and pretty brunette with pale freckled skin and very pale blue eyes. She wore a white macramé halter-top under a weird, shaggy blue coat that made her look like she had skinned one of the monsters on Sesame Street. There was a peace sign painted on her exposed and swollen belly.

"Oh, hey," Abby said when she saw them. "So great that you were able to make it. Roscoe will be thrilled." She leaned in. "You know how he gets if there aren't enough people at a show."

She held out the joint. Nina waved it away, but Walter accepted it.

"Thanks," he said.

"This is my friend Sandy," Abby said. "We're both due at the same time, around the end of next month. We were just wondering if we would have Libra babies or Scorpios. I'm hoping little Bobby will be a Libra.

Scorpios can be so resentful."

"Yeah," Sandy said. "But Scorpios are so brooding and sexy! Charles Bronson is a Scorpio."

"That just proves my point," Abby replied. "Look how he went and killed all those criminals after his wife was murdered. That's such a total Scorpio thing to do."

"So," Nina interrupted, looking vaguely annoyed. "Is the band set to go on soon?"

"They should be," Abby said. "Chick is late again."

All this talk about astrology was making Walter think of the Zodiac Killer, and how desperately they needed their crazy plan to work. It seemed like the marijuana was making him feel more edgy, and not less. He passed the joint to Bell.

Bell took a hit off of it and passed it back to Abby.

"You ladies want anything from the bar?" Bell asked.

"No, thanks," Abby said.

"You should have a beer," Sandy said. "The hops are supposed to help you produce more nutritious breast milk."

"Really?" Abby said. She turned back to Bell. "Well, then, we'll take two beers."

"Nina?" Bell asked.

"Whisky sour," she said. "Thank you."

"Want a beer, Walt?"

Walter shook his head.

"No thanks, Belly," he said. "I'm fine."

Bell headed over to the bar to get the drinks while Abby wet her fingers, put out what was left of the joint and dropped the roach into her tiny beaded purse.

"Oh, look," she said, pointing to a doorway at the back of the stage. "Here they come."

The band took the stage to enthusiastic cheers from the small but vocal crowd. Roscoe was dressed in a dragon-print Oriental jacket with no shirt underneath and white bell-bottom pants. He winked at Abby as he sat down at the keyboard and adjusted the mike to the level of his smirking lips. Behind him, Chick Spivy was wearing a dark green suede suit and snakeskin boots, slinging his famous hand-painted Les Paul over his shoulder and waving, a big stoned grin on his beaming face.

Next up were Oregon Dave and Alex, dressed twin-like in jeans and matching shirts. Dave's shirt was blue with red stars and Alex's was red with blue stars. Last up was Iggy, resplendent in royal purple bell-bottoms and a ruffled white shirt, open to his navel to unleash his thick, brambly chest hair.

He sat behind his drum kit and looked over at Roscoe, who in turn looked over at each of the other members, then nodded. Iggy clicked his sticks together and then they broke into a slower, dirtier, funked-up version of "She's Doing Fine."

Walter cheered freely, so happy in that moment in such a pure and uncomplicated way. It was a miracle to him that something as simple as music had the power to take away all his worries and anxiety, and transport him back to a better place. He'd been a college freshman when he first heard Violet Sedan Chair's seminal album *Seven Suns*, and it had opened his mind as surely as the acid he'd dropped for the first time that same year.

Life had seemed so different back then, so full of magic and potential. He'd been convinced that things were really going to change for the better, that love and music really could defeat fear and war. But then, somehow, it had all turned dark and ugly. Acid, mushrooms, and marijuana had been replaced with speed, cocaine, and heroin. Hippies were replaced by Hell's Angels. The gentle, open-minded spirituality and self-exploration of the late sixties had degenerated into the hard-partying glitter and hedonism of the seventies.

Their musical idols were dying, and being steadily replaced by plastic corporate pop stars and super groups.

Yet here Walter was, basking in the musical genius of one of his personal heroes, on a par with Tesla and Einstein. The incomparable Roscoe Joyce was in rare form on stage, coaxing new resonance and meaning from old hits and exploring uncharted territory in selections from a complex and profoundly spiritual rock opera that Walter had never heard before.

He glanced over at Bell, unable to stop smiling, and noticed that his friend seemed a little bored by the concert, checking his watch and looking impatient as Iggy thundered off into yet another ten-minute drum solo. Didn't Bell appreciate the layered complexity and meaning in this music? He'd seemed to like the band well enough when Walter had first played "Seven Suns" for him back in 1966. And he'd been intrigued by the rumor of the lost track "Greenmana" and its supposed hallucinogenic effect.

Now, he just looked annoyed.

Walter felt a sudden hot rush of embarrassment, and even guilt. Of course Bell was impatient. Walter should be, too. They weren't in the club to enjoy music. They were there to convince Roscoe and the band to help them defeat a dangerous killer.

"Thank you!" Roscoe howled into the mike, fist in the air as he got up from his keyboard bench.

"Thank God," Bell muttered under his breath as the band put down their instruments and left the stage. But Walter knew they would never end the set without doing

"Seven Suns." That was their one commercial hit, the one song that they were best known for. Besides, if they were really done, they would have taken their instruments with them.

Sure enough, less than a minute later the band came back up onto the stage, hands in the air. The small crowd made up for their lack of numbers with wild enthusiasm, cheering and chanting.

"Se-ven Suns! Se-ven Suns! Se-ven Suns! Se-ven Suns! Se-ven Suns!"

"You have *got* to be kidding," Bell said, rolling his eyes.

"You can't get rid of us that easy," Roscoe said, grinning into the mike. "This song is a little ditty I wrote a few years back. Maybe you've heard of it."

Alone on the keyboard, he broke into the first bar of "Seven Suns" and the crowd went crazy, hollering and cheering. The rest of the band joined in and the crowd started to quiet down, swaying together as if hypnotized. Abby and her pregnant friend Sandy sang along, loud and off-key, as the song ebbed and flowed like a tide over the ecstatic crowd.

Bell and Nina were the only ones who were unswayed.

Walter found himself wondering if the Zodiac might have been so brazen as to follow them into the venue. He couldn't see the bespectacled killer as he scanned the faces of the crowd, but that didn't mean he wasn't there.

He wondered if the killer was enjoying the music, too, or if he was even capable of enjoying anything other than killing.

On the album, Walter was pretty sure that the song was about four minutes long, but more than fifteen minutes had passed and the band showed no signs of wrapping it up any time soon. He actually found himself getting impatient, and if that was the case, Bell must have been crawling out of his skin.

It was nearly a full hour and six encores later when the band finally gathered up their instruments and left the stage for good. With Walter and Bell in tow, Nina immediately pushed her way through the crowd and through a beaded curtain to a doorway that led backstage.

"Backstage" was probably a fancier name than the area deserved. The band was hanging out behind the stage, so Walter had to give it that, but his idea of what it might be like to be "backstage" with his favorite band wasn't anything like this.

It was more like a vestibule with a crooked mirror bolted to one wall and crates of booze and beer kegs lining the other. A forlorn yellow plaid loveseat that was missing all but one of its threadbare cushions had been shoved into a corner, and a trio of spindly wooden folding chairs had been placed beneath the mirror.

The guys were all laughing and joking and putting away their instruments. Several joints were being passed both directions around the room. Two of the girls from the large group had found their way backstage and were giggling and flirting with Alex and Chick.

Abby was there, too, arms locked possessively around Roscoe's skinny waist.

"Little Bobby loves 'Seven Suns'," she was telling him. "He always kicks when you play it."

"Hey," Roscoe said when he spotted Walter and Bell. "It's the professors!" He grinned and passed a joint to Walter. "Did you dig that last song? It's called 'Gateway,' and it came to me during that amazing trip we had with you guys. Just came to me, to all of us like it was already written. We barely even had to rehearse, we just knew it, man. We *felt* it—you dig?"

"That's fascinating," Walter said, taking a hit off the joint. "Do you have any plans to record it? I'd love to study the structure in depth."

"Walter," Bell said, taking the joint out of his hand and raising his eyebrows.

"Ah, yes," Walter said with a slight frown. "Well…"

He had thought that Nina was going to talk the band into helping, since she was already friends with them. He'd had no idea that he would be called upon to do the convincing.

"Say, professor," Roscoe interrupted. "You got any more of that righteous special blend of yours? I feel like 'Gateway' is just the tip of the iceberg, man. I can sense a whole concept album in there, just waiting for me to plug in, you know? I feel like this is exactly what the band needs to take us to a higher level."

Walter looked over at Nina and Bell, shaking his head in disbelief. This was almost too easy.

"I tell you what," Walter said. "We're planning another telepathy experiment tomorrow."

"We were wondering if we could use that old cabin that belongs to Chick's parents," Nina said. "You know, the one up in Fairfax?"

"Oh, yeah," Chick said. "My folks never go up there this late in the year, it'll just be sitting there empty."

"Perfect," Nina replied. "We'll head up there first thing—what do you say?"

"That sounds groovy," Abby said. "Can me and little Bobby come along?"

"Not for this one, Abby," Nina said. "This particular

blend has certain ingredients that may not be safe for unborn children."

"Oh," she said in small voice. "Well, I could just help out then…"

"While we appreciate your offer," Bell said, using his deep, soothing voice to maximum effect, "in this particular experiment, we've had problems with preexisting relationships affecting the telepathic connections that are formed under the influence of the blend."

"Yes, yes," Walter agreed, thrilled with what Bell had contrived. "We can't risk one of the subjects bonding with a mind outside the circle. For experimental purposes, we need to make sure that no external influences are allowed to skew the results."

"It's okay, starshine," Roscoe said, pushing a lock of Abby's hair behind her ear. "You stay here in the city and keep the home fires burning. And when I get back, I'll sing you a new song."

"Okay," Abby said. "Can we get pancakes now?"

"Pancakes," Walter said. "Splendid idea."

Alex and Chick took off with their two new lady friends to hit a different bar down the street, but Roscoe, Abby, Iggy and Dave, along with the other pregnant girl Sandy, all walked a few blocks to an all-night diner called Plucky's Waffle Inn. The place was jam-packed with disco queens and hippies alike, and the ancient and unflappable woman who was the only waitress in the place seemed equally amused by all of them.

Not that it really mattered to Walter, but over the course of their late-night, early-morning breakfast, he found himself trying to figure out which, if any, of the band members might be the father of Sandy's child.

She seemed equally flirty and friendly with everyone, including him. He wasn't so uptight as to be scandalized by an out-of-wedlock pregnancy, but he had to admit he was curious.

Not curious enough to come right out and ask her, though.

Besides, it was far more enjoyable to discuss music and mind-expanding drugs. Roscoe was ferociously smart, and full of new ideas in how the two can be combined to intensify the effects.

"Music is primal," he was saying. "It plugs directly into that central core of human consciousness. It goes beyond language, beyond any division between the self and the other."

"There's been some really exciting work done on the effect of music on catatonic patients, as well as those suffering from severe forms of dementia," Walter said. "Are you familiar with the L-DOPA trials performed on patients with encephalitis, by a young neurologist named Doctor Oliver Sacks? He published a book about it, came out just last year. Absolutely fascinating stuff."

"I'll have to check it out," Roscoe replied. "Who's got the boysenberry syrup?"

"I do," Walter said, holding up the little jug and giving his pancakes an extra drizzle before passing it over.

He would have been happy to stay all night in that diner, discussing a wide variety of intellectually stimulating theories and enjoying good, home-style food, but he couldn't forget what they were planning to attempt tomorrow—today, actually. How everyone would be at risk, and how much was riding on their success.

Roscoe and the other band members continued to joke and horse around on the walk back to Nina's place, but Walter found himself quietly introspective, lagging a little bit behind the others. Until he remembered that the Zodiac Killer was probably still following them.

He quickened his pace to catch up with Nina and Bell.

28

The next morning—more like afternoon, actually—Nina shook Walter awake again, this time with the typewritten note for the killer in her hand.

"It's time," she said. "You have to plant the note before we leave for the cabin, or none of this is going to work."

"Right now?" Walter said, rubbing sleep from his dry eyes.

"Yes," Nina said. "Right now. Remember, there is no prearranged drop spot, so it doesn't matter where you leave the note. Just make it look like you're trying to be secretive. Make sure you go slow, and be obvious enough to be easily followed."

He sat up and noticed that Abby, bless her, had made tea for everyone. He helped himself to a steaming cup as he slipped his feet into his shoes.

"All right," he said, shuffling toward the front door. "Right now. I just hope this works."

Allan watched from across the street as the curly haired hippie in the baggy tweed jacket left Miss Nina Sharp's house alone, and headed west. He hesitated, just for a moment, then followed. Of the three, this was the one who interested him the most. The one to whom he'd felt the closest that night at Reiden Lake. The one he planned to kill last.

The hippie was clearly up to something. He was anxious, constantly scanning the street and jumping every time a car passed, but Allan wasn't worried that he would be spotted. He lingered nearly a block behind, blending into the crowd. They passed a busy hamburger stand, a beauty parlor, and a head shop, around a series of seemingly random corners, and then doubling back.

But Allan was a seasoned hunter, and couldn't be shaken that easily.

Then the hippie suddenly dashed across the street and down a narrow alley. Allan followed at a safe distance, leisurely and unruffled as if he had all the time in the world to get to his destination. He strolled slowly past the mouth of the alley, peering casually down its length.

The hippie had his back turned to Allan, and seemed to be counting barred windows as he walked very slowly down the alleyway. When he arrived under the seventh window, he stopped, crouched down and slipped something under a concrete block. Then he stood and continued on until he was out the other end.

Allan waited a few beats before entering the alley himself, then made his way over to the seventh window. He lifted the concrete block and spotted a folded note and a wrinkled map.

He unfolded the note. Read it. Smiled.
Things just got a whole lot more interesting.

29

Walter was still so tired that he wound up falling asleep in the back seat of the rented tan Buick LeSabre, before they even made it out of San Francisco. When he woke they were on a narrow winding road, passing through deep, green woods. It felt almost like time travel, as if he'd fallen asleep in 1974 and awakened in pre-colonial times, before the intrusion of European industry into the primeval forests of America.

The day was sunny, the windows were down, and the sharp, piney scent of the clean crisp air was uplifting and refreshing. He found he could almost forget about all the pain and death and madness.

Almost.

Nina turned off the main road and onto a bumpy, unpaved dirt track that bounced Walter around like popcorn in the back seat. He clung to the back of Bell's seat, peering anxiously over his shoulder. The brightly painted bus carrying the members of the band was no longer following them.

"Are you sure this is the right road?" he asked.

"We can't very well park right in front of the cabin,"

Nina said. "The killer would see the car and know someone was inside. Even though he wouldn't recognize the rental, the cabin still has to look empty. So we'll ditch the car down below, and walk up."

"What about Roscoe and the band?"

"They're headed straight up to the lodge up on the top of the ridge," Nina said. "Once we have the killer bound and sedated, we'll contact them via the walkie-talkies and have them join us for the gate-opening trip."

Nina pulled the big beast of a car into a weedy turnout in front of the burnt-out husk of some kind of structure. She killed the engine, and the three of them just sat there quietly for a minute, listening to oblivious birds and the soothing shush of wind in pine branches. It seemed so strange to Walter that the world around them just kept on keeping on, everything ordinary and normal, as if they weren't about to commit this unthinkable offense against the very fabric of reality.

He rolled up the window and got out of the car, slinging the duffle bag full of supplies over one shoulder.

The walk up to the cabin was steep and roundabout, zigzagging back and forth along the safest, most stable ground. Nina took the determined lead, with Bell right behind her and Walter bringing up the rear. The bag on his shoulder was growing impossibly heavy by the time they reached the low, sloping back yard.

It was less like the old-fashioned log cabin Walter had pictured in his mind, and more like a small, rustic house. It was long and narrow, with a mossy stone chimney, weathered, grayish siding and a tall, A-frame roof.

They followed Nina around to the front door, which she opened with a large, old-fashioned key.

Inside, it was dim and dusty, furnished with minimal, utilitarian furniture that included a pair of tough plaid chairs set next to an oversized fireplace, and a hand-hewn wooden table. There was a really hideous lamp made from antlers, but Nina stopped Walter from flipping the switch to turn it on.

"Leave it," she said, taking a small flashlight from her purse and thumbing it to life.

The curtains were closed, so the light was dim. The weak yellow illumination from the flashlight made the interior of the cabin seem *more* gloomy, rather than less. Dust spun and danced in the beam as Nina crouched down in front of the fireplace and pried up the third flagstone from the left.

When it finally came loose in her hand, she blew away the dust and replaced the stone loosely and slightly crooked.

"So," Bell said. "He comes in through the door…"

"Right," Nina said. "He comes in through the door and goes right for the fireplace. We should wait there." She pointed to a dark doorway. "In the bedroom. When we hear him come in…"

"I grab him from behind," Bell said.

"And I'll put the rag with the chloroform over his mouth and nose," Walter said.

"Then I cuff him and bind his legs together with duct tape," Nina said.

"While I prepare and administer the sedative," Bell finished.

"What's through there?" Walter asked, gesturing to a second dark arched doorway.

"Kitchen and back door," Nina replied.

"So that's that," Walter said. "We are as ready as we can be. All we have to do now is wait."

30

Waiting, however, turned out to be more difficult than they had anticipated. With no real idea of when the killer would arrive, and no way to watch for his arrival without exposing that they were there, the three of them were forced to sit in the bedroom, away from any windows, and try to remain on alert for what soon started to feel like an eternity.

For the first hour, none of them could relax enough to do anything but sit and stare distractedly at each other. Nina on the bed, Bell in an old rocker, and Walter sitting on an old leather trunk with a musty moth-eaten blanket folded to form a meager cushion. They jumped at every sound, the settling of the cabin or the creaking of a tree branch outside.

By the second hour, Nina was flipping through old issues of *Field & Stream* magazine that she had found on the bedside table, while Bell and Walter were playing chess on a pocket set Bell had brought. They were so distracted by listening to the sounds of the cabin that they kept forgetting whose turn it was.

By hour three, Nina lay on the bed with an arm

flung over her eyes, though judging from her breathing and body position, Walter didn't think she was actually asleep. He and Bell had finally given up on chess after three stalemates. Bell had read through all the *Field & Stream* issues and had resorted to searching for the hidden pictures on the back of a copy of *Highlights* magazine for children.

"Is that a fish?" he asked. "Or a water stain?"

Soon dusk fell over the little cabin, and Nina was anxious that any light would give them away. So they were forced to sit in the dark, waiting.

Walter tried to nap, but his brain would not allow it. Instead, he pulled the musty old blanket over his head and turned on the flashlight, like he used to do when he was a boy, up late and reading under the covers long past bedtime. He knew that if even the tiniest sliver of light appeared, Nina would take it away from him.

He took out the photocopies he'd made of the pages from the killer's notebook and laid them on the floor around him, trying to figure out the key for that last fragment of text.

He got nowhere.

He had hoped that the keyword was in some way related to the word for the already translated page, whether phonetically, thematically, or structurally, but if it was, he could not discover the connection.

Then he went back into the file from Iverson, and starting reexamining the original cryptogram included in the August 1969 letters—the ones that had been sent to the newspapers. The code that had been solved by the teachers.

I like killing people because it is so much fun.

At the end of that message, a grouping of 18 extra

letters whose meaning or significance had never been determined.

EBEORIETEMETHHPITI

Strange, when the rest of the message had been based on a relatively simple substitution code. But the way these last letters were grouped, there was no way they fit in.

In fact, the more Walter stared at them, the clearer it became that this segment had been created with a code so complex that each letter had more than one meaning. That first E was clearly an I, but then the second and third E seemed to have a totally different meaning.

I am? Could those first three letters spell out "I am?"

Walter concentrated on that third E. If there was a sliding key being used, then what was the numerical distance between the letter I and the letter M? Five. Move five more letters down the alphabet and you get R. But then at the fourth E, the key seemed to switch again, leaving him with a D.

Frustrated, he went back to the O-R-I, and after several false starts and aborted attempts, he wound up with S-C-H, which he added to the letters he'd already deduced.

I AM SCHR_D _ _ _ _ _ _ _ _ _

That couldn't be right. It seemed as if he was stuck with too many consonants in a row, and couldn't think of any English words that began with SCHR. He decided to tackle the last three letters, I-T-I.

If the Es did not have the same value, then the Is must not, either. It seemed to Walter that the last I was actually a T, but the neighboring T seemed to be an A.

The number of three-letter English words ending in AT was enormous. Bat, rat, mat, sat, hat, fat, cat...

Cat.

I AM SCHR _ D _ _ _ _ _ _ CAT

Like lightning, it hit him. There was only one thing it could be, only one way to make those seemingly unrelated letters spell something. Something eerily apropos.

I am Schrodinger's cat.

"My God," he said out loud, throwing the blanket off his head and shoulders.

Bell looked up, squinting at the sudden light. Nina raised her head from the pillow and opened her eyes.

"Are you crazy?" she hissed. "Turn that off!"

"What is it?" asked Bell.

Walter ignored both of them and grabbed the photocopy of the final page in the killer's diary, honing in on the final untranslated chunk. Using the word *Schrodinger* as the key he tore through the final segment, feeling the hair on the back of his neck prickle as he translated.

Walter held up the translation, his hands shaking.

"It's details of his next murder."

Nina took the translation from Walter and read out loud.

"I think I shall wait until the following Monday night. Pretty little Miranda Coleman, usherette at the Roxie Theater, works late on Monday nights. She leaves at eleven thirty and walks alone to the lot where she parks her car on Hoff street. She will die at 11:40 p.m. next Monday the twenty-fifth of September."

And those same English words scratched furiously into the page.

BY KNIFE

Bell stood, setting the rocker rocking.

"Why that's..." He looked at his watch. "A little more than two hours from now."

Nina jumped up from the bed, letting Walter's translation seesaw through the air and land at his feet.

"Then we have to go," she said. "Now! We have to stop him!"

"But what about…" Walter gestured around with pleading hands. "What about the plan. The trap. He…"

Nina rolled her eyes.

"Don't be a fool, Walter," she said. "Why would the Zodiac disrupt his plans for us? Unless he's desperately impatient, there's no real reason he would need to come get the book today. If his next victim only works late one day a week, then he'd have to wait seven more days to kill her. Why would he do that, when he can just come up and get the book after she's dead?"

"Nina's right," Bell said. "Having intercepted our supposed note to Iverson, our killer will be confident that no one will be coming for it. Which means he doesn't have to hurry. He can retrieve the journal any time. Which means he's going to kill that girl in two hours, and we've been waiting in vain for him to walk through the door."

From the main room came the low, haunted-house sound of the creaky old front door swinging slowly open.

31

Walter jumped as if someone had stuck him with a cattle prod, and hooded the flashlight with his palm. Bell stepped back and nearly tripped over the rocker. Nina clamped a hand over her mouth then pointed at their tools.

"The chloroform!" she whispered. "Get it!"

Walter went to the duffle bag and traded the flashlight for the chloroform bottle and a rag. Soft steps and shifting noises came from the main room. He made certain the cap on the bottle was loose enough to open easily at the very last minute, but not loose enough that fumes could escape and overwhelm him.

His hands were shaking so badly, he was afraid he might drop the bottle. Nina grabbed the handcuffs and duct tape while Bell got out the syringe and started to prepare the chemical cocktail that would keep the killer unconscious long enough for them to put him through the gate.

"Ready?" Nina whispered.

"I suppose so," Walter said.

"Come on," Bell said.

Walter crept to the door, chloroform and cloth held together in one hand, reaching for the knob with the other. They had deliberately left it open a crack so that they would be able to surreptitiously peer into the main room and see when the killer was bending to check under the flagstone.

Walter looked through the crack.

The light had been switched on in the main room, but no one was at the fireplace.

Where was the killer?

There was a footfall just on the other side of the door. Walter stepped back, his breath catching, and bumped into Bell.

The door swung open and Chick stuck his head in.

"Hey, hey, cats and kittens," he said. His gaze dipped to the handcuffs in Nina's hands and he flashed a wink and a sly smile. "Oh, wow, kinky!"

Walter couldn't imagine what he was referring to, but clearly both Nina and Bell did, since they turned matching shades of magenta.

Nina elbowed past Walter and shoved the newcomer back into the living room.

"Never mind, Chick," she said. "What the hell are you doing down here? We told you to stay up in the main lodge until we called you on the walkie-talkies."

Chick looked sheepish.

"Well, you know," he said. "You told us we were gonna get some more of your special acid, but we were getting bored just sitting around waiting. You said it was only gonna be a little while, and it's been ages. So we thought we'd come down and see how things were going. I didn't mean to…"

"We?" Nina said.

Chick shrugged toward the front door. Roscoe and

Alex were standing on the porch sharing a joint. Out in the rocky front yard, Dave and Iggy were playing with a glow-in-the-dark Frisbee, missing more often then they caught it. Alex had an acoustic guitar slung over his shoulder and gave a little wave, smiling the slow sleepy grin of the perpetually stoned.

"We didn't want to bug you, man," Chick said. "But we didn't want to miss the party either."

The other band members snickered and elbowed each other, and Walter realized they were *all* stoned out of their gourds. While he and Bell and Nina had been down here in the small cabin, chewing their nails to the quick with tension, up in the lodge, the band had been getting apocalyptically hammered.

Nina started shooing Chick toward the door.

"I don't care how bored you are," she said. "You guys can't be down here right now. We're still getting things ready. Now go back up and wait until we…"

"Getting things ready with handcuffs and chloroform?" Some real worry was cutting through Chick's stoned bemusement. "I thought this was supposed to be some kind of peaceful shamanistic mind-expansion thing, so we could see into…"

He was cut off by a booming megaphone splitting the quiet mountain air, and a voice as deep and loud as the cartoon voice of God.

"*This is the FBI,*" it said.

Walter knew that phony snake-oil-salesman's voice. It was Special Agent Dick Latimer.

What the hell is he doing here? How could he have found us?

"The cabin is surrounded," Latimer said. "Step onto the porch and stay there, keeping your hands where we can see them."

32

The disembodied order elicited exactly the opposite of the intended effect. It was like firing a shot at a tree full of pigeons. The guys in the band flew every which way at once, their sleepy calm instantly shattered and twisted into pot-fueled paranoia.

Iggy, the drummer, shoved past Nina into the cabin, swearing and hurrying for the bathroom.

"Gotta flush my stash!" he said.

Roscoe and Chick raced back up the path to the lodge. Alex and Oregon Dave ran in the opposite direction, down the gravel road that led to the state highway.

Men in dark suits burst from the bushes and swarmed after them. The door of the cabin slammed open and two agents came in, guns drawn. Walter ducked back into the bedroom, but the two agents ignored him and started to bang on the bathroom door instead.

"Occupado, man!" Iggy yelled from the other side. "Occupado!"

Walter and Bell stared at each other in fear and disbelief.

"How... how did this happen?" Bell asked. "Our note to Iverson was a fake. And even if it wasn't, the killer got it, right? Not the FBI."

"He must have realized it was a trap," Walter said, figuring it out as he said it. "He knew we would be waiting for him, and so he dropped a dime to the feds, so to speak. Telling them we were here, knowing we would have the acid."

"Well, I'm not sticking around waiting to get arrested," Nina said, pulling the gun from her purse. "Come on, you two. Put everything in the duffle and let's go. We've got to get to the car."

"But... but..." Walter stuttered. "But we're surrounded!"

"They're busy chasing after the guys in the band," she insisted. "This is our only chance."

Walter put the bottle of chloroform aside and then snatched up his photocopies, notes, and Iverson's file, and stuffed them into the duffle bag. He checked around the room for any other personal items as Bell tossed in the cuffs and sedatives, zipped the bag up, and slung it over his shoulder.

"Right," she said. "Through the kitchen and out the back. Let's go."

"The back? There are FBI agents..."

"I told you, they've got their hands full," she said. "Come on."

Walter almost forgot the chloroform and grabbed it at the last second before following Nina and Bell out of the bedroom.

She did seem to be right about the agents having their hands full, struggling with the vociferous Iggy inside the tiny bathroom.

"I got nothing, man!" he was shouting. "Nothing!

See? There ain't no call to be hassling a man while he's on the crapper!"

Walter looked over Nina's shoulder as she paused at the back door, peering out through the gingham curtains of a nearby window.

"Damn," she hissed. "Two more out back."

Walter looked out through the gap in the curtains. In the ambient light cast by the moon, he could see that she was right. Two more figures stood in the back yard, guns drawn, covering the back door. One of them was recognizable as the gray man who had picked up Walter and Bell at the Howard Johnson.

Walter still had the bottle of chloroform in his hand.

"Nina," he said, holding up the chloroform. "Do you have any nail polish remover in your purse?"

"Acetone?" Her eyes went wide. "Genius!" She fished a small bottle from her purse and handed it over.

"Duct tape!" he called, like a surgeon asking for a scalpel.

Bell pulled out the tape and slapped it into Walter's hand. Walter tore off a large strip and used it to bind the two bottles together. He loosened the cap on the nail polish remover in the hopes that even if the bottles didn't break on impact, at least the caps would be knocked off, allowing the two chemicals to mix and react explosively.

The use of chemistry to make weapons flew in the face of his principles, so he'd never actually tried this before.

But theoretically it should work.

"Get the door on three," Walter said to Bell. "One... Two..." His hands were sweaty, making the bottles slick and difficult to hold. *"Three!"*

Bell pulled the door open and Walter threw the makeshift bomb out into the back yard. The two agents dove for cover as the bottles came sailing out and plopped down in the center of the yard.

Nothing happened.

The agents got slowly back to their feet, cautiously eyeballing the object. Both bottles were intact but leaking, generating a thready plume of foul-smelling toxic smoke, but no big exciting explosion like the one Walter had hoped for.

"Good try, Walter," Nina said, hand on his shoulder. "Now get back. Away from the windows."

Walter did as she suggested as she aimed her gun out through the crack in the door.

"You can't just shoot FBI agents!" Bell said. "That's got to be a felony or something!"

"Who says I'm going to shoot any FBI agents?" she replied with a smirk.

She shot the bottle of chloroform.

That did it.

The resulting explosion rattled the old windows in their frames, and bathed the whole back of the cabin in bewitching blue-white light. The sound was flat and hollow, like someone dropping a fifty gallon drum off a skyscraper.

"*GO!*" Nina shouted. She shouldered the door open, jumped down the back steps, and started running straight for the woods. Bell was right behind her, and as scared as Walter was, he wasn't about to be left alone.

Out in the scorched yard, the two agents were down on the ground, arms flung up to protect their faces. He couldn't tell if they'd thrown themselves to the ground on purpose, or had their feet knocked out from under them. There was a large circle of grass burning in the center of the yard, and it looked almost cheerful, like they should gather around it and toast marshmallows.

The fire turned their shadows into long leggy monsters as they ran.

They all made it into the trees with no shots fired.

"Which way?" Bell asked.

"Down and left!" Nina said. "Hurry!"

The two men plunged after her down the leaf-slick slope, dodging mossy trees and jutting boulders as someone—presumably one or more armed agents—thrashed through the ground cover behind them. Walter had no intention of looking back to see who it was.

He was glad Nina seemed to know where she was going. He remembered they had parked the car at the end of an overgrown track that led to that burnt-out shack, but he didn't have the slightest clue where that was in relation to the cabin. It was hard enough to avoid getting lost in the familiar halls of MIT. Out in the dark woods, he was worse than useless.

From behind and above, Latimer's voice squawked through the megaphone again.

"No point in running, Bishop! Bell! We know where you live. We know where you work. You've got no place to go. All you're doing is prolonging the inevitable!"

"Just keep going," Nina hissed.

Walter was panting like a dog, his heart hammering. The running. The panic. It was too much. He didn't think he could take it anymore.

Nina slid down an embankment and stumbled on ahead. Walter and Bell crashed down after her, clinging to each other to keep from falling. When they reached the bottom, teetering and pinwheeling their arms for balance, an agent stepped out from behind a tree, flicking on a flashlight, his gun drawn.

He was surprisingly young, with lots of fluffy blond hair that vigorously defied whatever grooming products he'd used to try and tame it, but his face was cold and serious.

"Drop your weapons," he said, tipping his chin at Nina's pistol.

They were caught. Their backs were against the U-shaped embankment they'd just tumbled down, and the only way out was past the agent.

33

Nina let her gun drop to the leafy forest floor and slowly raised her hands. Walter felt a terrible desperation welling up like bile in his throat as he thought of Miranda, the usherette at the theater who would die in less than two hours if they couldn't get to her first.

There was a quick blur of movement between the trees. The blond agent crumpled first to his knees, then awkwardly to his side.

Behind him was the shadowy form of Special Agent Iverson, trench coat flapping open and a gun held butt-first in his right hand. He knelt beside his pistol-whipped associate and checked his vitals.

"He'll be fine," Iverson said. "Go on."

"Thanks!" Walter said. "How can we ever repay you for saving us again?"

"You want to repay me?" he asked. "Whatever you do, don't let Latimer capture the Zodiac. He's become obsessed, and can't be reasoned with. He thinks Zodiac is the ultimate nuclear weapon, and all he cares about is controlling him. It's up to you three to prevent it."

The fallen agent groaned, eyelids fluttering as he struggled to regain consciousness.

"Now go. Run!"

The enormity of what Iverson was saying barely had time to sink in before Nina grabbed Walter's hand and pulled him away.

"You heard the man," she said. "Come on, Walter. *Run!* We're almost there."

A moment later, Walter could hear Iverson's voice up above.

"They have another accomplice!" he cried. "Caucasian male, thirties, about six one and bald, with a beard. I saw him sap Davis, and then the four of them ran off, that way!"

There were more agents thundering through the trees, but farther back and up the slope to the left, misled by Iverson's ruse. Walter lurched after Nina and Bell, chest heaving, as they dodged through a thick stand of young elms. He saw something dark ahead of them, beyond the trees, which quickly resolved itself into the blackened timbers and tar paper walls of the ruined shack. The nose of the rented car stuck out from behind its far corner.

They ran to it, hopping over charred debris, opened the doors and threw themselves in, Nina and Bell in front and Walter in back. Nina jammed the key into the ignition and cranked it.

The big V8 roared to life.

She dropped the shift into drive and stomped on the gas. It was too much. The tires spun in the leaf mold and mud, going nowhere.

Two agents were crashing through the elms. Walter could tell by the glint of moonlight that they had guns out.

"Easy," Bell said.

"I got it," Nina said. "Got it."

She let up on the accelerator and tried again, more slowly this time. The wheels caught. They were rolling.

An agent grabbed at the car, catching a side-view mirror and smacking the driver's side window with the butt of his gun, starring it. Nina sped up, roaring down the narrow track, and the agent let go as a tree threatened to scrape him off. The other agent skidded to a stop behind them and fired.

Walter and Bell ducked, but Walter heard no impact, and the next second they had taken a curve. The agents were out of sight.

"Not out of the woods yet," Nina muttered.

Walter frowned, thinking it a very obvious thing to say, then realized that she meant it metaphorically.

"Those guys are going to catch us in a matter of minutes," she said, "if we don't find some way to slow them down."

The paved road appeared ahead of them. Nina swerved out onto it in a spray of gravel, then rocked back into line and sped down the hill. Walter looked behind. He couldn't see anything at first, but then he could. Headlights raced under the trees, reaching out for them.

"They're coming," he said.

Nina barreled down the gravel road at a terrifying speed. This was no Volkswagen Beetle, but she didn't seem intimidated by the Detroit behemoth, and slung it along the twisting track with an admirable—if heart-stopping—fearlessness.

At last they came to the state highway. Nina bumped up onto it without braking, then roared west with her foot pinned to the floorboard. The highway was smooth and clean, but almost as twisty as the smaller road. They were screeching around the curves.

"This is where they'll catch us," she said.

"Then what do we do?" Walter asked. "What's the point of running?"

"For a scientist," she replied. "You have very little imagination."

Another dirt road was coming up rapidly on the left side of the road. Nina glanced in her rearview mirror, then swerved toward it, killing the LeSabre's headlights. Bell hung on with both hands. Walter grabbed the door handle and looked back. The FBI cars still were out of sight behind the curve of the highway.

The big car slammed down onto the dark dirt road at speed, almost smashing Nina's head into the ceiling as the jolt sent her bouncing out of her seat. She drove forward about ten yards then hit the brakes and skidded to a stop in the muddy gravel.

She, Bell, and Walter looked back. A narrow sliver of the highway was just visible through the trees. One second. Two seconds. Three. Two sets of headlights howled by, and then two seconds later, a third.

"Is that all of them?" Bell asked. "How many were there?"

"I didn't see," Nina said. "But if there are any more, they're probably still up at the cabin, trying to catch Roscoe and the boys. Time to go."

She turned the headlights back on, put the LeSabre in reverse, and backed out of the side road onto the highway. But instead of going east, she went west.

"You're going the wrong way," said Bell. "The connector to the Five is west."

"They're going to turn around eventually, William. I don't want to be behind them when they do. We'll take the 101 back."

"Didn't you say that took longer?" Walter asked. "We need to get back to San Francisco as soon as possible."

"That's okay," she replied. "I'll just go faster."

Walter exchanged a look with Bell, then put his seatbelt on. It was going to be a long trip.

34

Miranda was wrapping up her shift at the Roxie, sweeping cigarette butts and scattered popcorn out from under the seats and turning out the lights inside the candy display cases. She tossed out the last of the sad, mummified hot dogs that had been spinning on the hot rollers all day, and wiped down all the spigots on the soft-drink dispensers.

It wasn't the best job in the world, but it certainly wasn't the worst, and she got to see all the movies for free. She'd proved herself to be so reliable that she'd been given a set of keys, and the added responsibility of locking up every Monday night. She took that responsibility very seriously.

Monday nights were usually pretty dead, anyway. They were closed on Tuesday, and Wednesday was when they changed the feature, so by Monday night, pretty much everyone already had the current film.

Besides, who goes to the movies on Monday night?

This past week they'd been running this French animated film called *Fantastic Planet*, which she had to admit she didn't really understand. Clearly she wasn't the only one, since it hadn't been very popular, and this last late show had been nearly empty—except for a young couple who were way more into each other than the movie. And that same creepy guy with the glasses who'd come in alone every Monday night for the past month.

For some reason, that guy had left early, twenty minutes before the end of the movie, and Miranda wasn't sorry to see him go. She always had the feeling that he was watching her when she wasn't looking.

As she reached into her purse to get the keys to lock up the theater, her fingers brushed against a bottle of Miss Clairol Born Blonde hair bleach. She'd been carrying it in her purse for a full week now, trying to get up the nerve to use it. On her way through the lobby, she paused to look at her own reflection in the mirror behind the candy counter.

Skinny, no kind of body at all beneath her polyester uniform. Freckles. Stick-straight brown hair. Such a blah-bland Breck girl. No wonder Matt barely even noticed that she existed.

Matt MacIntyre was the shift manager. He was twenty-five, and knew every single movie ever made. He had a bleach-blond shag haircut and an earring in one ear. He liked Ziggy Stardust and the New York Dolls, and made all his own clothes, or bought them from thrift stores and ripped them up, embellished them, and remade them so they looked way cooler than anything you could buy in the trendy boutiques.

She once complimented him on a purple scarf he was wearing and he'd smiled and wrapped it around her neck, telling her she could have it, that it matched her "Liz Taylor eyes." That had been the best day of her entire life.

She wore that scarf every single day, and when it stopped smelling like him, she'd gone over to the Liberty House department store at Union Square and secretly doused it with the spicy cologne he wore—Halston Z-14 for Men.

When she went home, she wrapped that fragrant scarf around her face and listened to "Bad Girl" by the New York Dolls, over and over again, imagining that she was that bad girl in the song. The kind of girl that guys would beg to be with. A tough, sassy blonde, with glitter eye shadow and platform shoes, and attitude to spare.

The kind of girl that Matt would notice.

But every time she'd take that bottle of bleach out of her purse and set it on the edge of the sink, she'd chicken out at the last minute. What if it didn't come out right? What if she ended up looking stupid, like Rita Bianchini back in eight grade, who'd tried to dye her black hair blond and turned it a terrible frizzy orange. Rita had to wear a hat for the whole rest of the year, and everyone teased her mercilessly about it. Miranda couldn't take that kind of humiliation.

As she left the theater, walking alone down 16th Street toward Hoff, she decided that it was time to take the plunge. No more girly indecisiveness. She would bleach her hair that night, as soon as she got home. Of course, her mom would flip out, but so what? She was a grown woman now, just turned eighteen and ready to move out of her parents' suburban house and find her own apartment in the city.

It was time for her to be her own person. She'd been a good girl for way too long.

Miranda was ready to be bad.

The ride back was a nightmare.

Nina drove like a maniac, flooring it the whole way, and Walter sat rigid in his seat, afraid at every second that she would wreck the car, or kill somebody, or attract the attention of the police. And he didn't understand why she was trying. There was no way they were going to make it. It was too far, and there wasn't nearly enough time.

Then, as they neared the city and he checked his watch, the nightmare got worse, because somehow she had managed it. She had driven so fast that the theater was within reach. As they came off the Golden Gate Bridge and started south into the steep hills of Divisadero Street they still had thirty minutes to spare.

That's when they hit some kind of traffic jam that had everything snarled up for as far as they could see. Walter's fingers dug into the seat as they crawled through the Fillmore district. Nina leapt at gaps, jerking the big car forward one second, then stomping on the brakes the next. But there was no point. There was nowhere to go.

Ten minutes later, they were only at Haight Street. And a few blocks later, when they turned left on 16th, it got even worse, as a large multi-car accident was revealed at the intersection with Market.

He checked his watch as they inched past the pile-up and headed into the Mission District. Two minutes. Maybe the killer would be late. Maybe the girl wouldn't show up. Maybe they would make all the lights and get there on time.

But four minutes later the bright marquee of the Roxie came into view. Nina pulled up in front and Walter jumped out of the back seat before the car had come to a complete stop, stumbling and catching himself at the last minute as he ran to the glass doors.

Locked.

He banged on the door, cupping his hands to peer inside, but he didn't see anyone.

"Hello?" he called. "Hello!"

Nothing. No response. They must have just missed her.

Walter ran back to the car and dove into the back seat, rifling through the file for his translation of that last page of the Zodiac's notebook.

"...she parks her car on Hoff Street," Walter read out loud. "Where the hell is Hoff Street?"

"There," Nina said, pointing through the windshield and stomping on the gas, cutting off a honking Dodge Dart. "Just a few blocks down."

"For God's sake," Walter said. "Hurry."

When Miranda turned down Hoff, a sudden cold wind whipped the ends of Matt's purple scarf up into her face. She clutched it tighter around her neck and quickened her step, making a beeline for the parking lot where she kept the hated Honda CVCC she'd received for her birthday, instead of the cute Beetle she'd wanted.

"So much more practical," her father had said. *"And better gas mileage. Next time OPEC pulls another oil embargo, you'll thank me."*

Which pretty much summed up the entire 18 years of her life so far. Practical. Carefully thought out in advance. She was so ready to break out of that expectation. To be extravagant and wild. To *hell* with oil embargos.

She had her hand half raised to wave at Dio, the friendly parking lot attendant, but when she looked over at the little booth where he always sat, she was surprised to see that it was empty, the door left hanging open. Maybe he'd gone to the bathroom or something, but it seemed kind of weird that he would just leave the door open like that.

She took a step closer, frowning.

Inside the booth, Dio's little portable heater was

running at the foot of the stool he sat on. His transistor radio played the crackly religious station he always listened to. There was a half-eaten Zagnut bar sitting on top of the radio. A faded snapshot of Dio's five daughters had fallen off the shelf and landed against the grate of the little heater, dangerously close to the glowing coils within.

She figured that she'd better move that photo before it caught on fire, and was bending down and reaching toward it when she noticed the blood.

There was a small red smear, about the size of a man's shoe, on the floor to the left of the stool. Could have been anything, ketchup or maybe raspberry jam, but it was enough to turn Miranda's own blood to ice.

She backpedalled, heart racing and thinking that she ought to try to call the police or something, but the nearest pay phone was two blocks back on 16th, and she was only a few feet away from her car.

The lot looked empty. No one was passing by on the street.

She should get in her car and get away, right away. Then she could maybe stop at a gas station and call the police. That was the sensible thing to do, and despite her fantasies to the contrary, Miranda had been raised to be a sensible girl.

Rooting through her overstuffed purse for her car keys, she walked around her little white Honda to the driver's side.

There she found Dio.

He was dead, that much was clear, slumped up against her car as if propped there like a rag doll, ready for a tea party. His neat white shirt and navy blue uniform jacket were soaked with blood, but that wasn't the worst thing about him. The worst thing about it was his face.

He didn't have one.

Where his face should have been was a charred red crater lit from within by a strange pale glow emanating from a network of fissures in the red ruin that used to be his features.

Then she quickly realized that it wasn't the worst thing after all. The real worst thing was the note.

A handwritten note, stuck to the center of his chest with a small folding pocket knife.

HELLO MIRANDA

Her purse fell from her numb, shaking hands, spilling its contents across the asphalt as she stood, frozen in horror. That's when she started to notice her lips tingling unpleasantly, a weird itchy feeling that spread deep into her gums and tongue. There was a sensation sort of like heat radiating from the faceless corpse, causing her skin to tighten and pulse all along the front of her body.

That's when a hand clamped down over her mouth. A large, calloused hand crawling with sparks. The sparks leapt from his fingers and burrowed like hungry maggots into her tingling skin, burning trails of excruciating agony deep into the meat of her cheeks.

She screamed against the muffing hand, but the sound was reduced to an impotent squeak. Then the fat blade of a large hunting knife appeared before her tear-blurred eyes. The terrible sparks flashed and reflected in the blade, then the knife buried itself in her vulnerable throat.

When Nina turned into the parking lot, she slammed on the breaks so hard that Walter banged into the back of Bell's seat.

"Look," she said.

In the pool of yellow cast by their headlights, Walter could see a pair of thin female legs in tan pantyhose, sticking out from behind a white Honda CVCC. One shoe was off, lying a few feet away.

Walter had one hand on the door handle and was about to jump out of the car and rush over to the fallen girl when Bell grabbed a fist full of his shirtfront and shook his head.

"We're too late," he said.

"Maybe she's just hurt and needs help," Walter said.

Nina ignored him, swiftly reversing and squealing backward out of the lot.

"Hey!" Walter shouted, wrenching himself free from Bell's grasp and looking back at the receding parking lot through the rear window. "What the hell is the matter with you two?"

"What the hell's the matter with *you*, Walter?" Nina asked. "Have you forgotten about the gamma radiation the Zodiac leaves behind?"

"We're clearly too late to save her," Bell said, "but not more than three hours late. Remember, Iverson said that the radiation lingers for approximately three hours. We can't afford to jeopardize our own lives, especially when there's clearly nothing we can do."

Walter slumped down in the back seat, feeling utterly defeated.

What's the point of all of this? he thought morosely. The killer was clearly way ahead of them at every turn. They just weren't cut out for this kind of thing. *We might as well just admit defeat.*

When they arrived back at Nina's, they parked several blocks away and cased her house from a distance, on the lookout for feds, the killer, or both. There was no one. The feds may have had Walter and Bell's personal info, but they clearly hadn't traced them back to Nina. Not yet, anyway.

The weary trio stumbled in through the door and found Abby in the hallway.

"Oh, hey," she said with a big stoned smile. "You just missed your friend."

Walter didn't think he had any more adrenaline left in his glands, but they somehow managed to pump out just enough to make him feel sick and light-headed.

"What friend?" Nina asked, scowling.

"He didn't say his name," Abby replied. "But he was very polite. He just stopped by to pick up his notebook. He left a note for you."

She reached into a large decorative pocket in her dress and handed a folded piece of paper to Nina.

35

Nina opened the note, revealing several lines of code and the familiar cross hair symbol instead of a signature.

"Abby," Nina said, not taking her eyes off the page. "Your parents are in Santa Cruz, right?"

"Yeah," Abby said. "Why?"

Nina handed her the keys to the rental car.

"Do me a favor," Nina said. "Take my rented LeSabre and go visit them. Stay for a few days. A week maybe."

"Gee, that's awfully nice of you," Abby said. "Roscoe and I will head down first thing in the morning."

"Abby," Nina said. "Go now."

"Now?" A cute little frown creased Abby's brow. "But it's after midnight, and my folks go to bed real early. Besides, I can't leave without Roscoe. Where is he, anyway? I though he was with you guys?"

"He can take the train down and meet you tomorrow," Nina said. "Please, no more questions. Just go."

The frown deepened, not so cute anymore.

"Hold on a minute," Abby said. "I think maybe something funny is going on around here. Where's Roscoe?"

"You're right, Abby," Walter said. "Something funny is going on around here. Something dangerous. So please, if you value your life and the life of your baby, you'll do as Nina says."

Abby looked from Walter to Nina and back again, still unsure.

"Is Roscoe okay?" she asked in a small child's voice.

"Of course he is," Nina answered without batting an eye. "Now please, go."

Walter looked away, unable to meet Abby's pleading gaze. Reluctantly, she took the offered key and pulled her shearling coat down off a peg by the door.

"Okay," she said. "But you'll tell Roscoe to call me as soon as he can. He knows my parents' number."

"I will," Nina said, opening the door for her.

"Well, all right then..." Abby said, trailing off. She turned and walked away.

Walter, Nina, and Bell just stood in the doorway, watching her make her slow and steady way down the slanted street, waiting until she got into the car and drove off.

They were all thinking it, but Bell was the one who said it.

"Now what?"

The coded note was almost insultingly simple, based off the same keyword as the final section of the last page in the notebook. Walter felt no sense of accomplishment as he dutifully translated it for Nina and Bell to read.

> *It would have been so easy to kill the pregnant cow. She is so trusting and so open. Almost too easy. Here's what I will do instead.*

I will shoot everyone on the Golden Gate carousel at noon on September 25th.

Have fun trying to stop me.

"This is completely pointless," Bell said. "What can we possibly do to stop him? Every single thing we've tried has been a complete and utter failure."

Neither Walter nor Nina had an answer. It just felt so hopeless, like trying to stop a river from flowing with their bare hands.

Walter paced, folding and unfolding the killer's letter over and over.

There had to be a way. There just had to be.

Then, just like that, it came to him.

"What if…" Walter paused, pushing his fingers through his hair. "Just bear with me for a moment, but what if we were to, for lack of a better metaphor, bring the mountain to Mohamed? After all, we know exactly where the killer will be, and at what time, right?"

"So what," Bell said. "You're suggesting that we try to open the gate there?"

"Exactly," Walter said. He grabbed another sheet of paper from Nina's desk. "See, what we would need would be three teams, each one consisting of two trippers and one ground control." He started to sketch a rough triangle. "We'd place the alpha wave generator here at the center—" He pointed with the pencil. "—and we could use three smaller slave units to boost the signal."

"Right," Bell said, but he didn't sound as skeptical. Walter could see the excitement building in his face. "Right, of course. Then we sync the teams, triangulate the signal and…"

"Open the gate." Walter tapped the center of the triangle. "Right here."

"Well, I hate to rain on your little eureka moment," Nina said, "but where the hell are we going to get these teams you're talking about? I don't know if Roscoe and the rest of the band have been arrested or not, but I'm pretty damn sure they aren't going to want to participate in any more of your 'exciting experiments.'"

"Fair enough," Walter said. "So who else do you know who might be willing to help?"

"Ideally," Bell said, "it would need to be people who are intelligent, open-minded, and familiar with the use of biofeedback techniques."

Walter immediately thought of the lovely May Zhang, with her charming, gap-toothed smile and bright, brainy banter.

"How about volunteers from Doctor Rayley's Institute for Bio-Spiritual Awareness?" Walter suggested. "Students, maybe, or other test subjects who have worked with Rayley in the past."

"Great idea," Bell exclaimed. "Nina, what do you think?"

"I suppose we could ask," she replied with a grudging shrug. "But let's say we are able to recruit enough people for these teams you have in mind. Then what?"

"Then it plays out just the way we planned," Walter said. "We chloroform him..."

"You'll need to get a new bottle," Nina reminded him.

"Yes, yes, but let's say we have—then we just chloroform him, cuff him, and sedate him like we originally planned. Once he's under, we radio the teams to start the mental synchronization, and when the gate opens..."

Nina and Bell both nodded, silent and thoughtful.

"What about the psychic bleed through?" Bell asked. "We can't risk allowing the same kind of deadly telekinetic phenomenon to endanger those innocent people in the park!"

"When you were in the trip," Walter said, struggling to remember, "didn't you notice, about a minute after the gate opens, that it starts to grow these... well, tendrils?"

"Yes," Bell said. "I saw that, too."

"Well," Walter said. "I'm almost positive that's the moment at which the psychic side effects begin to manifest. If we could set up some kind of failsafe that would stop the trip and close the gate the moment those tendrils begin to appear..."

"A valium injection, perhaps," Bell suggested.

"Yes, that would be perfect," Walter said.

"Of course," Nina said, "that leaves us with a pretty short window of time to get the killer through the gate."

"It's the only way!" Walter insisted. "We can't let this monster continue to threaten—or, God forbid—succeed in killing more victims."

"He's right," Bell said.

Nina didn't respond, but Walter could tell by her grim expression that she agreed.

"We should prepare individual doses of the special blend," Walter said. "A sugar water suspension, maybe. Simple to hand out and easy to ingest."

"And we'll need to borrow additional equipment from Rayley," Bell said. "Do you think he'll be amenable?"

"I think we need to get some rest," Nina said, weary hand over her eyes. "We can head over to the Institute the first thing in the morning."

36

The drive out to the Institute in Nina's Beetle was tense and quiet, a weighty sense of anxious expectation like a fourth passenger inside the little car.

There were so many ways their scheme could go apocalyptically wrong, and only one way for it to go exactly right. Walter had been unable to sleep a wink, even though he was so tired he felt as if his eyeballs were made of sand. All he could do was think and rethink the plan, turning it over and over in his mind, searching out flaws and weakness.

Although if he stopped to really think about it, he knew, the whole thing was absolutely crazy. Impossible.

Yet it was their only hope.

When they arrived at the Institute, there was no one at the front desk. Walter couldn't help but feel a little disappointed that May wasn't there. They found the good doctor in his lab, brewing herbal tea in a large Erlenmeyer flask. He was wearing nothing but fuzzy pink slippers and boxer shorts under his lab coat.

"Well, isn't this a nice surprise?" he said with a childlike grin. "Would you like some tea?"

He gripped the neck of the flask with tongs and poured the tea through a strainer, into several small beakers. He handed a beaker to each of them and then took one for himself.

"Now, to what do I owe this pleasure?" he asked.

After much debate, the three of them had agreed to let Nina do the talking this time, since they already had an existing friendship, and Nina was by far the most socially adept out of the three.

"We've been getting the most extraordinary results in our early trials of the psychic biofeedback alpha-wave theory," she said.

"Is that right?" Doctor Rayley said, leaning one hip back against a tall stool and taking a sip of his tea. "Do tell."

"Fascinating stuff," Nina said. "We've been able to achieve near perfect synchronization within a dual-subject model. Including several verifiable incidents of parallel ideation."

"Why, that's wonderful," Doctor Rayley said.

"Isn't it?" Nina smiled over the rim of her beaker of tea, turning up the charm.

"So what's your next step?" Doctor Rayley asked. "Something on a larger, more ambitious scale perhaps?"

"Exactly," she agreed. "We have a plan worked out for a large scale, wide-ranging experiment that, if successful, could very well shatter all preconceived notions of human brain function. But…" She batted her lashes, going in for the kill. "But where could we possibly find such a large number of appropriate and willing subjects?"

Walter took a swallow of the strange, medicinal tasting tea to cover his excitement. Nina was playing this brilliantly. Setting Rayley up to think helping them was his idea.

"Why, my morning class on nurturing bio-spiritual

wholeness has more than a dozen students," Rayley replied. "Bright, young, and open-minded, every one of them. I'm sure you could find plenty of willing volunteers from within that group." He winked and patted Nina's arm. "I'll tell them it's an extra credit assignment. You three are welcome to sit in on the class. It starts in about thirty minutes."

"Jeremey, you're the best," Nina said, leaning in to kiss his cheek. "Thanks!"

Rayley flushed and grinned.

"My pleasure, my dear," he said. "Now if you'll excuse me, I need to prepare my notes for the class. Help yourself to any parts or equipment you may need for your experiment. And have some more tea, if you like. It's specially formulated to encourage digestive regularity."

Walter frowned into his beaker as Doctor Rayley shuffled off into another room. Bell arched an eyebrow. Nina smiled and held out her open hands.

It almost seemed as if they could do this.

While Bell stayed in the lab to make the necessary adjustments to the various machines, Walter sat in on Doctor Rayley's lecture.

Rayley seemed like a genuinely decent, intelligent, and progressive man, full of controversial ideas and bold, thought-provoking theories. But his teaching style left something to be desired. He seemed to wander aimlessly from one topic to another, motivated by pathways of internal logic unfathomable to anyone but himself.

Whenever he seemed about to touch on a topic of particular interest, such as the role of putative neurotransmitters like dopamine and serotonin in empathic spiritual bonding, he would become sidetracked by some irrelevant tangent, and end up talking about the health risks of wearing pants that were too tight.

So Walter found his mind worrying at the details of their plan, like a dog chewing a bone. Thinking and rethinking every detail they had mapped out, and searching for weaknesses. All he succeeded in doing was increasing his anxiety.

The lecture just went on and on, and even though the Zodiac wouldn't be anywhere near that park for more than another two hours, every passing second felt excruciating.

He tried to distract himself by studying the faces of the students in the large round lecture hall. It seemed like an interesting and intelligent group. A little bit more than half male, almost all college age, all white with the notable exception of the lovely May Zhang, who was taking dutiful notes in the far corner.

She was wearing a dress instead of the pant suit Walter had seen her in before. Her legs seemed too delicate for the clunky brown boots she was wearing. She didn't seem to notice him, as she was completely engrossed in Doctor Rayley's baffling lecture.

"So in closing," Doctor Rayley said, "using bio-spiritual connectivity to stimulate the production of empathy inducing neurochemicals is the only viable way to break through the jaded modern malaise, and know the kind of pure and unadulterated love for which the human brain was intended. For you see, we must never stop learning, never stop questing into the heart of the mysterious and unknowable.

"And so I leave you with a quote from the great Albert Einstein. 'The most beautiful thing we can experience is the mysterious.'"

The members of the class gathered their books, stood,

and had begun breaking into small, chatting groups when Rayley waved his hands in the air. Bell appeared in the doorway that led to the lab, wiping his hands on a rag.

"How was the lecture?" he asked Walter.

"Interesting," Walter replied. "But a little frustrating. I think—"

"Ah yes, just a moment class!" Doctor Rayley called, cutting Walter off. "If I could just have your attention for one more minute."

The students quieted down and turned back to him.

"An esteemed colleague of mine is visiting from... MIT, is it? Yes, yes, that's it. Anyway, he's been conducting some fascinating experiments involving alpha wave synchronization and telepathy." Rayley paused dramatically, letting the word *telepathy* resonate through the lecture hall. "He's had some truly extraordinary results. Just extraordinary. So, without further ado, please welcome Walter Bishop."

Walter looked around, startled. He hadn't been expecting to be called upon to speak, and had nothing prepared. Nina gave him an encouraging smile as he shuffled nervously up to the front of the room.

"Um..." He stuffed his hands in his pockets. "Thank you, Doctor Rayley. I... we... well, that is to say..."

Pull yourself together, Walter, he told himself. *Everything is riding on this.*

He cleared his throat and took his hands out of his pockets.

"We're looking for participants in an important experiment," Walter said. "Nine bright, open-minded people who want to be a part of neurochemical history. This isn't just hyperbole, I assure you, we are attempting something that has never been done before. We will be using a combination of hallucinogenic chemicals and biofeedback technology to link multiple minds in multiple locations. If you are intrigued, please join my colleagues and me in the lab for a complete briefing.

"Thank you."

To Walter's surprise, the first person to approach him was May.

"I'll admit," she said, "I'm intrigued. Where do I sign up?"

Looking at her, with her charming gap-toothed smile and clunky boots, Walter felt deeply conflicted. Of course, he would love to work with her, to get to know her better. But involving her in this deeply dangerous endeavor made him feel queasy. As did the realization that if he didn't want to involve someone he liked in this experiment, how could he with good conscience involve anyone at all.

After all, human beings aren't lab rats, to be used, tested, euthanized, necropsied, and disposed of, he thought to himself. Didn't May and her fellow students deserve to know what they were really getting into?

Looking over at Bell, Walter knew what his friend would say. Bell would say that they needed to think of the Zodiac's victims, that sometimes sacrifice was necessary to defeat a greater evil.

And he was probably right, but that didn't make Walter feel any better about it.

37

A small curious group gathered around Walter and May.

"Come on into the lab," he said, motioning for the students to follow him. Once they were there, Nina counted heads. Amazingly, they managed to gather exactly nine students. Five men and four women.

"Let's all introduce ourselves first," May suggested. "Most of you know me already, I'm May Zhang."

She held her hand out to the man standing at her left. A handsome young man with a scruffy attempt at a mustache, shoulder length dirty blond hair parted on the side and piercing blue eyes.

"Yeah, hey," he said with a roguish smile that probably got him a lot of action with the ladies. "Gary Keyes."

"Simon Tausig," the next man in the circle said. He was British—a dapper, slightly effeminate lad with neat, trendy sideburns and large ears. The man to his left was a quiet, studious type with heavy black glasses and dark hair just starting to recede on his high, round forehead.

"David Zweibel," he said, eyes on his shoes.

Next up was a skinny and slightly anxious young

woman with an unflattering bowl haircut and restless hands.

"Judy," she said. "Judy Rusk.

"Payton Jarvis," the next guy said. He looked like any of hundreds of students they might have seen at a American Biochemical Society meeting. Socially inept, questionable hygiene, mismatched socks. Walter liked him immediately.

"Kenneth Van Hoften," the next guy in the circle announced, barely waiting for Payton to finish before jumping in with his hand out to Walter like a campaigning politician. "But my friends call me Van." He was expensively dressed, his thick dark hair professionally disheveled. Likely a child of old money, Walter guessed, trying to shake up his square family with drug use and consciousness expansion.

He had a girl with him, a beautiful young thing with a sleek chestnut ponytail and a sensuous mouth. Her body was tall and lean, all legs. That fact was accented by a micro-mini skirt.

"This here is the lovely Miss Susan Keswick," Kenneth said, as if showing off a new pair of shoes. She smiled gamely, though it was clear that she wasn't even really sure why she was there, let alone why she had been volunteered to participate in some crazy experiment.

"Leslie Elowitz." This from the last student, a woman. She said her name like a target shooter cracking a skeet plate in half. Quick, precise, and to the point. She was studying Walter with dark, skeptical eyes behind large round glasses.

Her thick curly brown hair had been unevenly chopped into a shortish non-style that would have been equally forgettable on a man or a woman. She wore no makeup and was dressed in baggy, androgynous clothes, including a frumpy tweed jacket that could have been the twin of Walter's own beloved Norfolk.

"It's good to meet you all," Walter said. "And thank you for agreeing to participate in our experiment today. Time is of the essence in this particular endeavor, so I will get directly to the point."

He looked over at Doctor Rayley, who winked and grinned.

"To begin, we will divide into four groups of three," Walter said. "Each group will consist of two test subjects, who will ingest our special hallucinogenic formula, and one team leader, who will act as ground control, monitoring the subjects, communicating with other groups, and taking all precautions to ensure the safety of the subjects."

Bell stepped up beside Walter.

"The first test group will consist of Walter and me," he said. "With our associate, Nina Sharp, functioning as control. And, since Doctor Rayley knows you all much better than we do, I will be asking him to choose the members of the other three teams."

"Ah, yes," Rayley said. "Excellent. For starters, I would suggest May Zhang, Leslie Elowitz and Kenneth Van Hoften as team leaders."

Walter glanced over at Kenneth, curious about Rayley's decision to choose him over, for example, Payton Jarvis, who seemed to be a far more appropriate choice. But Rayley knew his students better than he did, and Walter was always the first to admit that he wasn't the world's best judge of character.

"Fine," Bell said. "Leaders can I have you all here by me, please?"

"As for the rest of the teams," Rayley said. "Gary and David, you're with May. Simon and Judy, with Kenneth."

"Hold on a sec there, doc," Kenneth said. "I really think Susie should be on my team."

Rayley shook his head.

"From what I've been told, we can't have a pre-existing relationship coloring the results," he said. "Susan and Payton, you're with Leslie."

To Walter's surprise, Susan gave a thoughtful nod, then walked over to stand beside Leslie. Kenneth looked stricken, as if his cat had just decided to go sit in someone else's lap.

"Okay, listen up," Bell said, once everyone had repositioned themselves in their assigned groups. He unfolded a map and spread it open on the table. "Here's how it's going to go."

38

After Bell had finished outlining the basics of the plan to the students, he looked over at Walter, signaling him with a wordless nod.

Walter opened the little case he'd been carrying and looked at the small, stoppered vials that lay within. The individual doses of their special blend that he and Bell had prepared. Danger, death and madness lurked within the clear, innocuous liquid, but also salvation for those people in the park, and for all of Zodiac's future victims.

Or so Walter hoped.

He looked up at Doctor Rayley and the gathered groups of students, and put on what he hoped was a reassuring smile.

"Here it is," he said, setting the case on the table beside the rumpled map. "This is the mixture with which we have had all our previous successes, and which I hope will give us the ultimate proof we are seeking this afternoon." He started handing out the vials as Bell cleared his throat and held up a cautionary finger.

"I want to make sure that we're all clear on what we're doing and where we are going," he said. "Leaders, can you confirm your destinations, please?"

May spoke up first.

"Gary, David, and I," she said, "will be in the middle of the Sharon Meadow, just north of the playground. We'll pretend we're having a picnic lunch, and keep the feedback machine in our picnic basket." She poked at the map with a slender finger. "We will be there and set up no later than 11:45."

"Payton, Susan, and I," Leslie said, "will be in the parking lot of the lawn bowling club on Bowling Green Drive, also no later than 11:45."

"Good," Bell said. "Kenneth?"

"I still don't see why the time is so important." Kenneth shrugged. "I mean, there's no real reason we can't just take our time, is there? It's an acid trip, not a bank robbery."

"It is a scientific experiment," Walter snapped. It made him feel sick to have to keep lying to the students, but it was imperative to impress the importance of timing upon them. "And we must treat it as one. If we do not want to be dismissed as a bunch of spiritualist phonies, our methodology must be precise, and our standards exacting. The experiment will begin at the stated time, the duration will be recorded to the fraction of the second, with all our impressions recorded immediately.

"Timeliness is of the essence," he concluded.

Kenneth looked sullen.

"Whatever you say, professor," he muttered.

Walter still wasn't sure why on earth Doctor Rayley had chosen him as a leader.

Bell cleared his throat again.

"Kenneth," he said. "Can you please give us your destination?"

Kenneth scowled, but nodded.

"We'll be parked on Kezar Drive," he said, "just north of the stadium." Then he added, "At 11:45."

"Good." Bell nodded. "And our group will be here at the center." He tapped the map with a capped pen. "Inside the burnt-out Sharon House. Walter?"

Walter inclined his head, then turned back to the students.

"Right," he said. "Here we go. If the six subjects will ingest their doses now, along with Bell and I, and if the monitors would please record the time of ingestion, then we will be on our way."

Walter handed Bell one of the vials and took the last one for himself. When he unstoppered it, so did the others. Some of the students grinned nervously.

"The things we do for science," Simon said.

"To science," Gary said, as if toasting friends in a bar.

And with that, they all tipped their heads back in unison and let the ounce of sugar water spill over their tongues. After they had all swallowed, they paused and looked around at each other.

"It will be precisely fifty-four minutes," Walter said, "before you begin to feel any effects. So it is imperative that we all get ourselves settled in place within a forty-five-minute window, before initial onset.

"Now, I would ask the team leaders to please try to remember that the safety and peace of mind of the test subjects will be in your hands. Nina, May, Kenneth, Leslie, we are depending on you. Take good care of us."

The four team leaders all gave a solemn murmur of assent, and Walter smiled.

"Good," he said. "Now, if you're all ready, lets get the cars packed and get underway."

▲

The lab phone rang as the students gathered their packs and jackets and started loading the biofeedback machines onto lab carts. Dr. Rayley answered it, then frowned, turning to Walter.

"Er, Doctor Bishop. It's for you."

Walter blinked. It *couldn't* be for him. Nobody but the people in this room knew he was there.

He looked at Bell and Nina. They looked as scared as he felt. He stepped to the phone and reached for it like it was a live cobra, then brought it to his ear.

"Hello?"

"Bishop. Iverson. Listen to me. Latimer is coming for you. At the Institute. I wish I could have warned you sooner, but I was being watched. You have ten minutes at the most. You have to get out *now*."

39

"But..." Walter stammered. "But how did he... I mean..."

"Rayley's been on a watch list for years," Iverson said. "And once your descriptions got passed around the office, after the fiasco up at the cabin, his surveillance picked you up. You have to go to ground. Whatever you're planning, just drop it and go. It has no chance of success now. Go!"

There was a click, and Walter was listening to a dial tone. He looked around to see Bell and Nina staring at him, questions in their eyes. Rayley and the students weren't paying attention. They were pushing the loaded lab carts toward the door.

"It was Iverson." Walter swallowed. "Latimer's on his way. We were seen here. He said we have ten minutes to get out."

Nina swore.

"Then we better get on the road," she said, turning resolutely toward the door. "Come on."

Bell nodded.

"Right," he said. "Let's go."

Walter didn't move. He shook his head.

"No," he said. "No, not again. This was already so dangerous, and morally problematic. Now? With the federal authorities involved? No. I feel bad enough about what may or may not have happened to Roscoe and the rest of the band. But…" He looked over at May, who was smiling and laughing with Gary. "We just can't ethically involve any more people without letting them know what they're really getting into. They deserve to be told the truth of what's going on."

"Walter." Bell's voice was a warning growl. "You can't be serious."

"Even if I thought that was a great idea," Nina said, "which I don't, you said it yourself, there's no time."

"There has to be." Walter stepped past them and raised his voice. "Doctor Rayley. Testers. Can you all come back, please? I have one more thing to say before we go."

"Damn it, Walter." Bell and Nina groaned in unison.

Looking curious, Rayley and the students all made their way back to the lab table and peered expectantly at Walter. He wiped his coat sleeve across his lips, then closed his eyes.

"We… I… Well, we haven't been completely honest with you. Not that we've lied, we just haven't told you the whole story. And now I'm going do that. As much as I can anyway. This is going to sound completely crazy, but I hope that, once you know exactly what we are up against, you will still be willing to help us today."

He paused for a moment, looking into the curious and expectant faces. Weighing exactly what to tell them and what not to tell them.

He looked over at Bell, who was frowning, arms crossed.

Then at antsy Nina, who gestured to her watch.

"We aren't just conducting theoretical experiments," Walter said. "We are fighting to stop a killer. And we can't do it without your help." He let that sink in for a few heartbeats, then continued. "There's no time to go into detail and answer all the reasonable and relevant questions you may have. Because the federal government is also after this dangerous, murderous man. Only they don't want to stop him, like we do. They want to capture him and use him as what would undoubtedly turn out to be one of the most deadly nuclear weapons ever unleashed against humanity."

Expressions on the faces of the students ranged from skeptical to angry to amazed. But he had no choice but to keep going. Time was not his friend.

"Worse, these same federal agents will be here in just a few minutes to arrest, interrogate, and violate the civil rights of every last one of us. And while we're in their custody, the killer will be free to shoot everyone on the Golden Gate carousel in exactly…" He looked at his watch. "Sixty-two minutes."

"Shoot them?" Kenneth frowned. "You don't mean… the Zodiac Killer?"

Walter didn't answer, but he didn't have to. Suddenly the mood in the lab went from casual skepticism to intense interest. So he just nodded.

"What we are planning is very dangerous," he said. "With potentially lethal side effects for all of us, and everyone around us. But there are deadly consequences for the killer's future victims should you chose not to participate. So, while I cannot make you help us, if you are unwilling, I sincerely hope that you will."

"It's no choice at all," May said, stepping forward without hesitation. "I'm in."

"Right," Leslie echoed, stepping up beside May. "In."

All the other students swiftly gathered around them. All of them in.

Walter hung his head, humbled and grateful.

"Thank you," he said. "This is a wonderful thing you're doing."

"Yeah, fantastic," Nina said. "But we're not going to do it at all if we don't get going. Now, come on. Let's move!"

She clapped her hands and the students all hurried back to the lab carts and rolled them out into the hall. Walter let out a long, shaky breath and started to follow, but Nina put a hand on his arm and gave it a squeeze.

"Way to go, Walter," Nina said. "You should have been a politician. Ask not what science can do for you…"

Bell nodded in agreement.

"Honestly," he said. "I can't believe you managed it."

Walter shivered, suddenly chilled.

"I almost wish I hadn't."

They hurried into the hall and down the stairs.

Walter looked uneasily around the parking lot of the Institute as he followed Nina and Bell out. He was afraid they would find unmarked black cars, filled with Latimer's men, blocking the drive. But everything seemed quiet. The students were loading the individual biofeedback machines into their vehicles and scrambling into their seats. May was driving a tan Ford station wagon. Kenneth drove a teal Volkswagen microbus, and Leslie drove a white eight-seat passenger van owned by the Institute.

"Maybe we made it," he said, more to himself than to anyone else.

Nina climbed into the driver's seat of her Beetle, and fired it up as Walter got into the back seat, and Bell slid in beside her. Before Walter had a chance to get buckled in, she was surging toward the drive and pulling out into the street.

"Easy," Bell said. "The last thing we want to do is draw attention to ourselves."

"Yeah, yeah," Nina said. "But Walter's little speech cost us some precious time. We've got just under an hour to get to the park before that psycho starts his rampage."

"Still," Walter said, "we'll be even more delayed if we get stopped for speeding."

"Okay, okay," she replied. "I suppose you're right." She slowed reluctantly as the bus, the van, and station wagon swayed out of the Institute lot and fell in behind her. They trundled down Stanford Avenue toward the Bay Bridge at a reasonable thirty miles an hour, while Walter and Bell swiveled their heads in every direction.

Walter was positive that he was going to spot a line of unmarked black Fords following them, or coming to intercept them.

And finally, just when he had begun to hope they might have made it into the clear, the dreaded black cars cruised into view.

40

The Beetle was just coming down the ramp on the San Francisco end of the Bay Bridge when Walter heard Bell suck in a quick breath, and he turned to look.

There, on the opposite side of the highway, starting up the ramp that would take them to the east-bound lower tier of the bridge, was a line of unmarked black cars in the middle of heavy traffic. In the driver's seat of the first car, he saw a recognizable face with a square jaw and Hollywood tan.

"Oh, hell," Walter said. "It's Latimer.

Nina turned and looked, then laughed.

"This is *great*," she said. "Look at them. They're stuck. They won't be able to turn around until he gets to the Oakland side of the bridge. And he won't know that we've left the Institute until—"

She cut off when, as though he had heard her, Latimer turned his head and looked right at them. He did a double take and stomped on his brakes, nearly causing the cars behind him to rear-end him.

"Damn," Walter uttered.

"No, no," Nina said, knuckles white on the wheel.

"We're still good. He still can't turn around. He still has to go all the way to Oakland."

Bell shook his head.

"But he can call it in, can't he?" he asked. "And I'd be willing to bet that's exactly what he's doing right now."

Walter craned his neck as the black unmarked cars started to disappear under the upper tier. Latimer was, indeed, on the mike. He was shouting, the cords of his neck standing out like cables, obviously putting out an all points bulletin, or whatever they called it.

He was alerting the cops.

All of a sudden the maze of San Francisco wasn't just a puzzle of traffic snarls and one-way streets. It was a trap, poised to close on them.

Nina swerved the Beetle into the left lane and started speeding up. Walter turned to her, but Bell beat him to it. He put a hand on her arm.

"Steady," he cautioned. "We still can't give ourselves away."

She slowed again.

"Sorry," she said.

"The good thing is," Walter said, "Latimer can't possibly know where we're going. He'll tell them we're headed west. Change directions and we'll throw them off."

Nina whipped around a corner, still too fast, and started heading north. Walter slammed against the door, then pushed himself upright.

"Nina…"

"Sorry. Sorry."

The walkie-talkie crackled. Leslie's sharp, whip-crack voice came through the static.

"Everything okay?" she asked. "What the hell just happened?"

Walter looked out the back window. He could see her

at the wheel of the passenger van, holding the walkie-talkie and looking a bit surprised. The others were swinging into the street behind her, swaying a bit on their wheels.

Nina grunted and picked up the walkie-talkie.

"Everything's fine," she said. "Almost missed my turn, that's all. Nothing to worry about."

"Not for them," Bell muttered. "The police won't have descriptions of them."

"Fine," Leslie said over the crackly speaker. "But give us more warning next time."

Nina let out a breath, and put down the walkie.

"With luck," she said. "There won't be a next time."

She took them up the side street to Market, then turned west again, which deposited them into the middle of mid-afternoon traffic. Bell scanned for police cars. Walter reflexively checked his watch.

"Plenty of time," he said, seemingly half to himself. "Plenty of time. We'll get there. We'll hide the car. Everything will be fine."

But as they passed Stockton Street, the walkie-talkie squawked again.

"Nina? Bell? Come in?" Leslie said. "We have to find a bathroom. The dose isn't agreeing with Payton's digestion."

A crackle and a laugh interrupted Nina as she tried to respond, then a loud scraping noise and Gary's voice, singing loud and off-key.

"Plop, plop, fizz, fizz! Oh, what a relief it is!"

More shuffling noise, then May's calm voice replaced Gary's.

"Knock it off, Gary!" she said. "Sorry about that, Nina."

"No problem." Nina clicked off, then keyed in again. "Okay, Leslie, find a bathroom. Just get to your location as quickly as you can."

"Roger," Leslie said. "Over and out."

Behind them, Walter saw the white passenger van peel off and take a left at the next street.

"We shouldn't be splitting up," Bell said. "It just multiplies what can go wrong."

"Like herding cats," Nina said.

Two blocks later, a red light stopped them. Walter looked out his side window and found himself staring at a cop in the next lane. The officer was an older man, with a thick salt-and-pepper mustache and aviator glasses, sitting in the passenger seat of a cruiser and talking with his partner, who was driving. Walter nearly jumped and drew back, but forced himself to move slowly, so as not to draw their eye.

He leaned back in his seat, hiding his face.

"Don't look, but there are police next to us," he said out of the side of his mouth.

Nina and Bell looked anyway, then turned back.

"Crap," Nina said. "He's looking."

"Green light," said Bell.

Nina nervously hit the gas too fast, and they surged forward. Then she eased off, and drove up the street with her hands white-knuckled on the wheel. Walter angled his head to look in the rear-view mirror. The cruiser was easing in behind them, putting itself between them and Kenneth's Volkswagen bus, and the cop in the passenger seat was talking on the microphone.

"That's it," Walter said. "We're sunk."

"What should we do?" Nina asked. "Abort?"

"Keep driving," Bell said. "Nice and slow."

Another block of agonized crawling, with Walter's fists clenched so hard his knuckles creaked, and finally the cop in the passenger seat nodded to the driver, and the driver flipped a switch. With a whoop that made all of Walter's hair stand on end, the siren and lights came on, and the cop's voice came through the cruiser's megaphone.

"Please pull to the side and turn off your engine."

"No way," Nina said. "We'll never talk our way out of this and even if we could, there's no time!"

"But…" Bell began.

"Sorry, baby," she said.

Nina stomped on the gas just as the light ahead of them was turning red and roared across the intersection to a cacophony of blaring horns. The cruiser leapt after them, but had to swerve and brake in order to avoid crashing into the crossing cars.

It was through in another second, but Nina had bought them a block and a half lead.

Walter put a hand to his chest. He could feel his heart thumping through his shirt, like an angry prisoner protesting unfair treatment.

Bell was clutching the door handle and the dash to stop himself from being thrown around.

"You're out of your mind," he said. "You can't outrun the cops. It never works in real life. Never! Especially not in a goddamn Volkswagen Beetle!"

"Maybe not for long," Nina said. Teeth clenched, she barreled through another red light and kept going. "But hopefully long enough. I have an idea."

"Oh, God," Bell muttered.

On the seat beside her, the walkie-talkie was a confused clutter of voices. Kenneth's nasal whine won out in the end.

"What the hell was that?" he asked. "What's going on?"

Nina snatched up the walkie-talkie, driving one-handed as she barked into it.

"Kenneth!" she said. "May! Listen to me. Don't do anything stupid. They don't know any of you guys. Just keep driving up Market. Act normal. I'll check back in with you all as soon as I can."

"Are you sure?" May asked.

"No," Nina replied. "But do it anyway, will you?"

"Well, okay," Kenneth said. "If you say so…"

He didn't sound so sure. This could all go to hell at any moment. There were too many factors, too many variables.

Walter looked back. The police car was swerving through another intersection, and gaining.

"What are you going to do? What's this 'plan'?" he asked.

"Shut up," Nina snapped. "I'm working on it…"

Bell hissed as she narrowly missed a car in an oncoming lane. Nina cried out so suddenly that Walter flinched, afraid they were about to hit something, but she was pointing excitedly ahead. Walter looked forward, following her gesture.

Down a long green mall that angled due west on the north side of the street, he could see the domed neoclassical massiveness of San Francisco's city hall. And in front of it, what looked like a massive throng of people, all waving signs and banners.

"Perfect!" she cried.

She tore onto the next side street, Grove, which bordered city hall on the south, and roared toward the edge of the crowd that was spilling out of the plaza and into the street. Walter could make out some of the signs now. In fact, they were becoming clearer by the second.

Transportation Workers on Strike!

We Want a Living Wage!

Bell's feet stomped the floorboards as if he could work the brakes from the passenger seat.

"What on earth are you doing!" he asked.

"Losing our tail," Nina said. "I hope."

41

Walter looked behind them. He didn't see how it was possible. The police car was fishtailing after them into Grove, only a block and a half behind. There was no way Nina could lose them, when they had line-of-sight on her.

"Okay," she said. "Be ready to get out. And don't leave anything behind. Sorry, Nitida." She patted the Beetle's dashboard. "But we won't be coming back."

Bell looked incredulous.

"We're getting out?"

"Stay if you want," Nina snapped. Her foot was still all the way to the floor. "But I'm not coming to visit you in jail."

Walter gripped the seat back.

"Nina," he called. "Look out!"

Several seconds beyond the last possible second, Nina stomped hard on the brake, sending the car into a screeching skid that stopped just inches from the shrieking, scattering crowd.

"Out!" She grabbed the walkie-talkie and shouldered out through her door. "*Out!*"

Walter and Bell threw open their doors and staggered

out as Nina ran around the car and hooked arms with them.

"Into the crowd. Come on!"

Walter looked back as he followed her, and saw the police car skidding to a stop right behind her Beetle. The two cops spilled out, guns raised.

Nina raised her voice.

"Don't let the pigs through, brothers!" she called. "They're here to bust up the protest!" The crowd roared and seemed to fuse into a single, solid organism behind her as she dragged Walter and Bell through it and across the plaza.

Bell looked over at Nina, face lit from within with admiration and other, more complicated emotions.

"That… that was brilliant."

She shook her head.

"Not unless we get to the park, it isn't." She raised the walkie-talkie and clicked in. "Kenneth. Are you there? Have you reached McAllister yet?"

"Uh…" A long crackly pause. "I don't think so."

"Well, take it when you reach it, and keep an eye out. There's a protest going on at City Hall. A lot of traffic and a lot of people. When you arrive, look for us."

"Uh, okay."

"What about me?" It was May's voice.

"Just head over to the park on your own, May. And just stay calm. We'll meet you there."

"Roger."

Walter pulled up short, hauling the others back.

"Cops!" he hissed.

Nina and Bell looked around. A line of policemen stood and blocked off the steps of the city hall, and more were walking through the protest, keeping an eye on the picketers.

Nina slowed her step and took a deep breath.

"It's okay," she said. "They're not looking for us. As

long as we don't stand out, we're fine. Just take it slow, and try to look like you're here for the protest."

A crowd of men and women in bus driver uniforms marched past in the direction they wanted to go, all shouting and raising their fists. Walter, Bell, and Nina followed in their wake, chanting along with the rest.

"More say! Higher pay! More say! Higher pay!"

The marchers turned at the north side of the square, and started south again, but Walter, Bell, and Nina left the train and melted into the crowd that had gathered to watch it all.

They were almost to McAllister Street.

"Kenneth," Nina called in on the walkie-talkie. "Where are you now?"

"I'm on McAllister, about a block from the plaza," he replied. "You sure this is where you want me to be? It's completely jammed."

"That's fine," she said. "Just keep coming."

Nina squeezed through to the street side of the crowd, then pulled back. There were cops there, trying to move everybody onto the sidewalk, but people were streaming across the street in both directions, weaving through the cars and slowing traffic to a standstill.

"Do you see them?" she asked.

Walter craned his neck and looked east, but all he could see were people's heads.

Bell, however, nodded.

"He's moving, but it's slow."

Walter looked back into the plaza, scanning for the cops that had chased them there. He couldn't see anything in that direction either, and the shouting of the protesters drowned out all other sounds. He felt as if he was in a cornfield on a windy night, with wolves prowling somewhere nearby. He'd never know they were on him until he felt their teeth in his leg.

Nina ground her teeth, frustration creasing her brow.

"All we've got to do is stay here and stay calm," she said. "Just stay calm." But she looked about as calm as a chihuahua in a firecracker factory. All that adrenalin still seemed to be churning through her veins. Walter was feeling anything but calm, himself.

He looked east, going up on his tiptoes.

"Another half block," he said. "Almost there."

He looked behind again, and his heart seized up. Through a gap in the crowd he could see the cop with the salt-and-pepper mustache. He and his buddy were striding across the plaza, scanning for them. He grabbed Bell's arm.

"Duck down!"

"What?" Bell frowned.

"The police are here!" Walter said. "You're too damn tall!"

Bell crouched down, dropping his head between his shoulders. There was a guy holding a huge sign to their left. Walter pulled Bell and Nina behind it, then snuck a look around it and back toward the plaza.

The two cops were walking along the edge of the crowd, heads moving constantly. Walter pulled back, heart hammering, just as the one with the mustache started to look his way.

Had he seen?

Was he coming?

"There's Kenneth's bus. Come on." Nina took his arm.

Walter turned toward the street and followed Nina and Bell as they stepped off the curb. One of the cops in the cordon stepped up to stop them, but Nina pointed past him.

"Our ride's here," she said sweetly. "We're just trying to get out of this mess."

The cop waved them by and kept pushing the rest of the crowd back. In the minibus Kenneth, Judy, and Simon were looking for them. Judy saw them first and threw open the side doors.

"What happened?" she asked, her little ferret face looking even more anxious than usual.

"Tell you later," Nina replied, pushing past her onto the back bench and lying down with her hands over her head. "William. Walter. Lie on the floor."

Walter squeezed down between the seats under Judy's feet while Bell did the same under Nina's.

"Close the doors!" Nina said. "Quick!"

Judy pulled the doors closed again and looked down at Walter.

"Don't look down!" Nina whispered. "Pretend we're not here! Act natural! Relax!"

Judy raised her head, quivering, and kept her eyes front.

"Anybody coming?" Walter whispered.

"Not yet. Not..." She pressed a thin spidery hand to her mouth. "Oh, God. They're right outside. They're—" She held her breath for a tense moment, then let it out. "They're crossing the street. They're looking through the crowd over there."

Walter closed his eyes and let out his own held breath.

"So what happened?" Kenneth asked over his shoulder, keeping his eyes on the street. "Why did the cops chase you?"

"Why do you think?" Nina asked. "Keep driving."

Kenneth grunted, annoyed, but did as he was told. It took ten more minutes to get through the crowd and get moving again. Walter thought it was the longest ten minutes of his life.

42

Leslie sat in the idling van. They were in the parking lot of a fast food joint called Butchie Burger, waiting for Payton to come back from the bathroom. The restaurant's mascot was an anthropomorphic Boston Terrier in checkered pants and a bow-tie, holding a huge hamburger. He seemed to be leering down at Leslie with a maniacal grin.

She looked at her watch, even though it had been less than a minute since the last time she'd looked at it. They were bleeding time at an alarming rate.

She had no idea why she'd wound up being assigned the weakest team members. She liked to think it was because she was the strongest leader, and Doc Rayley figured she could handle shepherding these two lame ducks. But she was afraid it was more likely a kind of subtle punishment for her refusal to dress and behave in a traditionally feminine manner.

"Do you think Payton is going to be okay?" Susan asked.

Speaking of traditional femininity, Susan was the dictionary definition. Cloying floral perfume, perky smile, vapid gaze. But Leslie didn't want to write a sister off just because she'd been brainwashed by patriarchy. Never one to miss out on an opportunity to encourage free and radical thought among women, she reached into the inner pocket of her coat and pulled out a mimeographed flyer.

"He'll be fine," she said, handing the flyer to Susan. "Listen, if you're not doing anything tomorrow night, why don't you stop by my place for the weekly meeting of our feminist consciousness-raising group."

Susan looked dubiously at the flyer.

"What kind of group?" she asked.

"Consciousness raising," Leslie repeated. "It's nothing uptight or structured or anything like that, we just meet once a week to share our experiences and feelings and talk about the ways in which we have been oppressed by the male-dominated culture."

"Oh," Susan said. "Um… thanks."

Payton picked that moment to show up, sipping a large strawberry Butchie shake. Leslie frowned at the shake as he slid open the back door and climbed into the van.

"Are you sure that's a good idea?" she asked. "If your stomach is upset…"

"It's better now," Payton replied.

"If you say so," Leslie said, shoving the van into drive and pulling out of the parking lot. "But I'm gonna tell you this right now, if you toss your cookies back there, I'm not cleaning it up."

A huge tan '68 Chrysler Newport skewed across the driveway of the burger joint, smoke pouring out from under its hood, and blocking the only way out.

"You have *got* to be kidding," Leslie said. She laid on the horn and stuck her head out the window. "Hey, move that boat out of the way, will ya? We gotta be somewhere!"

The driver got out of the Newport. He was a tubby,

red-faced guy in a pair of skin-tight white pants that did extremely unfortunate things to his nether region. He threw his hands up in the air.

"Engine no good," he said, with a thick, Eastern European accent. "Is overheat!" He made a pushing motion with both meaty hands. "You help?"

"Oh, crap," Leslie muttered. "Come on," she said over her shoulder, checking her watch again. "The sooner we get this guy's car out of the way, the sooner we can be on our way."

"What?" Susan looked at her as if she'd lost her mind. "I'm not pushing anybody's car. That's a man thing. Let Payton do it."

Leslie restrained herself from raising Susan's consciousness with a boot to her skinny little ass, and got out of the van.

"Payton, you coming or not?"

"Okay," he said, following her like a reluctant child.

"Thank you, thank you," the man said when the two of them approached. "I steer, you push, yes?" Leslie nodded, struggling not to look down at his catastrophically squashed and all too visible crotch.

"Right," she said, grabbing Payton by the arm and dragging him around to the rear of the enormous vehicle.

She placed both palms on the trunk.

"Don't just stand there," she said.

Payton put his hands on the car like he was petting a Doberman of questionable temperament. Leslie rolled her eyes.

"Now," the man called, putting the car in gear and then getting out to steer with one hand and push with the other. "*Push!*"

Leslie did so with all her strength, but the massive beast of a car was so heavy that even with the three of them, it rolled up the driveway slower than a slug. Not that Payton was doing much in the way of pushing. More like just resting his hands on the car.

"Come on, push!" Leslie said. "We're already nearly ten minutes behind. The other teams are depending on us!"

Payton put a little more effort into it and the Newport started moving a little faster, rolling into the parking lot. The man in the tight pants guided it into an empty parking place and then came back to shake both of their hands, thanking them and offering to buy them a couple of Butchie burgers as a reward.

"No time," Leslie said. "But thanks anyway."

Payton, who had started to look a little green as they were pushing the car suddenly lurched off to the left and threw up the strawberry milkshake into a nearby trash can.

"Gee, imagine that," Leslie said. "Who knew?"

Payton continued to retch, while Leslie crossed her arms and checked her watch again.

They were never going to get out of this parking lot.

43

As May worked her way through the snarled traffic around City Hall, dipping down into the Lower Haight to avoid the worst of it, she heard her mother's voice in her head, criticizing her every move.

So aggressive, the way you change lanes. No wonder you don't have a husband.

May hadn't seen her mother in over a year, estranged as she was from her large family, but that voice was alive and well in May's head. She could still hear the sharp little tooth-sucking sound of disapproval she would always make, wordlessly cutting May to ribbons over some unforgivable moral transgression, like wearing a short skirt or taking too much food for herself at the family table, instead of making sure her brothers all had enough first.

Ever since she got the job at the Institute, May felt as if she'd found a brand new family of open, like-minded people who accepted her for who she really was, and didn't think she was a whore because she took birth control pills or failed to live up to some antiquated stereotype of how women should behave. But the ghost of her disapproving mother wasn't so easily exorcised. And whenever May was worried or anxious, that voice came back to remind her of what a disgraceful failure she was at every single thing she did.

She distracted herself from the critical ghost by thinking about that guy from MIT, Walter Bishop. There was something about him that she found appealing, with his terrible coat and wild hair and gentle, curious eyes. He didn't seem at all intimidated by her intelligence, and shared many of her most passionate interests. She had been deeply moved by the bravery and determination he'd showed in choosing to fight against the Zodiac Killer and was exhilarated to be a part of that fight.

And she'd always thought she was the only one in the world who actually liked Necco wafers.

"I don't feel a thing," Gary said, leaning his head out the window like a dog. "Are you sure this stuff is gonna work?"

"Remember," May replied. "It's supposed to take fifty-four minutes to kick in. It's only been…" She looked at her watch. "Thirty-seven."

"Do you believe all that business about the Zodiac?" Gary asked. "I mean, what if that's just a part of the experiment? Testing to see how we react when an element of danger is added in to the mix."

May hadn't thought of that.

"I suppose that's possible," she said, heading up Divisadero to Fell. "I mean, it sounds a lot more plausible than the idea of fighting a psychic serial killer, doesn't it?"

"No," David said quietly from the back seat.

"No?" May asked, looking up into the rearview mirror. But his head was down, gaze aimed at the floor. "No, it doesn't sound more plausible?" she said.

"No, that's not what's happening," David said. "This is real."

"What makes you say that?" Gary asked, turning back with one arm thrown over the top of his seat.

"I just…" David looked away, out the window. "I can just tell. Ever since I was a kid, I've always… known things. And as soon as I saw Doctor Bishop, I knew that this was real. That this, being a part of this, is what I was meant for. All of us, we *have* to be a part of this."

"Wow," Gary said, turning back around. "That's heavy."

"I see men," David said. "Watching me."

May frowned, looking up into the mirror again, and then down at her watch.

"Right now?" she asked. "You shouldn't be hallucinating yet."

"No," David said quietly, speaking to his folded hands in his lap. "All the time. They wear hats. Like Alain Delon in *Le Samouraï*. And they never say anything, they just… watch."

May looked over at Gary, who smirked and pointed a very unsubtle circling finger at his temple. This revelation was actually deeply worrying to May. David was clearly suffering from some type of mental illness, probably schizophrenia, and the idea of linking minds with a person like that seemed like a spectacularly bad idea, especially with so much at stake.

Yet, many progressive thinkers had recently suggested that so-called mental illness was really nothing more than freedom from culturally imposed restrictions on the mutually agreed upon "reality." It was possible that May was being too uptight in her thinking. She should allow herself to be more open about unconventional views of reality.

After all, just because she couldn't perceive them, who was she to say that mysterious men with fedora hats *weren't* actually watching David?

Still, she had no way of knowing how David's unconventional view of reality might effect the experiment.

Only one way to find out.

44

Walter, Nina, and Bell stayed lying on the floor the rest of the way to Golden Gate Park, but even hidden Walter felt as if the whole of San Francisco was watching him. He kept thinking he heard police sirens coming after them, but every time he strained his ears they seemed to fade away again.

He had to keep wiping his face.

Sweat was soaking his collar.

"Paranoia," he murmured. "I've never noticed paranoia as a side effect of our special blend before."

"It isn't paranoia if they really are after you," Bell said with a smirk.

At last they were turning off Fell onto Kezar drive and entering the park, the lush green of the trees and lawns swallowing up the noise and visual chaos of the city and enveloping them in soft shady silence. But what should have calmed him down only made Walter more tense.

They might have escaped the scrutiny of the police, but they were closing in on a much more fearsome adversary, and a much riskier enterprise. Their showdown with the Zodiac was only minutes away. Their chance to get rid of him once and for all. Or perhaps to perpetrate the greatest disaster in San Francisco since the Great Earthquake of 1906.

Kenneth pulled off the road and parked just south of the playground that lay adjacent to the carousel. Walter rose up cautiously and looked around.

"Have we heard from Leslie lately?" he asked.

Nina picked up the walkie-talkie.

"Leslie?" she said. "Report in please."

Leslie's voice popped from the speaker.

"Going a bit slow," she said. "Payton is really feeling the bumps. Don't know if he's going to be okay for this."

"Damn delicate flower," Nina growled. She keyed the mike. "Well, get there as soon as you can, please. The clock is ticking."

Bell shook his head.

"Our blend should have no impact whatsoever on the digestive system," he said. "It has none of the impurities of mushrooms."

"It's fear, Belly." Walter pressed his dry lips together. "Garden variety. I'm feeling pretty sick to my stomach myself."

Leslie barreled down Fell Street like a race car driver on speed, pushing the crotchety old van to its limit, swearing out the window and cutting off cars with the horn blaring. Lucky for them, Payton didn't seem to have anything left inside him to throw up, but he still looked pretty queasy.

To Leslie's surprise, Susan seemed exhilarated by her aggressive driving, even letting out a little cheer when she finally cut in front of a cigar-smoking cabbie who was being a jerk and wouldn't let her into the lane. Leslie was even more surprised when Susan gave the cabbie the finger as they passed. Maybe there was hope for her yet.

"I don't know if this is such a hot idea," Payton said.

"That milkshake wasn't such a hot idea," Leslie snapped. "But you survived, didn't you?"

"I think this is fun," Susan said with a big happy grin. "It's like being in a cool spy movie or something. And I didn't even want to come to this class in the first place, because I thought it would be boring!" She patted Payton's arm. "You'll be okay. Just visualize peace inside your stomach, like Doctor Rayley says."

"Uh… okay," he said with a wan smile. "You're probably right."

Leslie tried not to be bothered by the fact that men always listened to women like Susan, and almost never listened to women like her. There was too much on her mind to let something like that get to her.

She drove into the park, searching for Bowling Green Drive. She'd never driven in the park before, since she normally rode her bicycle everywhere, so she got a little bit flummoxed by the one-way streets. The ticking clock made each minor mistake seem epic, and she hated to make *any* mistakes in front of Susan. It was important for her be perceived as a strong, competent leader, especially given the stakes of this particular mission.

She forced herself to remain calm and double back without comment, searching for the entrance to the parking lot for the lawn bowling club.

May parked the station wagon on Stanyan Street. Gary ran around to the back and grabbed the picnic basket containing the biofeedback machine, along with a folded plaid blanket. David just stood quietly waiting at the curb.

"How are you feeling, David?" May asked as they waited for a break in the traffic.

"Good," David said, a little half smile playing over his lips. "I feel good."

"I don't feel good yet," Gary said. "But we should be feeling good any minute now, right?"

"Right," May replied, crossing the street and motioning for the two men to follow. "Any minute now."

The Sharon Meadow wasn't too crowded when they arrived. There was a birthday party taking place in the far northern corner, and several trees had been decorated with cheerful, brightly colored balloons and streamers. All the revelers were gathered around a picnic table, clamoring for slices of a large pink cake being doled out by a tiny, grandmotherly woman in a sweater that was almost the exact same color as the cake.

A pretty young woman with a long black braid that hung nearly to the backs of her knees played fetch with a brindle Boxer puppy. An earnest young Latino man was playing an acoustic guitar while two female friends sang in harmony. On the far southern end, a young couple was enthusiastically making out on a blanket, willfully oblivious to everyone else in the park. The wide center of the meadow was basically empty, with the majority of the population sticking to the shady parts.

It wasn't a ton of people, but there were more than May might have preferred. In fact, a public park seemed like a pretty risky place for a dangerous experiment. If it really was dangerous.

Was this all just part of the test, like the famous Milgram experiment in which students had been told they were delivering painful electric shock to subjects, when in fact they themselves were the ones being studied?

As May and Gary spread out the blanket for the three of them to sit, she could see the burnt-out shell of the Sharon House through the trees, and wondered if Walter and his friends were in place yet. Real or not, dangerous or not, the experiment would begin in just ten short minutes.

45

"Alright," Bell said to Kenneth. "Are you good to go?"

Kenneth looked a little unsure, but did his best to cover it with a mask of cocky confidence. Judy and Simon sat side by side in the back seat of the bus with the hushed expectation of kids waiting for a puppet show to begin.

Walter checked his watch. In about three minutes, the special blend of acid would be kicking in.

"Excellent," he said, without much conviction.

"Start the biofeedback machine," Nina said to Kenneth. "As soon as we're out of sight."

"Let's go," Bell said. "We have to be in place before the killer arrives."

He headed north, through the trees, toward the carousel. Nina followed close behind him. Walter cast one last glance back at the bus and its occupants before hustling to catch up.

When the carousel came into view, the three of them paused and hung back, scoping the area for any sign of the killer. The carousel itself was open and running, with a small group of people waiting for the current cycle to end so they could have their turn. The organ music was cheerful and upbeat, accented by excited, high-pitched squeals and laughter. A little less than half of the colorful menagerie animals were occupied.

Beside the carousel stood the Sharon House, a Romanesque stone building stained with soot. It had been closed down and fenced off after a fire gutted the place. Many of its tall arched windows were broken and boarded up. There was a large, charred hole in the north side of the roof.

Just as they suspected, this burnt-out building would be the perfect hiding place for a sniper who wanted to shoot people on the carousel. It was also perfect as the epicenter for their psychic web, a place where they could open the gate in private, away from curious bystanders.

When they circled around the back of the building, they spotted a large slit cut into the chain-link.

Bell put one hand on the fence, eyebrow raised.

"He must have beat us here," Nina said.

"Could have been kids," Bell said. "Or vagrants."

"Should we go in?" Walter asked. "Or..."

A scrawny black kid about sixteen years old sidled up to them. He had an impressive Afro, sunglasses and an orange leather jacket that he had clearly borrowed from a much bigger friend.

"Hey, man," he said. "You from Reiden Lake?"

Walter and Bell exchanged a look.

"Who are you?" Bell asked.

"Your friend said you'd be here," he said, instead of answering. "He gave me five bucks and asked me to give you this note."

The kid held out a slip of paper. Walter frowned, scanning the tree line. No one. The deep sense of unease in his belly twisted like a knife.

"You want the damn note or not?" the kid asked.

Walter took it.

"Did he say anything else to you?" Walter asked.

"Nope."

The kid strolled away, uninterested now that his job had been fulfilled.

"Well," Nina said. "What does it say?"

Walter unfolded the note. It was written in code.

"God *dammit*," Walter said. "We don't have time for this. We're going to start tripping any second now!"

"Look," Bell said, pulling a pen from an inner pocket. "He's obviously using Reiden again as the key. He *wants* us to read this." He drew up a quick Vigenère cipher and started laying out the key on the back side of the note. The message was short, and once the key was established it translated swiftly.

My dearest friends,

I have taken a hostage, but I am growing tired of this world. Leave Miss Nina Sharp behind and come to me so we can talk. Come around to the north side of the house. If I see that redheaded bitch I will kill the hostage. If you come alone, I will let the hostage go.

I want to go home.

Again, the note was signed with the infamous cross hair symbol.

"I don't trust him," Nina said immediately.

As Walter stared at the cross hair symbol, it seemed to swell and welt up on the paper like a fresh brand on raw flesh.

The acid was starting to kick in.

"Belly?" Walter asked.

"Yeah," Bell replied. "Me, too."

Nina rolled her eyes.

"Oh, this is just great," she said.

"What are we going to do?" Bell asked.

"Look," Nina said. "Here's the plan. I'll go into the building from this side, set up the central biofeedback rig, and then I'll come through to the north end from the inside, and cover you two with Lulu. Agreed?"

"We don't seem to have much of a choice," Bell said.

"You have the extra walkie-talkie?" Nina asked Walter.

He checked inside the bag that contained the chloroform and handcuffs. The extra unit was there, right we're he'd left it. He turned it on.

"Good," Nina said. "If you get into trouble, use it."

"Seems like a probable outcome at this point," Bell said.

"Maybe he really does want to go home," Walter suggested.

Nina turned away from them and squeezed through the slit in the chain-link fence.

"Go find out," she said.

46

Nina followed the tan stone wall around the corner of the building, and slid alongside one of the boarded-up windows. The lowest board had been pried loose on one end and if she got down on her hands and knees, she could just wiggle through.

She looked around to see if anyone was watching. The sound of the carousel was clear, but from this angle she couldn't see it. That meant all the people there and in the neighboring playground couldn't see her, either. She pushed the canvas messenger bag in through the window frame ahead of her, and then squeezed in after it, loose nails scratching at her skin like metal claws.

Inside, the building was dim and redolent of char. Nina could see the cloudy sky through the hole in the roof, reflected in tarry puddles on the ruined floor. She remembered reading about the fire in the paper, something to do with glass blowing or kilns or something, but whatever the cause, the devastation was extensive. The interior had been burned down to the bones, nothing left intact but the exterior stone walls.

She could still hear that happy organ music from

the carousel, an eerie counterpoint to the lonely, haunted house feeling inside the burnt-out building. She had never been a superstitious person, but found herself wondering if anyone had been killed in the fire, and shuddering at the thought.

Shrugging off the childish willies, she surveyed her surroundings and selected a spot near a descending staircase that seemed close enough to the exact center of the building, She unloaded the biofeedback rig and set it up, thumbing the power switch. Satisfied that it was working at maximum capacity, she drew Lulu from her purse and, barrel pointed at the damp floor, made her cautious way toward the north side, to check on Walter and Bell.

The big open space echoed her footfalls back at her, multiplying them and making it sound as if someone was following her. She paused for a moment, scanning the hazy corners and archways around her as the echo died off. Her eyes strained to separate the dim, sooty shadows. Pale ash kicked up by her feet swirled in what little light managed to find its way in.

Nothing. No one.

She continued, skirting another large black puddle and making her way toward a window on the north wall—a window with a single missing board.

Walter and Bell stood on the north side of the fence that surrounded the burnt-out building. The acid was really starting to make itself known, and shadowy figures seemed to lurk at the far edges of Walter's peripheral vision. But if the killer was there, he didn't make himself known.

"What should we do, Belly?" he asked, gripping

his friend's upper arm to steady himself. "We can't wait here forever. The synchronization must begin in less than a minute!"

"I don't know," Bell replied, staring intently at the ground between his shoes. "I simply don't know."

That's when Walter noticed the folded note tucked under the edge of the chain-link fence. He bent to pick it up, almost reluctant to unfold it. The paper seemed to pulse with a feverish infection in Walter's hands.

"Do you see this?" he asked Bell.

"Yes," Bell said. "But that doesn't mean it's real."

He opened the note and found a message in plain, uncoded English.

I never had a hostage. But I do now.

The cross hair symbol winked at Walter like an eye. He dropped the note, wiping his hand on his pant legs as if it had touched something rotten.

"My God," Walter said. "He's got Nina!"

Nina reached the window with the missing board, and peered out. She could see Walter and Bell on the other side of the fence, waving their arms and having some kind of intense debate. No sign of the killer.

She checked her watch. Time was running out.

She was about to call out to them when she heard a stealthy, sliding footstep behind her. She spun, gun raised. The dappled shadows taunted her with a dozen hiding places, but she couldn't see anyone.

"Show yourself!" she called.

Her echoing voice disrupted a brooding pigeon, who took off through the hole in the roof with a noisy flutter. A single white feather seesawed down from the ceiling and landed at her feet.

She waited.
Nothing.
No one.

Her ears rang with listening, eyes wide in the dim, shadowy building. Outside, the carousel started up again, taking a new batch of excited children for a ride with a burst of jaunty music.

The walkie-talkie in her purse crackled with static, causing her to jump, startled. Then Leslie's voice.

"Nina? Nina, do you read me?"

She took out the unit with her left hand and keyed the mike.

"Everything okay, Leslie?"

"We're in place," she said. "I didn't think we were going to make it, but we're in place here at the parking lot. Ready when you are."

Nina looked at the walkie-talkie in one hand and the gun in the other. No point scaring the students. Their only option was to proceed as if everything was normal. Stick to the plan.

"Roger that, Leslie," she said into the mike. "Get your equipment set up, and begin the synchronization."

"You got it," Leslie said. "Over."

Nina hoped she was doing the right thing. She put the walkie-talkie back into her purse.

That's when she was grabbed from behind, the cold blade of a knife biting into the exposed flesh of her throat.

"Drop the gun, sweetheart," the killer whispered, his breath hot against her ear.

47

"What are we going to do?" Walter asked.

Before Bell could answer, he heard a sharp piercing whistle. When he turned toward the sound, he saw Nina's pale face in the lower corner of a partially boarded window. Her expression was masklike and unreadable. Then Walter noticed the gloved fist twisted into her red hair, and the knife pressed against her throat.

"He wants you to come inside," Nina called, lips barely moving, her voice a flat monotone.

Bell took a step toward the building, hands clenched into shaking fists, but Walter gripped his shoulder.

"If we do what he says," Walter said, "what's to stop him from killing Nina? Once he has us, he won't need her any more."

"But what other choice do we have?" Bell asked through gritted teeth. "The bastard has the upper hand here."

The walkie-talkie in Walter's bag crackled and squawked.

"Nina?" It was Kenneth. "Nina do you copy?"

Walter dug out his unit and fumbled with it for a

moment. It seemed to have far too many buttons, many of which were weirdly organic looking, like clusters of shiny spider eyes.

Bell snatched it out of his hand and hit the button.

"Bell here," he said. "What is it?"

"A bunch of black Fords just pulled up behind us on Kezar," Kenneth said. "And a bunch of guys in suits got out. I'm pretty sure they're feds, and they're headed your way!"

"Copy that," Bell said. "Stick with the plan, no matter what. Do you hear me?"

"Will do," Kenneth said. "Good luck."

Walter looked back through the trees and saw the agents headed their way, but there seemed to be thousands of them moving in robotic lockstep, like mechanical Nazis. This was really the worst possible time to be tripping.

"They're coming, Belly," he said. "We have to go into the building, like it or not. This is our last chance before the feds turn this whole thing into a fiasco."

Resigned and resolved, the two of them ran for the hole in the fence.

"Attention team leaders," Bell said into the walkie-talkie. "Tell your subjects to visualize a gate, and to open it! Do you copy?"

"Copy," Kenneth replied. "A gate."

"Will do," Leslie said.

"Got it," May said.

"And stand by with the tranquilizers," Bell said, folding his long body nearly in half to squeeze through the slit in the fence. "Be ready to stop the trip if I tell you to do so. Over and out."

Walter followed Bell through the hole, but when he looked back at the feds, he saw Latimer front and center.

Worse, Latimer saw him.

Or did he? Was Latimer even there at all, or just a figment of his chemically enhanced perception?

There was nothing to do about that now, though. Either the man was there, or he wasn't. And he would either catch them, or he wouldn't. They had no choice but to try and go through with the experiment. Stick to the plan, and hope they weren't too late to save Nina.

When Walter caught up, Bell had pried a loose board off one of the windows and was climbing through. The remaining boards looked disturbingly skin-like, and the hole Bell was crawling into seemed like a giant wound. Its edges oozed and pulsated, making Walter pull back with disgust.

"Come on," Bell's voice called from inside. "Hurry!" So Walter closed his eyes and climbed into the gaping wound, trying not to notice how feverish and slick the edges felt.

Inside the dim, char-stinking interior of the burnt-out building, Walter felt completely disoriented. He could no longer trust anything he was seeing, but he definitely didn't see any sign of the killer—or Nina. Although in his current state, that didn't mean they weren't there.

Then he heard the killer's voice.

"Here we all are," he said. "Just like old times."

The stocky man with the reddish-brown crew cut stepped out of the gloom and into a shaft of light that streamed through the broken roof. He was like an actor taking the stage, arm around Nina's neck and the knife pricking the skin beneath her left ear. A trickle of blood seemed to flow out into the air between them, floating in weightless globules. A gory lava lamp.

"Okay," Bell said, palms held up and out. "Okay, just take it easy."

"Tell me," Zodiac said, "since I just can't seem to figure it out. Which one of you is nailing her?"

The killer turned Nina's body toward Walter, then toward Bell.

"Ah," the killer said to Bell. "It's you, isn't it? But…" He leaned in over Nina's shoulder, squinting. "It's not just that, is it? You're not in love—no, this is much more… complicated. Mmmmmm." He pressed the knife harder into Nina's neck, eliciting a stifled hiss and a more vigorous flow of blood. "I can't wait to see how you react when you watch her die."

"Wait," Bell said, taking a cautious step forward. "The FBI is on our heels. They'll be in here any minute. If you kill her, you won't have a hostage to use when you negotiate with them."

"Nice try," the killer said. "But I don't need this bitch as a hostage. The FBI, they know me. They know what would happen if they hurt me." He waved his left hand in an expansive circle. "I'm holding this whole park hostage!" He grabbed a fist full of Nina's hair and cranked her head back, stretching her pale throat taut. "Say goodbye, sweetheart."

"No!" Bell cried.

A sharp crack sounded in the hollow space, and for a moment, Walter was sure someone had been shot. Maybe even him.

"Freeze! FBI!"

Bright light washed over Walter and he realized that the door had been kicked in. Three dark, backlit figures stepped into the building, two ahead with guns drawn and one slightly behind. He felt as if he really should do something about this turn of events, but nothing was coming to mind. In fact, he *still* wasn't even sure they were real.

But the killer was, and reacted to the arrival of the newcomers far more swiftly and efficiently. He let go of Nina's hair and drew a gun from his waistband, drawing a bead on the figure in the center.

Having been released, Nina ran to Bell. The two of them seemed to melt into each other like conjoined twins, outlines blurring and blending. Walter shook his head, struggling to keep it together.

"Don't shoot!" Bell cried. "If you shoot him, you'll kill us all!"

The dark figure in the center stepped forward, features resolving out of the sticky, viscous light.

Latimer.

"We don't want to kill you," he purred, ignoring Bell and approaching the killer with open hands. "We want to give you a job. We have a lot to learn from someone like you."

The killer let out a contemptuous bark of laughter.

"I'm nobody's lab rat," he said, gun aimed between Latimer's eyes.

"Shoot me if you like," Latimer said. "There are a dozen more just like me right outside that door. You're coming with us today. It's up to you if you want come willingly, or…"

"Or what?"

Walter still couldn't trust what he was seeing, or what he thought he was seeing, but he was pretty sure that the other two agents had begun a slow creep around either side of the killer.

He knew it was real when the killer shot them both, first left, then right, with blinding speed and precision.

They dropped almost in tandem, uncapped syringes falling from their twitching hands. One rolled across the floor and bumped against the killer's muddy boot. He looked down at it with a smirk, then lifted his foot and crushed it under his heel.

"Plan B?" he asked Latimer.

Latimer started backing away.

"I didn't think so." The killer started to strip the gloves off his hands, revealing the swarming sparks flowing over the surface of his skin. "You want to study me? Learn about me? Find out what makes me tick? Take a good long look, Agent Latimer."

He stepped in with the smooth, fearless grace of a boxer, but instead of throwing a jab, he reached out and grabbed Latimer's face.

The agent let out a horrible, muffled scream as the killer's fingers sank into the burning flesh. The skin bubbled and split around his fingertips, peeling back in charred flaps. Latimer's exposed skull started to effervesce into the air around him, emitting a sparkling cloud of atomic particles.

48

Walter was staring at this hideous display with his jaw hanging open when Nina grabbed him and shoved him toward the open door—the one that led to the stairwell. She pushed so hard that he nearly fell, dropping his bag. It slid across the floor and landed in a large puddle.

"What the…"

"Get into the basement *now*," she said. "Or we're all cooked!"

"But the chloroform!" Walter cried, taking a step toward his soaked bag.

Over her shoulder, the sickly green glow from Latimer's melting face was spreading outward like ripples in a pond, until it was just inches away from the back of Nina's head.

"It's too late," she said. "Just GO!"

Walter didn't need to be told twice. He could feel the burning heat on the back of his neck as he dove for the basement stairs. In mere seconds, the upper level of the building would be awash in deadly gamma radiation. They had to get to the relative safety of the solid stone basement.

Bell went pounding down the stairs ahead of him as Walter half-fell and half-ran right behind him. Nina was reaching out to pull the heavy old door shut behind them when a powerful blast of energy slammed it, knocking her down the stairs and into Walter's arms.

The two of them nearly smashed into Bell, who was standing awestruck at the bottom of the stairs.

The gate had opened.

It was to the left of the stairs. Still just a glittering slit, but bigger than ever before. Nearly eight feet tall and bulging in several places along its length, like a gecko's pupil. As Walter watched, the bulges dilated and joined together to form one larger opening, swirling and pulsing at its heart.

"How long do you suppose the gate has been open?" Nina asked, looking at her watch.

"There's no way of knowing," Walter said. "Just watch for the formation of tendrils around the outer perimeter. That's your signal to call the teams and tell them to end the trip."

"But what if we haven't had enough time to get him through?" Bell asked.

"Doesn't matter," Walter said. "I won't risk any more innocent lives."

Flickering images of carousel horses seemed to be careening through the air around Walter's head. He waved at them, as if they were pesky insects, and struggled to keep himself focused.

"Look," Nina said, pointing to the gate.

Sure enough, tiny threads were appearing around the top, growing and stretching.

Nina pulled out the walkie-talkie.

"Talk to me, team leaders," she said. "How's everyone doing?"

"Rocky." May's response was immediate. "Both of my guys have been really agitated. I'm doing my best to keep them calm, but I don't think they can take much more."

Another voice.

"This is Leslie. My trippers are... well, they aren't moving at all. They seem almost comatose. I hope they're okay. Also..." She paused. "I'm starting to get this weird headache, almost like I'm getting sucked into the psychic link."

"Me, too," May said. "But I get a lot of headaches, so I figured it was just me."

"We have to stop this," Walter said. "Stop it now."

"One more minute," Bell insisted. "We need to try and lure the killer into the basement."

"And how the hell are we supposed to do that," Walter snapped. "Stop it *now*, Nina!"

"Kenneth?" Nina said into the walkie-talkie. "Kenneth, do you copy? Are you and your team all right?"

"Can I play, too?"

The Zodiac stood at the top of the stairs, head cocked and curious. His hands were slick with half-cooked gore, but otherwise normal.

He started down the stairs, gun in hand but pointed at the floor.

"You think you can get rid of me like this?" he sneered. "That I'll just stroll right out of this world like a good little boy. Idiots."

He reached the bottom of the stairs. Walter backed away, while Bell put out an arm to push Nina behind him.

"I have a better idea," the killer said. "How about you three go through that gate? See how well you can do in *my* world."

He raised the gun and pointed it at Walter.

"You first," he said.

At that moment something unexpected happened. Walter felt like he'd been hit by a psychic truck as the remote teams suddenly linked minds with him and Bell. The strength and power of that connection started to pull the killer in, revealing that ugly soulless void that was the mind of the Zodiac, struggling against their influence.

Walter could feel Bell close by, and the other minds—all intimately connected, sharing a kaleidoscopic cascade of personal memories and images.

A chubby dark-haired woman with a black eye and a sad smile.

An illicit kiss from a fellow student in the stairway of an all-boys high school.

A music box with a twirling ballerina.

An old woman in a casket, dressed in a frilly, dated frock.

A turquoise parakeet, perched on a child's finger.

A man turning away, utterly uninterested in a drawing of two smiling stick figures, holding hands.

A backlit silhouette standing in a bedroom door.

All these memories, each one so deeply personal and fraught with significance, felt overwhelming. They distracted Walter from the task at hand. He struggled to shut out all the psychic noise, and hone in on the mind of the killer.

But at the same time as the killer's dark consciousness was being drawn into the circle, like a snared and panicking bird, Walter could feel Bell's mind slipping away, lured by the lone bright flame of Nina.

"Belly," he thought he said. "Stay with us!"

But then, Bell was gone—and in his place, the dark, ferocious psyche of the killer.

Just like that night at Reiden Lake, the world dropped

out from under him. Walter felt as if he was plunging through cracked ice, and into the arctic water below.

Then the hallucination changed. The room around him ceased to exist as he plummeted down through a spinning tunnel of images, dragging the linked group of minds behind him like tin cans on a string.

A paper cup full of pills.

A lab filled with children's toys.

A strange device shaped like a window.

A blond woman with a gun.

But whose images were these? Not the killer's this time, he didn't think. Maybe the other members of the group?

Then, just as suddenly as they started, the whirlwind of images stopped, and Walter was in a child's bedroom, sitting on the edge of a little boy's bed.

The room was decorated with a space theme. Posters of rocket ships and planets, and a hanging mobile of the solar system over the high-backed wooden bed. A calendar on the wall featured fun facts about astronomy.

It was dated 1985.

Under a striped comforter and propped up on several pillows, was a small boy with a pale, drawn face and dark hair falling over shadowed eyes. He was looking up at Walter with such love and trust that it made his heart ache.

This was his boy. His son.

When they joined minds at Reiden Lake, the Zodiac had shared the most powerful emotional moment in his future. So, too, was this a profoundly significant moment—one from Walter's future.

He looked down at his open hand, and saw that he was holding a coin. A silver dollar. He looked back up at the little boy. The boy offered a wan smile.

"Will you wake me for dinner?" the boy asked. "I don't wanna miss it."

Walter could feel the other minds there, poised like an audience, watching him. The killer's consciousness was front and center, like a darkening bruise.

The boy reached up his skinny arms, asking for a hug, and Walter was suddenly hit with a terrible realization. The boy was sick. He was dying. And although he couldn't imagine why, Walter was sure that it was his fault.

He hugged the boy—too hard, but he couldn't help it. The sweet smell of freshly shampooed hair mingled with a powerful odor of medicine. Walter's heart felt as if it was shattering into a million pieces.

The boy's breath hitched and then let out, long and slow. His heavy little head sagged against Walter's shoulder as Walter waited from him to inhale.

He never did.

The boy was dead in his arms.

Raw howling anguish flooded Walter's mind, echoed and amplified by all the linked minds in the chain. The vision of the lifeless boy and his cheerful room disintegrated into ash, but that bottomless grief followed Walter back into the real world, resonating to the depths of his being and making him feel as if his chest had been torn wide open.

He staggered with the weight of that terrible emotion, crushed and so consumed by it that he thought he would die. Then he opened his eyes and saw the killer, standing less than a foot away, gun pointed at the floor. The Zodiac had a hand over his eyes and was swaying as if he was about to faint. An emotionless sociopath, suddenly broadsided by empathy, he had been devastated by unknown emotion.

Meanwhile, the tendrils around the edges of the gate

were reaching critical mass. It was now or never. Walter didn't have a second to think.

He threw himself at the disoriented killer, driving them both toward the undulating gate.

49

Nina had been struggling to stay alert, and focused on the gate, but the narcotic comfort of linking minds with Bell again was so tempting. He was standing about six feet to her left, facing away, but she could feel his consciousness inside her, like a twin heartbeat.

She would snap out of it for a second, gripping the walkie-talkie so tight that her knuckles ached, and ready to call a stop to the experiment. But then she would find herself drawn back in to the seductive Möbius strip of the psychic connection.

Meanwhile Walter and the killer were almost nose to nose, both frozen and locked into some psychic encounter Nina couldn't even begin to comprehend. Their eyes were closed and twitching beneath their lids, as if they were dreaming.

Then, just as she felt herself starting to slip away again, Walter suddenly *tackled* the insensate killer. He ducked down, driving one shoulder into the killer's chest and wrapping both arms around his waist.

They fell together toward the gate, Walter on top and the killer on the bottom. Nina screamed Walter's name, but it was too late. They were both certain to fall through.

What happened next was so astonishing that she could hardly process what she was seeing. The top third of the killer's head entered the opening, disappearing up to the bridge of the nose, as if plunged underwater. Then in the blink of an eye, the gate seemed to destabilize. It disintegrated into something that resembled jagged, whirring fan blades that sliced the killer's head to ribbons, filling the air with a fine mist of blood and brain matter.

His death was instantaneous. It had to have been.

The rest of the killer's body—along with Walter, whose head was tucked down and pressed against the man's shoulder—were thrown violently backward, as if from an explosion.

Nina could almost feel her connection with Bell tearing and bleeding as she ran to help Walter. Bell seemed to feel it, too, and he turned toward her, shaking his head and squinting as if reacting to a persistent loud noise. When he saw what had happened, he joined Nina at Walter's side.

The killer's heavy, headless body had fallen on top of him, and so Nina and Bell worked together to move the dead weight. He was spattered with the killer's blood, and clearly disoriented, but seemed otherwise unharmed.

"Walt," Bell said. "What the hell happened? Why did the gate suddenly close."

"I..." He wiped his lips on the back of his hand and looked up at the two of them. "I have no idea."

Two Observers stood beside the carousel, watching the FBI agents escorting handcuffed Walter, Nina, and Bell away from the Sharon House.

"They aren't ready to know," one said to the other.

"Not yet," the other replied, adjusting the brim of his fedora.

Together they turned and walked toward Kezar Drive.

"What about the rest?" the first Observer asked.

"They are necessary casualties," the other said, gesturing toward the group of FBI agents who were removing three bodies from a Volkswagen minibus. "We had no choice but to close the gate. As a result, catastrophic timeline disruption has been effectively averted."

The two watched dispassionately for a few minutes as the bodies were bagged and loaded into a waiting vehicle.

Then they were gone.

50

Walter and Bell sat together in the same featureless interrogation room where Walter had first met the late Dick Latimer. Nina had been taken elsewhere.

They were both shaken and exhausted—Walter even more so, because he couldn't get that dying boy out of his mind. He told Bell everything, every detail of his terrible vision, and how that powerful emotion and helped him beat the killer.

"The future isn't set in stone, Walt," Bell said. "Linda's grandma and all the other passengers on that bus are alive today because of you. You saw her die, but she didn't. You changed the future. You saved her life—you saved all of their lives." He put his hand on Walter's shoulder. "Don't you see? Just because you saw your son die, doesn't mean you can't still save him."

"My God," Walter replied. "I hope you're right."

The door opened and, to Walter's surprise, Iverson walked into the room.

"Gentlemen," he said. "I had to pull more strings than the Howdy Doody Show, but you're free to go. However, I'm afraid you're on the map now. We'll be keeping a close eye on both of you." He gave them a wry smile. "Who knows, we might even offer you a job someday."

Walter and Bell stood, and Bell reached out to shake Iverson's hand.

"What's going to happen to you, now that Latimer is out of the way?" Bell asked.

"Well," Iverson replied, "it looks like I get my paranormal investigative unit after all. Although it will probably take years to develop it into a workable division. It's not like we have a precedent to follow."

"Good luck with it," Bell said.

"But Agent Iverson," Walter said, "there were several other students involved in this experiment. A young woman named May. Is she… are they okay?"

Iverson's expression turned grim.

"They didn't make it," he said.

Walter staggered as if punched in the stomach. If Bell hadn't been there beside him, he might have collapsed to his knees.

"All of them…?" he asked.

"Strangest thing," Iverson said. "The bodies were entirely unmarked, with no sign of any injury or trauma. They were just dead, as if their lives had been switched off like light bulbs."

"Did… " Walter was reeling, devastated. "Did we kill them?"

"No way of knowing, really," Iverson said. "I'm sorry."

Walter thought of smart, charming May, picturing her gap-toothed smile as she took a purple Necco wafer from the roll he had offered.

Just moments earlier he had felt so shell-shocked and numb, he was sure there was no way he could feel more grief. Yet there it was, fresh and stinging like a brand new paper cut.

He barely heard Iverson's goodbye, barely reacted when Nina was released with them, and said nothing on the whole ride back to her house. It was as if he was under water, everything icy cold and distant.

They had survived, and they had beaten the killer. But at what cost?

51

Nina unlocked the door to her house, almost unable to believe that it still existed. That her normal day-to-day life was still there, just the way she had left it. Food in the fridge. Bills to be paid. Her half-read book on her bedside table, waiting to be finished.

The world was going on with its mundane business as if none of this had ever happened.

But it had, and Nina knew in her heart she had reached a critical crossroad. That the life she might have had if she had just met Bell that one time, and then never seen him again, was no longer an option. That whatever complex endeavor she might be engaged in with Bell was well on its way to becoming a reality.

Her two companions followed her in like a couple of refugee war orphans, devastated by everything they'd been through. When the phone rang, they both nearly jumped out of their skins.

Nina grabbed the receiver of the wall-mounted phone in the front hallway.

"Hello?" she said, tucking the receiver between her shoulder and ear as she took off her coat.

"Hi, Nina," a familiar voice said. "It's Abby!"

"Hey, Abby," Nina replied, stretching the spiral phone cord as far as it could go, to hang her coat on the hook by the door. "Is everything okay?"

"Sure, fine, no problem," she said. "I just wanted to thank you for letting me borrow your rental car. Roscoe is here, and I bet you'll never believe what happened to him."

"I bet I will," Nina said.

"He got *arrested*. By spooks!" she said. "The FBI, who totally hassled him for no reason, and kept him for twelve whole hours. The fascists!"

"Really?" Nina said. "Imagine that!"

"He says they asked him a bunch of questions about your two friends," Abby continued. "But he didn't tell them a thing, did you honey? Anyway, it's all fine now."

"Glad to hear it," Nina said. "Everyone else in the band okay?"

"They nailed Chick on possession," she said. "But he'll probably just cop a plea, like last time. Everybody else is totally fine." Nina could hear her taking a big hit off a joint. "But hey, listen. Me and Roscoe, we've decided to stay down here for a little while, just to take it easy and find our spiritual centers after everything that happened. We'll turn in the rental car and pay off the rest of what you owe, okay?"

"That's fine, kiddo," Nina said. "Thanks."

"What about your two friends?" Abby asked. "Are they okay?"

Nina looked over at Bell and Walter, who were standing together as if they were using every drop of their combined willpower not to fall flat on their faces. At that moment, she had no idea how to answer Abby's question.

"They're fine," she said, for lack of a better response.

"Okay, then," Abby said. "I better go. Mom's making coconut cake."

She hung up before Nina could reply.

Nina looked down at the receiver, and then put it back on the cradle. Although it didn't ameliorate the loss of all those innocent students from the Institute, it did make her feel just a little bit better to know that Abby, her baby, and all of the band members had escaped the madness unharmed.

Walter and Bell, on the other hand, looked far from unharmed.

"Come on, boys," she said, leading them into the living room.

Cat-Mandu, Roscoe's Himalayan cat, jumped down off the couch to greet Walter, demanding attention as if he were the center of his own little feline universe. Walter smiled and crouched down to pet him, but Nina could still see tension in his face.

Something was bothering him and not just the events of the day.

"Belly," Walter finally said, standing back up again and turning to Bell. "We have to destroy the formula for the acid. We must never, *ever* make that blend again."

"What?" Bell frowned. "That's insane! It's the single most significant breakthrough we've ever had! We can't just abandon such an important line of research. We need to study it. Refine it."

Walter shook his head vigorously.

"It's far too dangerous," he said. "The risks far outweigh the benefits."

"In it's current state, yes," Bell argued. "And I agree that further use of adult subjects would be ill advised. But with a few minor adjustments, we might be able to use it on subjects whose minds are more flexible and open. Like children."

"Have you lost all sense of ethics and *decency*?" Walter said. "We can't experiment on unsuspecting children! No, I insist that you destroy the formula immediately, and that we make a pact never to recreate it. The world just isn't ready for the kind of uncontrollable psychic power that it can unleash."

"Walter," Bell said, that deep, soothing voice of his, pitched low and gentle. "Why don't we sleep on it for a few days. After everything we've been through, we're not in any shape to be making important decisions about the future."

"My decision-making process has never been clearer," Walter insisted. "Destroying the formula is the only rational option."

"Well," Bell said, taking his little red notebook out of the pocket of his sport coat. "While I want it to be known that I strongly disagree, I supposed I have no choice."

He opened the notebook to the formula for the special blend and tore the page out, crumpling it into a tight ball.

"William, don't!" Nina said, hand on his arm.

He shot her a look and set the balled-up paper into an ashtray on a low coffee table. She withdrew her hand slowly.

"Give Walter your lighter," Bell said.

Nina narrowed her eyes at him, but he just nodded, expression serene. She did what he asked.

Walter took the lighter.

"This is the right thing to do," he said.

He sparked the flame and touched it to the crumpled paper. The page went up quickly, burning brightly for a moment, and then dying down to thin black ash.

For a full minute, no one said anything. The three of

them just sat there, staring at the crisp, delicate blossom of ash. Then Walter prodded it with the butt of the lighter, and it collapsed to powder.

"Well, I don't know about you, Belly," he said, setting the lighter down beside the ashtray and getting to his feet, "but I feel better already. It was the right thing to do."

"I suppose so," Bell said, his face unreadable.

"So," Walter said, clapping his hands together. "Who wants pancakes?"

"That would be great," Nina said, her curious gaze still locked with Bell. "Thanks."

Walter disappeared into the kitchen. Cat-Mandu followed, mewing in anticipation of Tender Vittles.

Nina stepped up beside Bell, silent questions in her eyes. He smiled and opened the notebook, revealing the formula for the special blend, unharmed on a previous page.

Beneath the complex chemical formula was a list of several potential brand names for the blend. The last one on the list was circled twice.

Cortexaphan.

That had a nice ring to it.

"He'll come around," Bell said. "Just give him some time."

Nina smiled. She knew that he was right.

Bell closed the notebook and put it back in his pocket.

ACKNOWLEDGEMENTS

The author would like to thank Al Guthrie, Steve Saffel, Anna Songco, JoAnne Narcisse, Angela Park, Noreen O'Toole, Rob Chiappetta, Glen Whitman, Joel Wyman, and Nathan Long.

ABOUT THE AUTHOR

Christa Faust is the author of a variety of media tie-ins and novelizations for properties such as *Supernatural*, *Final Destination* and *Snakes on a Plane*. She also writes hardboiled crime novels, including the Edgar Award-nominated *Money Shot*, *Choke Hold*, and the Butch Fatale series. She lives in Los Angeles. Her website is christafaust.net.

COMING SOON FROM TITAN BOOKS

FRINGE
THE BURNING MAN
By Christa Faust

As a child, Olivia Dunham is "Subject 13," exposed to the experimental drug Cortexiphan. It has strange effects upon her—effects that manifest when her stepfather assaults her mother—with dire consequences.

All of her life, Olivia hides the strange things Cortexiphan has done to her. But the older she gets, the more difficult it becomes to suppress them. And when faced with a life-or-death situation, she can no longer deny her true nature. For if she does, someone close to her will die.

July 2013

TITANBOOKS.COM